Wicked Words 3

A Black Lace short-story collection

Wicked Words 3

A Black Lace short-story collection

EDITED BY KERRI SHARP

BLACK
lace

Black Lace novels are sexual fantasies.
In real life, make sure you practise safe sex.

First published in 2000 by
Black Lace
Thames Wharf Studios,
Rainville Road, London W6 9HA

Check-Up	© Jacqueline Sydney
Tom-Kat	© Maria Lloyd
Public Washrooms, Private Pleasures	© Verena Yexley
Alien Sex Fiends	© Dr Ann Magma
The Shape of Venus	© Franciska Sherwood
I Like Boys	© Marilyn Jaye Lewis
The Good Girl	© Marilyn Jaye Lewis
The Bad Gal	© LaToya Thomas
England expects . . .	© Julie Savage
Temptations	© Airyn Darling
Wild Justice	© Jenesi Ash
Shoreline	© Lesley Wilson
Outmanoeuvred	© Juliet Lloyd Williams
Meeting the Bitch	© Jean Roberta
Esthely Blue	© Mary Anne Mohanraj
Hades and Persephone	© Ainsley Gray
An Inside Job	© Catharine McCabe
The Leather Lover	© Georgina Brown

Typeset by SetSystems Ltd, Saffron Walden, Essex
Printed and bound by Mackays of Chatham PLC

ISBN 0 352 33522 X

Contents

Introduction and Newsletter

❖ ❖

*I*sn't the cover to this compilation great? I was speaking to the photographer the other day and she told me it took five hours to get the model's hair just right. Obviously not a girl in a hurry – unlike me, who makes do with that 'tousled' look 24/7. But, to the matter in hand . . . stories, and lots of 'em. We're proud to bring you another cracking compilation of high-grade smut. A virtual distinction award has to go to 'Dr Ann Magma' for her *Alien Sex Fiends* – for the sheer craft of the piece, and for having such a sustained, wild imagination.

There's a wonderfully unrepentant feel to the stories this time. After kicking off with a fun-filled 'lady dentist on the job' story (and we do like a lady dentist), we're into serious girl/boy gender play in *Tom-Kat*, where the central female character explores the twilight world of gay cruising on Hampstead Heath, and all is definitely not what it makes out out be. It's good to get something like this from a British author. Almost all genderplay stories I receive come from the US, where there seems to be more of an established sub-culture of playing with sexualities and dressing up as someone else: another gender; a different set of values. Maybe it's because they have San Francisco and Pat Califia and an iconography that lends itself more easily to creative roleplay. Maybe the films, clothes and cars are just damn sexier. Whatever, hidden within *Tom-Kat*'s contemporary London location are the accoutrements of delinquent 50s America. Kenneth Anger would approve.

My three feisty lesbian stories, *Meeting the Bitch*, *Temptations* and *Hades and Persephone*, are all from the US and Canada, and all three are the real deal – not the soft-focus cheesy lesbian fantasies of men's magazines. Here we get leather, strap-ons, and humour; what more could a girl want?

The third story, again from Canada, is a no-holds-barred piece of unashamed perviness. No excuses, no apologies, just really bad behaviour, as a well-dressed, married couple engage in games of voyeurism and urolagnia. The author describes the two main characters as 'the Bonnie and Clyde of public toilets'. This story is a different, surprising and unusual tale of conspirators of bizarre pleasures.

North Americans are very present in this anthology. You'll notice which stories come from across the water by their spelling. This time I've decided to relax the stringent rules on spelling and allow our American authors their voice. Back to the UK and *The Bad Gal*, which is very London, and written with more than a dash of Jamaican slang and attitude. This one's told with a voice you're not likely to hear in the *Erotic Review*. There's room for all styles and voices in *Wicked Words* anthologies. As long as there's a twist or an unusual slant – something a bit different. A bit different is *England Expects* ... very cleverly written and a great example of inspiration from an unexpected source. *Shoreline*, too, is full of imagination; a bit softer than most Black Lace stories, but the gentle tone suits the dreamlike sea setting.

There isn't room to mention all the stories individually; suffice to say they're all marvellously entertaining and a big thank-you to the contributors – that wonderful group of you out there in cyberland. If only it were possible to meet you all!

The same diversity of stories will be reflected throughout this year's publishing programme. However you like your erotic fiction, Black Lace books will provide you with a stunning array of stories and authors. The next anthology is, you guessed it, *Wicked Words 4*, due for publication spring 2001. Until then, be wild, be wonderful, be lucky!

Kerri Sharp
May 2000

I'm always keen to see stories from women who write from the heart and the groin. Women who aren't afraid to be bad girls, and who want to translate their most outrageous fantasies into top-notch erotica stories. If you think you could write for us, send a large S.A.E. to

Black Lace Guidelines
Virgin Publishing Ltd
Thames Wharf Studios
Rainville Road
London W6 9HA

A first-class stamp is sufficient.

Check-Up

Jacqueline Sydney

Check-Up

❖ ❖

I had an erection the minute I entered the dental surgery. No one had told me my new dentist, Dr Maya, was female, and a total babe!

'Please, take a seat, Mr Sherwin,' she commanded, her voice smooth and melodious. 'Just a check-up today, I see.' Where was she from? Her accent suggested hot nights and spicy days far from London. Her skin was a tawny colour not usually seen during an English winter.

'Call me Nick,' I entreated. Her full lips curved into a lazy smile. My erection became more uncomfortable as I imagined them wrapped around my cock. I could feel my face become red. She was my *dentist*, for God's sake; here I was fantasising about her, with her nurse in the room!

'And you can call me Dr Maya,' she responded. Obviously this appointment was to be kept at a very professional level.

'May I ask, not being rude, but are you old enough to be a dentist?' I inquired. 'After all, you look about my age and I'm still a student.'

She raised a sardonic, perfectly curved eyebrow at

the impertinence of my question. 'And what do you study, Nick?'

'I'm in my final year of Sport Science at university,' I replied. 'Training to teach physical education.'

'You must be pretty fit to do that. Do you work out at a gym?' she asked, a mocking tone colouring her voice.

'No,' I said, squirming slightly under her scrutiny. 'Just lots of rugby.'

I had plenty of war wounds from playing scrum half. The last had been a broken nose, which I'd refused to have reset, hoping the locker-room name of 'Pretty Boy' would be abandoned. It hadn't.

'OK, Nick, shall we lay you back?' she said briskly, eyes trained on my trousers, which by now seemed to have a life of their own despite my best efforts to hide the evidence that I was horny as hell. 'And by the way, I'm twenty-eight.' The chair reclined until I was level with her full, luscious breasts, which gently pressed against the top of my head as she positioned herself behind me.

'Open wide,' she whispered close to my ear. I could feel her arrange herself until her legs straddled the dental chair behind me. I inhaled sharply as I realised how close I was to her exotic pussy, and opened my mouth. I'm quite proud of my teeth. A couple of years in braces and *voila*! A killer smile, or so I've been told.

A surgical mask obscured most of her face but revealed her eyes, sensuous amber pools with surprising flecks of green.

'You have excellent oral hygiene, Nick,' she said, meeting my gaze. She looked up. I could see the nurse was arranging instruments just feet away. 'And I know you've wanted to fuck me from the start of this appointment,' she whispered, barely audible. My heart lurched. Had she just said that? I hoped to God I hadn't heard her wrong. Abruptly, she sat up. 'Louise,' she said to her nurse, 'would you like an early lunch break? The patient needs a very simple piece of treatment so I'll finish up here.' I watched her blank expression as the nurse left the surgery.

Without another word she tore off her mask and kissed me hard. It felt so sexy to be the one dominated in a kiss. Her tongue, sweet and firm, plunged into my mouth with startling lust. I responded eagerly, probing the depths of her mouth, wanting to taste more, harder and stronger. Her cat-like tongue seemed to sweep parts of my mouth never explored by previous lovers, and I felt like a shy virgin in my responses. She was in control here.

I expressed my concern about the lack of a lock on the door. What about staff entering? My girlfriend was in reception waiting for me to finish. She could come in at any minute, wondering where I am!

Dr Maya smiled reassuringly. 'I usually take a nap at lunch, so the staff know better than to disturb me. And I don't think you will need your girlfriend for the next hour.' She drew away from me. 'I could feel you wanting to touch my tits, you know.' Her hand rested on my hair, lightly but firmly. 'The way your hair brushed against me. I've always preferred blonds, you know.' She rasped her hands through my sandy hair, her nails leaving exquisite raw tramlines through my sensitised scalp.

The most direct way to my cock is through my hair. Play with it, pull it, whatever. I could feel my hard-on strain to titanic proportions, rubbing eagerly against the fabric of my pants.

She continued the erotic massage for a time, then, as if sensing this would not lead quickly to personal satisfaction, she suddenly stopped. Movement again behind me. I could hear the sound of garments being removed. Please let it be the G-string that is restraining her glossy bush! But no, the next kiss I felt was that of her erect nipples being placed expectantly against my lips. My head exploded in a whirl of lust. Beneath the clinical white coat she had worn were the lushest curves I had ever seen. I couldn't have imagined them in my wildest fantasies. The tight buds of her nipples were as succulent as I had anticipated. I kept my eyes wide open, so I could have a front-row seat for a porno which lurked inside every man's mind: to be dominated by a foxy health worker.

As I eagerly accepted the plump nipple in my mouth, I could hear her sigh in a detached sort of way. It was as if having such a dull young puppy such as myself sucking on such a glorious pair of breasts was tedious in the extreme. Her nipple firmed up quickly as I caressed the plump bud with my fingers and tongue, unable to get enough of her, wondering when she would tire of me and withdraw herself.

'You're a bit keen, aren't you?' she said huskily. Was it just me, or was she as turned on as I was? 'Girlfriend not servicing you properly? I'll teach you how real women fuck.'

She gave me a head rush, speaking so filthily in that exotic accent. She was right about my girlfriend: she'd boycotted having sex with me since she found out I was going away on a rugby tour on her birthday weekend. I'd had a couple of wanks lately but I felt like my balls would explode if I didn't get release soon. And what a release this was!

Then she pulled the tight bud from my mouth, glistening with my saliva, and stood in front of me. Her breasts in full view were perfect. They curved luxuriously, tipped with honey nipples. More than a handful but still pert and firm. I reached out to touch one of the perfect globes but she sharply slapped my hand away and smiled scornfully. 'You will not touch me unless I say so! Do you understand?'

Not wanting to anger her, I agreed to do as she said,

although I wondered what she would be like when angry. I could imagine her all fiery, the cool clinical exterior fragmenting.

She then removed her trousers gracefully, her lush forbidden breasts swaying gently with each deliberate movement. Her glossy bush was held captive by a flimsy scrap of maroon lace that just begged to be pushed aside to reveal her creamy aroused lips. She was completely naked now, except for a pair of surgical gloves adorning her hands. A wedding ring glinted through the latex, momentarily disconcerting me. Kneeling down by my waist, she drew my hand into hers. 'Such artistic hands, Nick.' She breathed lightly on the tips of my fingers, sending delicious shivers up my spine. 'I can't imagine you tearing someone apart on the rugby field, but I imagine it would be quite exciting.' My forefinger was then inserted into that voluptuous mouth, embraced by its soft warmth. She drew her tongue up the side, toying with its length, enough for me to realise that she would be sensational at sucking cock. She then reached over and pulled out a further pair of the pale-coloured gloves and, expanding them to their full extent, tied my hands to the armrests. The latex bit deliciously into my skin, a smattering of hairs pulled from their follicles. Now I was trapped.

Dr Maya moved behind me again and lowered the headrest of the dental chair still further backward. She then straddled my head until her cunt was just inches from my face. Her gloved hand reached downward and spread her plump lips wide. Her pussy was so pretty, opening up like an Amaryllis lily, foreign and exotic. The musky smell of her sex intermingled with the smell of the latex. Her fingers probed deeper into the furrows, revealing her swollen clit that she rubbed with surprising force. Her other hand, lubricated with her abundant juices, slipped readily into her sex. My God, she was a horny bitch! If she thought I would sit back and watch her frig herself senseless, she had another think coming! I tested the rubber wrist bonds. No, they were firmly attached. I would have to let her do as she wanted and only hope it would involve my cock.

I raised my head slightly. One inch more and I could lick her slit that was creaming up nicely. I experimentally extended my tongue until it probed her lush swollen lips. A small gasp – of pleasure, I hoped – escaped her lips. She descended her pussy lower and allowed my tongue to burrow in the moist crease. She tasted fantastic; the metallic tang of her juices intermingled with the faint powdery taste of the gloves. I applied pressure to her clitoris and flicked my tongue leisurely across its hood. She gasped in earnest and grasped my hair roughly, holding my head in that position. Got her, I thought. But I wouldn't give her the satisfaction of coming straight away. I shifted slightly until I could plunge my tongue up her vagina, mimicking a fucking action. Her fingers returned to her clit and she rotated her hips to maximise the thrust of my tongue. Her arousal was obvious, only to be outdone by my own. Her perfumed juices spilt in abandon over my face.

Again I moved my tongue further backward. She seemed so adventurous – would she let me? I experimentally toyed with the rim of the puckered aperture on display. This move obviously met with her approval as she spread the firm cheeks of her arse to accommodate me. I played with the tight little rim for a little while longer, listening to her sighs of approval. God, this was exciting. When I had tried to get previous girlfriends to experiment anally, the idea had been met with horror.

Abruptly, she dismounted my tongue and stood back to admire the sheen of herself on my face. 'You've done that before, I see,' she said, irony dripping from her voice. 'Right let's liberate your cock before it breaks the fly on your jeans.'

She moved down and bent over to release my zip. The sight from behind was spectacular. Her arse was a perfect peach with a tattoo adorning her left buttock. A tiny butterfly winged across the dusky skin towards her dark cranny, which was streaked with my saliva and her juices. Finally, my shaft was free. She turned to face me, stroking its granite length softly.

'Not bad,' she said, smiling wickedly, 'but I know how we can improve matters.' She reached over and pulled out another latex glove. This, she tied firmly at the base of my dick. I watched as my cock, the length of which I am very proud, turned from an impressive size to the proportions of a male porn star. I said as much to her in what I imagine was a very ragged voice. I inhaled sharply as she teased her gloved hands along the tense veins that bulged obscenely. It felt like nothing I had experienced before. Sparks seemed to ignite along the entire length and up to my brain. I felt faint but my awareness was heightened to her every move. 'You like that, don't you, Nick? Looking like a porn star? Have you watched a lot of those?' she questioned sharply. I had to admit that I had, but find me a 21-year-old bloke who hasn't wanked himself dry over a filthy movie. But this was better than a porno. It was interactive.

She grinned, her luscious lips parted in her mocking smile. She then lowered those lips on to my straining cock. The sensation of her teeth lightly rasping over my glans to envelop my girth sent a spasm of pleasure throughout my body. Her tongue flicking unhurriedly over the tense surface caused me to thrust my hips forward. She met the challenge and I watched as she proceeded to deep-throat me, her fingers dipping into my hips viciously. I wondered how I would explain away the ten crescent-shaped scars from her nails flanking each hip. It would not easily be dismissed as another rugby injury! Her eyes never left mine. I wondered what she could see in my expression. Did she realise her lips were the best fuck I had ever experienced in my life?

I could feel activity near my balls as she lightly caressed the tight sac. Then I could feel a gloved finger probe between my cheeks. Oh my God, she was going to put her finger up my arse! Her finger snaked and probed until it was fully inserted. She moved slightly to caress a swelling that caused me to emit a sharp yell of ecstasy. I bit my lip frantically until I thought I would taste blood. The others must have heard that! But she seemed to be unflustered by the noise and continued to fuck me with her mouth and finger. God, I was enjoying the feeling of her finger up my arsehole. I fleetingly wondered if that made me gay or something. I imagined something as large as a cock invading my ring would feel even better. My helmet rubbed against her soft palate causing a wave of faintness to come over me. The start of my orgasm. I anticipated the deep shuddering ecstasy I would next experience.

She suddenly expelled my hard sex from her mouth. 'Don't think you are going to get your satisfaction that easily,' she said, smirking. 'I could taste you were about to come then. I think I have just the thing for your little problem.' She pulled the gloves off and opened a drawer, bringing out a tube of cream. 'It's an anaesthetic lotion. I usually use it to take the sting off injections but I'm going to use it to desensitise your cock.' She applied a liberal amount to my straining shaft. I could feel my balls answer in protest. If they became any higher or tighter they would disappear!

She was right. I could feel the sensations slowly lessening. She bent over to get something out of her bag and I could hear a ripping noise. Now I was curious. As she proceeded to apply her mouth back to my cock, working with a strange but definitely erotic sensation, I tried to identify what she had done. Her mouth finished its elaborate movements and withdrew, leaving a condom in place. My shaft looked good completely encased in rubber. I joked that I might leave with a fetish. She didn't laugh, but lay on top of me and kissed me hard again, her mouth salty with the taste of my pre-come. I squirmed slightly, trying to rub my hard-on against her naked pussy, attempting to maximise contact between our two hot bodies.

She sat up and slowly undid the buttons of my shirt, her eyes taunting mine. Her once severely neat hair fell over one eye in glossy abandon. She was the superior here, and I felt blissfully like her plaything. 'So you do keep fit,' she said, running a finger slowly from my six-pack to my smooth chest. 'I like a well-toned man. Or shall I say boy?'

Her fingers teased my erect nipples with delicate movements, sending electric shocks to my throbbing penis. I groaned, not caring now who heard me. I could tell she would not let me leave the surgery until she had teased me into oblivion. I could only hope my girlfriend would wait outside to give me a lift home, as I was sure my legs would not take me further than the front door. Her full lips lowered on to the tight bud, encircling languidly with her incredible tongue. She then nipped it lightly; sensations of part pleasure, part pain intermingling. I didn't want her to stop, but the idea of begging was too humiliating.

As if she had read my thoughts, she raised her sexy face. 'You love this, don't you, being my little bitch,' she purred. 'I'm doing things to you none of your prissy playmates would ever do. How will you ever go back to making love to your dull girlfriends after I've let you put your cock up my arse?'

I didn't know. It was like drinking champagne after years of water. I felt dominated, humiliated and completely turned on.

She pulled backward and said huskily, 'My turn now, slut.' She grasped my latex-enshrined rigid sex and straddled her honeyed flanks over its length. Lowering herself slowly, I watched as my dick slid into her creamy sex. God, it felt like a thousand fingers were kneading its length. She was so tight and deep.

Men are visual creatures, I know, and the sight of those swollen lips slipping over my sex sent goosebumps of pleasure over my body. Her head was thrown back in abandon, her glossy hair in perfect disarray spilling over her full, pert breasts. Her hands worked upward, moulding to her dusky curves, her fingers lingering over her erect nipples, pleasuring herself. I wanted to break the rubber bondage she had subjected me to and feel those dark breasts cupped in my hands and yet the feeling of being completely submissive, her whore, excited me to a higher level of sensation.

Her hips moved in a teasing motion when she rode me. Sometimes long strong strokes that engulfed my entire length, sometimes writhing just on the tip of my cock. Although the anaesthetic had delayed my orgasm, I could feel my hips rising, trembling, wanting her to fuck me harder and deeper. I felt like I was suffocating, and dry gasps of air wrenched from my throat.

'That's it, slut,' she said maliciously. 'Do you think you can handle more?' As she slipped off my tense dick, a musky scent filled the room, and the end of my sex glistened with her abundant milky juices. Smiling at my horror at being stopped from coming again, she turned away, straddling me with her heart-shaped, toned backside.

'I promised you I'd let you fuck me up the arse,' she reminded me. 'I expect you are a virgin at anal sex, am I right?'

I muttered affirmatively, barely able to speak now. I felt so used and abused, I never wanted her to stop. She positioned her backside over my cock and descended slowly downward. I heard her whimper slightly as my sex broached her tight ring. Her slickening pussy juices acted as a lubricant, but I could see that my girth, distended as it was by the latex cock ring, was going to struggle to fit into her. It was so exciting to see my rigid hot sex probing between her perfect cheeks. Please, I begged, keep going. That seemed to be all she needed. She scowled at me over her shoulder and, letting out a cry of triumph, rammed my cock forcefully into her puckered hole.

Slowly, with deliberate thrusting motions, she screwed me into submission with each movement of her arse. I could see she was stroking her clit, bringing herself off as I buggered her. The sight of her tender pink flesh drawing up and down my shaft was the horniest picture, and one I would remember all my life. Her cries of ecstasy matched my own and I didn't give a damn who heard me. Her hand moved frantically out of my sight but I could just imagine her slim fingers delving into her lush cunt.

'Hold off, damn you,' she commanded. 'Otherwise, I will find some way of making your life hell.' I took her at her word, thinking of anything but the fantastic sensations shuddering through my body. She finally yelled triumphantly, which I took as my sign to shoot my load. It was almost painful as I came, hot spunk shooting out of my throbbing cock in abundance. I almost fainted at the pleasure of release. Her arse seemed to rhythmically contract over me, or was I imagining it? But she seemed to be enjoying the ride as much as I was.

Dressing was difficult. My legs shook like a newborn lamb's and my fingers trembled as I did up my fly. I didn't know how I would explain coming out of the dentist's with raw bands around my wrists. We had been at it for only half an hour but I felt like I'd played a game of rugby against the All Blacks!

All I could think now was how I would increase my intake of sugar and stop wearing my mouthguard for sport, in the hope that I could see her sooner than in six months.

When I turned to speak to her, Dr Maya was impeccably dressed and completely in control. Not a single sign was displayed in her expression that just a minute ago I had been inside the most forbidden place in her body. She handed me a slip of paper.

'What's this for?' I asked, puzzled.

'Your bill for your check-up,' she said sweetly, with undertones of laughter. 'You may have been a great fuck, Nick, but I still have to earn a living.

Tom-Kat

Maria Lloyd

Tom-Kat

❖ ❖

So here I am in the darkness of Hampstead Heath, watching a sliver of moon rise over the distant orange glow of London. Leaves rustle overhead in an unexpected gust and I shiver, more from nerves than from the chill of the September night. I'm pressed against the rough bark of this ancient oak tree, and I watch its boughs creak overhead, trying to think of the beauty of the evening rather than the reason why I am standing here, dressed in jeans and a black polo neck, Doc Martens and a baseball cap.

Then Jerome whispers across to me from the next tree trunk.

'Soon be time for some action, Kat.'

I can just make out his handsome face now I've adjusted to the darkness. He looks like the ghost of a beautiful if decadent aristocrat. There is a cruel edge to his chiselled mouth, and a predatory glint in his eyes. But I already knew that side to him, didn't I? It's one of the reasons I am here.

Let me explain. Yesterday morning was the usual monthly meeting for freelance journalists, held by a

17

group of women's magazines I sometimes manage to work for. The head editor was trotting through the type of features she wanted for a new title launch, aimed at the riot grrrl. She proposed a regular page for women reporters who managed to infiltrate a men-only institution in the capital. One of the freelancers offered to sneak into a Masonic lodge, another to cross over into the men-only section of her club, and so on.

Then I heard myself say, 'How about a report on what goes down in the male cruising grounds of Hampstead Heath?'

The editor's eyes focused on me for the first time. She tapped out one of her Moore cigarettes and lit up. Interested.

'You could do that?' she asked.

'I look pretty boyish, don't you think? And I have contacts. One of my best friends goes there regularly. I'm sure he'll help out if the fee is generous enough.'

She nodded and smiled. 'Top rates,' she said, 'if you pull it off.'

The blood gradually seeped back into my face as the meeting moved on and I made some excuse so that I could bolt for the ladies to recover. I wondered what my crazy ambition had let me in for this time as I lit up a Marlboro in the cubicle. Hubris. I never learn.

That afternoon I met up with Jerome in the Soho coffee bar which is our lunchtime haunt. He wafted in, looking like a modern Bosie in his tweed suit and crisp white shirt, honey-blond hair immaculate, smelling of Aramis. It's hard to believe he works in the head office of a major accountants but he's got brains as well as beauty, Jerome. He's not just my best friend, he's my cousin, and often crashes at my place when he's between lovers. So he owes me one. Big-time.

'What?' he asked, spluttering away the foam of his cappuccino when I explained my proposition. 'You want to what?'

'C'mon, Jerome,' I wheedled. 'You've offered to do it with me thousands of times. You say I look just like you when I dress in your clothes. Especially if it's dark, eh?'

'But I usually say this at the end of a boozy evening, the same way some people say, "Look at that moon, let's jump over it." ' He shook his head, speaking slowly to explain my stupidity. 'Kat, I say, "I'm going cruising, d'you wanna come?" when I know you'll say no.'

I pouted, pushing my hand through my cropped blonde hair.

'OK, so don't do it. It's only enough money to pay both our rents for a few months if I manage to do this piece. It'll only do my career no end of good. And besides, I thought it might be . . . fun.'

He cocked his head to one side, his grey eyes suddenly thoughtful. He was appraising me. Really looking at me. Not as a girl. As how I would shape up as a boy. And suddenly there was a spark between us. Just like that.

Jerome is bisexual, you see. But he had never thought of us in that way before. Even though I have thought of us in that way before. More than once or twice.

He leaned across and cupped my chin with the long aesthete fingers of his right hand. Turned my face to the side to check my profile, and as he did so his knees brushed mine underneath the narrow Formica table. He swallowed, and I could sense he felt as hot as I did. Assessing the possibilities. His fingers were firm, slightly rough, and branded my skin.

'Well,' he said quietly at last, 'it may be possible. But you would be willing to go through with it all the way? The whole method act – the way a man would pick up his prey and suck that other man's dick? How is your cock-sucking action, by the way?'

'Pretty good,' I replied steadily, keeping eye contact.

19

I thought of how I would love to test it out on him if he gave me half a chance.

The thought must have crossed his mind too, because he shifted in his seat. One of his knees pressed against the inside of my thigh now – casually, of course.

'We could go to a place on the Heath where they're pretty gentle. First timers and such usually start there.' He smiled, warming to the idea. 'I have some regulars I meet. You can pretend to be me in the dark. By the time they notice any difference, you'll be making them come. Don't worry, it's quite safe. I'll point out the ones I know are clean and considerate. But you'll have to follow through, OK? No bolting halfway. Hell hath no fury like a cruiser scorned.'

'I won't let you down,' I said. I could feel myself getting wet in anticipation.

I finished my sandwich and dabbed my left thumb in the mayo on the plate. I sucked it clean and then began to circle its very tip with my tongue, searching Jerome's impassive features. His eyes followed the movements of my tongue. He licked his own lips furtively. Then he looked away with an effort, and glanced at his watch.

'I've got to get back to the office,' he said. 'Meet me at my flat, tomorrow at seven. We'll dress you up. We'll have a chinese take-away, and lots of wine. Then we'll do it before you have a chance to bottle out.'

'OK,' I said.

I cursed my bravado once again, until Jerome leaned over to kiss me goodbye. This time he gave me a French kiss, his teeth seeking out and nipping my lips and my tongue, punishing me for my attempts at seduction. He smiled when he saw how much I flushed at the sweet and horny shock of it.

'See you tomorrow,' he said.

So that's how I got here. Waiting with Jerome on the Heath for a passing stranger willing to let me go down on him. While Jerome watches for his own amusement, of course. It reminds me of the dares we made each other do when we were younger. Only this time I feel a little more is at stake.

There's another figure in the distance now. A big, burly silhouette. My eyes adjust. It's a man dressed in biker leathers. Six foot four, black hair, moustache and beard. He's pretty clumsy, and stumbles a little in the undergrowth as he gropes his way towards us. Then he stops near the third oak tree in our little copse. Waiting.

'Go on,' Jerome mouths to me. 'I know him. Go.'

I take a deep breath. My mouth is dry and my legs won't move. Then I gaze at Jerome, and I think, I'll show you what I can do. You'll want to be that punter by the time I'm through. Another breath, and I'm walking forward slowly, so as not to startle the stranger.

He turns to look at me. His brown eyes glint faintly in the dim light and he smiles.

'Oh, you're here. I'm in luck,' he says in a deep, soft voice.

I smile back as he takes my hand, kisses it in mock reverence and then holds my hand flat against his leather crotch. He's already got the most enormous hard-on. He moans softly as I stroke his tool slowly and possessively. This is what I've been waiting for this last half hour, the chance to fondle a stranger with no strings attached. I can feel my sex slowly melt into the crotch of my boxer shorts (borrowed from Jerome for added authenticity) just from caressing this man's thick, meaty pole through the soft leather of his trousers. He reaches for my buttocks and squeezes my tight little arse cheeks and I shiver at the risk in it. The danger turns me on all the more. I back away so he won't search for my prick and find me wanting.

'Suck my dick,' he entreats, and his hands rest on my shoulders, pulling me to him for a quick embrace – he smells of male musk and soap and leather – before he pushes me down on to my knees before him.

I unzip him and take out his stiff prick. It's circumcised and a thing of beauty. I pull his leather pants down to his ankles so I can admire its list. His balls hang like apples, big and hard and covered in thick black hair.

I press my face against his cock and balls, inhaling their sweet musk. His pheromones heat my blood to fever pitch. I just have to fondle this big, butch plaything. I am fascinated by his balls. They've got to be the biggest I've ever seen. I gently take each in my mouth to feel their weight, and softly suck. He groans, presses against me, pushes off my baseball cap and fondles my short blonde hair.

'I'm aching fit to burst. Bring me off quick, now,' he begs urgently, manoeuvring my lips across the shining tip of his cock. I let my lips advance down the shaft, taking as much as I can of that thick bounty into my mouth. I am engorged on dick. I let my tongue waggle against his tip, then I suck and tease and worship until I feel him tremor under my ministrations.

All the time, in the back of my mind, I'm thinking of Jerome watching. I wonder whether he's got his dick out yet, and whether he is ready to come.

A twig snaps behind us and suddenly my lover-boy springs back, jolted at the thought of being discovered. Then he peers down at me.

'You're not Jerome,' he says roughly.

'No, Dirk, I'm over here,' Jerome calls softly, and walks towards us. As I thought, he already has his erect prick in his hand, his unzipped fly barely containing its lavish size. I wipe my mouth and sit back on the grass, glad he has intervened before Dirk turned nasty, but bewildered by this turn of events.

'What kind of rent boy have you got sucking my dick?' Dirk asks fiercely. 'You know I play careful.'

'It's OK, Dirk. My boy is clean. I just thought it would be a change for you.'

Jerome puts an arm around Dirk's waist to placate him. Dirk takes Jerome's arm and twists him around, then grinds up against his butt. Jerome winks down at me.

'I ought to screw you in the arse right now for screwing with me,' Dirk hisses in Jerome's ear. I watch entranced as Dirk reaches for Jerome's cock and fondles it savagely. Jerome sighs with satisfaction.

'Oh, please,' he replies. 'That *is* the idea. As long as you let my boy suck me off while you do it. C'mon, Dirk, give it a try. I thought it might be . . . fun.'

The exact phrase I'd used to Jerome in the cafe. I'm focused again, like an electric shock has just coursed through me, and my clit is aching as I rub it through the silk of my boxer shorts. I wish I could fondle myself more openly but I cannot give away my absence of cock.

Jerome is staring down at me, smiling as he drops his pants to allow Dirk better access to his prick and balls. Jerome closes his eyes to appreciate the sensation as Dirk plays with him some more, stroking then giving him quick hard slaps to his arse.

Dirk smears his fingers with some juices from his own prick – mainly my saliva – and daubs them against Jerome's arsehole. Dirk starts to ease his prick between Jerome's arse cheeks. Jerome bends over, slightly braced, hands pressed against the thick tree trunk of the nearest oak. He grimaces then moans slowly as Dirk grinds into him, the pain quickly overtaken by pleasure. I love to see the look on his face, the openness of abandonment, the way he registers each stroke of Dirk's cock as it travels further inside him. Then he turns to look at me, still sitting on the grass.

'C'mon, boy,' he orders me. 'Suck my dick.'

I crawl across to do just that.

Jerome's dick is long and thick, and blond hair sprouts from his hard balls. I like the smell of his cock even better. I lick along the shaft, and around his balls, then I gobble up his cock, flailing his glans with my tongue. It feels so good, his hard cock. Its girth fits inside my mouth so perfectly. I think of how it would feel butting up against my cunt, gyrating inside me. I sneakily press my flat breasts against Jerome's balls so he can feel my bullet-hard nipples. I take my lips away, so his cock is left straining for my caress in the cool night air until I stroke it tenderly. Then I take it in my mouth once more and play up and down his shaft, swaying in time to Dirk's thrusts.

All the while I think of how this scenario was my doing. I sucked Dirk into this insane fucking frenzy. I tantalised him into penetrating my cousin with that rutting action.

Meanwhile, I finally get the chance to become intimate with my cousin's beautiful cock. It tastes of honey and apples and cinnamon. I become lost in its subtle textures, the musk and sweat of him. I grip Jerome's muscled thighs to anchor my mouth more firmly around him as Dirk's fucking becomes still more agitated.

I feel the tremor of orgasm rise in Jerome. I can hear Jerome's groans of abandon as Dirk shoots into him. I'm hungry for Jerome's juices but still he does not come and I suck him desperately.

Then as Dirk withdraws from Jerome's arse, my cousin grips my head and fucks my wanton mouth like crazy. I moan with delight as he governs how much of that delicious cock I am allowed to have in my mouth. His roughness means I take even more of its generous length than ever before. I am delirious; drunk on his sex.

'Get ready, I'm gonna come any minute,' he whispers, and my groin circles in time with his strokes as I feel myself approach orgasm. I'm crossing my legs and grinding my swollen clit against the rough seam of my jeans' crotch until my juices flow prodigiously and my body quivers in the familiar ague of passion.

Finally I guzzle his warm, sweet come as it floods down my throat. It tastes faintly of cumin.

As I pull away I swallow the last of his come and gaze straight into his beautiful grey eyes. His eyes are hooded now, and he gives me his special sneer-like smile that means I did well. Then he kneels down and kisses me, a long, slow kiss, so that he can taste his own juices still on my tongue and dribbling from my lips.

'Thank you, Jerome,' Dirk says happily. 'I enjoyed that after all. Maybe I'll see you and your boy next week? What is his name, by the way?'

'Tom,' Jerome replies. 'Tom-Kat.'

And I am in heaven thinking of what Jerome is going to do to me when Dirk has gone.

Fast forward two months. The memory of that whole evening has distilled into a slow burning tincture in my brain, in my blood. I have become addicted to the adrenalin rush of adventure. I can recall every thrust of my cousin's cock in my willing pussy, every rasp of the oak tree's bark on my bare skin as he rode me against its trunk. Indulging in hetero sex on the Heath, where we could be discovered at any moment, was the icing on the cake. I replay every image of caressing Dirk, caressing Jerome, at idle moments, and it always makes me hot.

It certainly inspired my muse. The editor heartily praised the article I delivered, and the magazine's readers were equally enthusiastic, judging from the amount of letters it provoked. The editor and the readers decided they wanted more of the same.

And so did I.

It wasn't just for the handsome fee or the career

kudos. I was obsessed with the look on Jerome's face when Dirk had fucked him from behind. I wanted to feel the way he had. I wanted to taste the ultimate sexual experience which my gender denied me. To be taken by a man, as a boy.

I pondered. I planned. Ultimately I hit upon the ideal opportunity.

There was one gay nightclub that Jerome frequented which he had never invited me to. I knew it was pretty hardcore, harder than the area of the Heath he had taken me to. My curiosity piqued, my envy aroused, I decided to try my luck there. Alone.

Hubris. I tell you. Nothing succeeds like excess.

I took to searching Soho sex shops, after my lunchtimes with Jerome, for the perfect cruising gear. When I spotted the double dildo, a strap-on with a thick black phallus which also nestled in the wearer, I had to buy it. Next time I wanted to at least look like I had a prick, and I wanted more stimulation than my jeans' crotch seam.

My second purchase was a pair of leather chaps, cut away to expose the arse cheeks provocatively. Rather passé, but I knew they were perfect. Looking over my shoulder in the changing cubicle mirror, I was gratified to see that, cupped by the stiff leather, my bottom looked distinctly masculine and inviting.

Next I found a long leather coat at Camden Lock Market, and finally a leather waistcoat and leather biker's cap at a motorcycle shop.

Then I waited. Circled a date in my Filofax at random and vowed it would be my date with the wild side. Itching for it, the excitement ticked away at the back of my mind.

That Friday evening, a bunch of us met up at our favourite lock-up pub in Islington, but as official last orders rang out I cried off, claiming I was too tired, and needed to catch the tube home.

'You'll have to run for it,' Jerome slurred over his pint of Murphy's and his whisky chaser. 'You can stow your gear in my car if you like. I'll be staying at Ivan's overnight.' He dangled his spare set of keys at me, and I took them.

'See you tomorrow.' I pecked his cheek, my secret plans making me affectionate. Whatever happened tonight would only add to my sensual understanding of my cousin-lover.

Then I made my way to the Ladies and changed into the gear. I inserted and strapped on the dildo, giving a squirm of pleasure as the slick black mini-truncheon slipped into my expectant sex. I dressed in the leather chaps. Beneath their stiff black leather crotch I looked and felt like a well-packed boy. The rigid leather waist-coat flattened my small breasts away (and felt deliciously constricting in the process) and its half sleeves beefed up my biceps. I covered the outfit with the long supple leather coat, and the cap completed the ensemble. Cramming my discarded clothes into my sports bag, I stashed it in the boot of Jerome's car (parked a few streets from the pub) and ran down to the Angel station.

I caught the last Northern Line tube down into the West End. I stood in one corner of the carriage, trying to sink into my role. As I jolted and rattled with the drunken passengers around me, I was aroused by the pressure of my dildo circling inside me, butting against my clit and pubis.

I felt a hand brush and cup my arse through the leather coat as most of the passengers disembarked at Tottenham Court Road. It was a Mohawk, eyebrow and lip pierced, who turned to look back at me invitingly. I was tempted to follow and see what would unfold, but I decided against it. I gave a slight shrug and half smile as the tube doors slammed shut, and was flattered to see his disappointed grimace before the carriage picked up speed.

At Leicester Square I hurried into the neon of the West End night. I made my way through China Town and cut down the shabby alley which I knew held the discreet entrance to the nightclub. I was in luck. A gaggle of drunken men, regular clubbers, had just joined the queue and I tagged along with them, laughing at their jokes enough to convince the bouncer that I was one of their party. He let me through with them. He didn't even give me a second look, nor did the ticket vendor, although my heart was thumping harder than any virus had ever made it pulse.

Once inside, the club was mercifully low-lit. The music was loud and relentless – Prodigy, Nine Inch Nails, Foetus – in keeping with my mounting lust and adrenalin high. The incessant beat shook my chest cavity as I strolled about, checking out each small dance floor, before I retreated to the bar and ordered two double vodkas. I downed one, left the empty glass on the counter, and made my way to a shadowy alcove to watch the talent.

It felt raw, being there on my own, yet liberating too. I was anonymous in the shadows, watching men dancing as the lasers and silver balls spangled light on their fit, gyrating bodies. Couples embraced and kissed in booths where night lights flickered romantically on tables. Nearby a young bare-chested man was going down on his moustachioed lover.

I had chosen the softer leather action floor, close to the Gents, so I could watch the flow of traffic.

Soon I spotted my quarry.

He was big. Over six foot, broad, well muscled. He wore leather trousers and a T-shirt, and had the iconic look of a young Brando. He did not have to dress to impress. His dark hair was collar length; his eyes were the colour of brandy. He had a strong jawline and brooding brows. When he walked he had the faint swagger of a boxer, and when he danced his strong flowing movements hypnotised.

Just looking at him made me horny. He stopped dancing and stood propped against the distant bar, illuminated occasionally by swathes of neon that swirled in time to the beat. It was hard to tell, but it seemed like he stared straight back at me. Returned my lustful gaze with arrogant challenge.

When he went to the Gents, I knocked back the last of my vodka and followed him in.

He was standing at one of the urinals, pissing, as I entered. The walls were blood-red, the lighting suffused, so that it looked like a scene from a Roger Corman movie. He looked up as I walked towards him. I pretended I was heading for the cubicle beyond. His look was searing; took me off guard. But I stared back squarely, the heat of the vodka making me bold. He shook off the final droplets from his prick and I brushed my hand against his tight arse as I passed behind him. I could not resist looking down at his broad hands and the handsome prick that nestled between them.

He did not need any further invitation.

He swung round, gripped my shoulders and propelled me against the red concrete wall, slamming his tongue into my mouth, grinding his body against mine. It felt so good, to let his mouth rape my mouth, to feel my strap-on cock digging into his crotch as I stroked his cock into full erection, my pliant fingers circling his heavy balls, his thick shaft.

Meanwhile, his hands moulded my body through the leather coat, then crept beneath the coat. He growled with satisfaction when his broad hands contacted my bare arse cheeks. His stubby fingers stroked and pinched and grabbed possessively, kneading the flesh into sensitive expectancy. His arms encircled me, pinning me to him, his barrel chest crushing my flat breasts.

Another couple came in to urinate.

' 'Scuse us, why don't you,' the skinhead said with a smile, looking us up and down.

'Let's go to the cubicle,' my man said, backing off a little, licking his lips. His brown eyes were fired and narrowed with passion, the jaw clenched in horny determination.

I nodded.

He locked the cubicle. We could hear the chatter of the other couple; the tinkle of the urinals beyond the cubicle's graffiti-ridden walls.

I gazed at him for a second, weak with lust, then sank to my knees on the tiled floor.

He swayed and gave a low groan of appreciation as I took his rigid cock into my mouth. I marvelled at the tensile solidity in his phallus. It seemed as broad at the tip as it was at the base. My eager lips inched my way further down the thick shaft, teasing the swollen head, and felt the answering leap of desire. It was a huge succulent cock and I wanted all of it. I was becoming a connoisseur of cocks.

He removed my biker's cap and raked his fingers through my short hair, then his hands gripped my scalp more urgently as he arched further into my soft, willing throat.

'Suck,' he hissed. His eyes closed in pleasure as I obeyed, drugged by the heat of his sweat and lust mingling with his lemongrass cologne. My hands weighed and played with his silken balls, which were stretched tight and high, and nestled with wiry dark hairs. I wrapped the tip of my tongue around his glans and tasted the pearl of salty sweetness which oozed there.

I wanted this to last for ever but my man had other plans. My bare arse had seen to that.

He dragged me upright, then turned me to face the cubicle door, my hands braced halfway down so my arse rode high in the air, the flaps of the leather coat parted to expose my nakedness.

'Exquisite,' he murmured, cupping the arse cheeks between his hands and squeezing them. Then he slapped each cheek with the broad of his hand, making me catch my breath with the shock of it. Each stinging stroke jiggled my secret dildo provocatively, and I circled my hips high in appreciation. I wanted him to hit me harder; to increase the initial jolt of pain which soon subsided into a wave of pure pleasure.

'Say chocolate if you want me to stop,' he murmured, grinning at me with a hint of mischief in his eyes, as I craned to look at him over my shoulder. I nodded, then tensed as another barrage of fierce slaps assaulted my rump. But I did not want him to stop, I wanted more. He was not holding back the way a man would with a woman. Each slap was a measure of his strength; the measure of my choice to let him have mastery.

Then I felt his hands guide my hips further back on to his tongue and groaned as he lapped at my arsehole. Looking over my shoulder, I could see him sitting on the toilet bowl, ploughing his fat wet tongue into my arse crack. Sometimes he licked my red stinging flesh and gnawed at my buttocks with his teeth. Meanwhile my hip gyrations meant the dildo circled and slicked further inside my hot, feverish pussy, and the strap-on dildo grazed against my stiff, sensitive clit.

'I'm huge, boy, as you know. Are you ready and aching for my cock yet?' he whispered as he cupped my arse cheeks and separated them for easier access. He smiled again, surprisingly tender, as he stood up to jab at my vulnerable buttocks with his bestial phallus. I nodded, feverish, wanting him inside me, then watched with awe as he began to slick a ribbed condom over the generous girth of his straining prick.

'Then turn around. I think someone wants to be your gag while I do the deed.'

I obeyed. I noticed there was a hole kicked in the cubicle door, about level with my lowered head, and jutting through it was a glistening, erect prick, covered with a translucent black rubber. It looked like a perverse artwork, set against the vermilion of the painted plywood door.

'Are you two married or can anyone join in?' the owner of the cock called. I recognised the voice of the skinhead.

'Stay and play, by all means,' my man called, forcing my face on to the disembodied cock.

I gobbled eagerly, feeling the opiates of extreme arousal coursing through me, flowing from my tenderised buttocks, my hot, twitching cunt, my leather-encased nipples. The condom tasted of liquorice, a contrast to the musk-salt of the skinhead's balls. The combination reminded me of a good Kentucky bourbon.

All the while I quivered, heart racing and loins slick with juices, waiting for my man to fill my arse with his cock. He was watching the show, making sure I was near my peak before he entered me.

At first the tip of his prick butted gently against my arse, teasing me, so that I began to long desperately for the tender onslaught. Then he parted my cheeks and smeared a cold, moist, spittle-covered finger into my arsehole, probing deeper and wider at every muffled moan I made. I circled my arse on to his digit eagerly, while my lips and tongue anointed the cock in front of me.

Then the huge sickle of his prick eased into me.

A quake of pain and then brain-altering bliss. There was a guilty joy in feeling his hairy balls rasp against my tenderised arse. His prick throbbed and pulsated as he almost immediately ejaculated inside me. My pussy dildo thrust in time with his gentle piston strokes, massaged my eroticised clit, and juddered a visceral flow of orgasm from deep within my abdomen.

It felt like my whole body quivered in shock waves from the spasm, releasing so much blistering sensation that I nearly passed out in a flood of blinding white light.

Sex nirvana.

Meanwhile, I was dimly aware that my man had gripped my shoulder and hip to steady me and had quickened his pace to finally come with a deep, guttural cry of satisfaction. I sucked long and hard at the slick pole in my mouth, feeling it twitch and spurt its load into its liquorice second skin as its owner moaned outside the cubicle door.

When it was over, the liquorice prick disappeared and the skinhead murmured, 'Thanks, boys.' My man remained inside me, feeling the last quiver and shiver of my body impaled around him. Then when he was semi-soft he withdrew, and slipped off the spent rubber.

He turned me around and embraced me, kissing me slowly and stroking the arse he had punished a few moments ago.

'Still hard?' he asked, stroking my crotch. 'Need me to finish you?'

'No, I came. I'm still semi-hard.' I backed away, shy. 'Even though I'm exhausted, you turned me on so much, my body's only gradually winding down.'

It was true. My heart still thudded, my ears surging with blood from my orgasm and the fresh fear of being exposed at this late stage. Hell hath no fury like a cruiser scorned, Jerome had said. Perhaps a cruiser misled would be even worse.

My man grinned, accepting my explanation. He seemed pleased.

'I've got to go now. I came here with someone else. But if you want to meet up again, I'm here most Friday nights.'

'OK.'

He kissed me once more on the cheek and was gone, banging the cubicle door behind him.

Weeks and another successful article later, my arse still flickered in tender memory of that evening. The exact identity of the nightclub remained a mystery, of course, which had increased the article's controversy.

One Friday night I was waiting late at the magazine office for a delivery of books to review. Lisa, the receptionist, fetched me a coffee and we chatted about our summer holidays.

The courier finally arrived, dumping the books on to the reception desk and handing me his chit to sign.

I felt alarm and amazement when he flicked up his crash-helmet visor to smile as I handed him back the note-board.

It was my man.

Of course, I had never returned to the club to meet him again. I may possess bravado but I'm not completely stupid. I had hoped to come across him one dark night on the Heath, though. I was shocked to see him again like this.

A frisson of nerves and renewed lust made me smile back.

'Thanks, love,' he said as he sorted the paperwork and left me a receipt. 'Sorry I was late. There was a gridlock down at Marble Arch.'

'No problem. Have a good weekend.'

'You too.'

He was already halfway out of the revolving doors, visor re-lowered. Of course, he had not recognised me. I was distinctly femme that day, dressed in a cashmere top, hippie skirt and kickers.

'Cute, isn't he?' Lisa said. 'He's new to this route. Only been delivering here the last week or two. I fancied him at first, but he's as gay as they come. I'm afraid you were wasting your time there, Kat.'

'I know.' I smiled in secret satisfaction, still gazing out of the window. Across the busy road he was swinging himself into the saddle of his motorcycle like a rodeo hand, before pulling off in traffic.

Hubris. Sometimes it pays off big-time.

Public Washrooms,
Private Pleasures

Verena Yexley

Public Washrooms, Private Pleasures

❖ ❖

K ate stood casually at the end of the hall leading to
the public washrooms. This was the first of three
they had located in the small mall, and they would get
to the others in due time. She scanned the area for
possible intruders while giving the appearance of waiting for some lingering companion. There was never any
debate about the need for a lookout of sorts – she
wouldn't actually attempt to stop someone else from
going down to use the facilities, she'd just watch the
action if it happened to be a woman. It was always so
much more exciting when a patron did come along after
she or Mike had begun their quest for stimulation. If he
were caught in the women's washroom she would
watch the fallout, or if it became too threatening she
would help him make a hasty retreat. They would
scramble away, becoming the Bonnie and Clyde of
public toilets!

As she waited, a woman came out of the ladies'
facility and walked calmly down the hallway, straightening her skirt and rearranging her bundles. She gave

39

no indication of being disturbed or upset as she walked past Kate, a sign that she had not discovered the man using the ladies' stall to take a leak. Kate knew there were only two stalls inside, meaning Mike had been standing beside this woman while he did his thing. She knew this also meant he'd be just that much more aroused when he came out, setting her own pulse speeding at the thought. If he had found it especially enticing, he might have risked keeping himself exposed while he washed his hands, on the off-chance that he still might be seen. Pushing the envelope like that would mean she had some pretty nasty work ahead of her when it was her turn to relieve herself. Their friendly competition could become quite tricky as they took turns seeing how far they could go, trying to top each other with the level of risk.

Mike sauntered out a few minutes later, looking for all the world like a cat who'd just tasted the pet canary. The smile on his face could only be described as beatific. As Kate walked toward him down the hall, she saw how his eyes shone and the light film of sweat beading his dark upper lip. He was a pretty ordinary-looking man most of the time, only 5' 11", well-tailored sandy brown hair, plain brown eyes and a fairly nondescript body, especially when he was in the business suits he favored when they played their games. But now, only minutes after satisfying his first stirring of need, he looked to Kate like a male model for some advertisement guaranteeing sexual satisfaction with their product. His brown eyes were already being eclipsed by his expanding pupils, giving him an air of danger when coupled with the dusting of dark stubble he never seemed to be completely rid of, even when he shaved twice a day. His body movements were always so much more fluid when he was getting turned on, but at the same time she could see how his chest and neck were expanding, constricting him within his shirt and tie.

He'd be positively explosive by the time they had made a complete circuit of the mall, so much so that he might want to get her naked before they even got home. How she loved this man!

When they were close enough to touch, Mike took her hand and led her farther down the hallway, toward the emergency exit a few yards away from the washroom doors. He positioned Kate against the wall and put one hand flat against it beside her head. Anyone looking at them would assume they were a couple having a serious conversation and would not be able to see Kate's face hidden behind his extended arm. They were having a serious discussion all right, it just wasn't what anyone in their wildest dreams could imagine two such middle-class professional people would be talking about.

Kate knew exactly what Mike needed her to say and she wanted to tighten the bolt holding his desires in check. He leaned his head toward hers and they shared a brief chaste kiss. When he moved his head away, Kate began to describe the woman who had come out of the washroom while Mike had been in there. A middle-aged lady, neatly dressed, with pantyhose and casual pump shoes wearing a longish wool skirt. She'd had on some indistinguishable blouse and a black jacket and was carrying a purse and a few parcels. She knew Mike didn't really want these details, although having to create an image of the woman was important sometimes. He was waiting to hear where this was leading.

'She probably had a really hairy pussy, Mike, don't you think so? An older lady like that, overweight and all, hustling around a mall on Saturday morning, trying to buy satisfaction when what she really needs is something nice and juicy in that hairy pussy of hers.' Kate all but whispered this description into her husband's ear,

41

occasionally letting a little more breath then was absolutely necessary escape her mouth and caress his face.

'If she'd known you were there, honey, she would have wanted to suck on you even while the pee was still streaming out your beautiful dick. You know how women really want that slick hard cock of yours. You know I want it, I want it all the time, especially when I can watch you use it to pee.' Kate was getting just as turned on as Mike from her addition to his adventure. This was her own specialty – being able to make up erotic story details on the spot.

Mike was positively glowing with lust as he looked down at his lovely wife while she told him the story of this anonymous woman who'd squatted beside his stall while he stood with his cock in hand and watched his stream hit the porcelain bowl. That he had been so blessed to find this creature, this soul mate, was a gift for which his gratitude would never be enough. Kate wasn't anybody else's idea of a stunning beauty, but for Mike she all but walked on water. He looked into her blue eyes and didn't see the dull shade someone else would see, he saw the rich deep blue of the ocean, and right now the pulsing black of her broadening pupils gave her an exotic look he loved. Her hair might be fine textured and mousy brown to the average glance of a stranger, but he knew how rich the colors were close up and how silky it felt as it slid over his naked body or tumbled through his fingers. A casual glance would indicate a woman of medium height, slightly overweight but well dressed in a business suit, the skirt tight to her largish hips, the jacket open, revealing an equally large bust straining under the button-up blouse. She looked most like a typically thirtyish Canadian professional woman, overweight and uptight. Mike was pleased by her deceptive looks; it made what they did together so publicly seem even more secretive because the woman he saw doing what she did was not who others saw.

Unless, of course, they caught her in the act. Then men were blessed with the vision of her Mike had every day. If the man were willing to watch and not touch he could be given a sight of pure rapture. Kate would change right before his eyes and become the vixen of sex the man most desired. She was so blatant with herself when caught and being watched, she was every man's dream of the perfect wife: looking straight-laced to any casual observer, but hiding a smoldering slut available only to him.

With these visions of her floating past his mind's eye, Mike ran his free hand across Kate's blouse and motioned for her to take her turn. They had both noticed the man who had just entered the facilities and he wanted Kate to get in before he had a chance to finish a quick evacuation. Before he let her leave, Mike bent his head to hers again and licked her lips with his tongue, leaving a trail of wet across her mouth. The contact streaked through both their bodies, making a straight line for their mutually aroused genitalia.

With a last smile at her adoring partner, Kate plunged onward and pushed open the door to the men's washroom while Mike stood casually against the closest wall outside. He would easily be able to hear if anything untoward was happening and could instantly be at Kate's side if she needed him. In actual fact, however, over all the years they had been developing their unconventional games, no man had ever threatened to censure Kate or call for assistance. When she was caught they always seemed rather eager to accept her story of either a flooded women's facility or a greater need to relieve herself than she could hold while waiting for room in the women's toilet. The eyeful of pussy she gave them was as much to blame for this as the purely erotic image they suspected most men enjoyed while watching an

43

unknown woman pee, most especially if they were handling their own cocks. No, Mike wasn't at all worried. Kate could handle herself just fine and he could always quite legitimately enter and pretend to be an innocent bystander himself, something they did if the facility was very large.

When Kate first pushed open the door, the man they had seen minutes earlier was standing with his back to her, directing his stream into one of two urinals. She watched his flow for a moment, delighting in the heat the sight elicited between her already damp legs. She walked with ease over to the single empty stall to the side of him and was rewarded with an unintelligible noise as he noticed a woman gazing at his arc of urine. With a smile that would put the Mona Lisa to shame, she looked the stranger straight in the eye and innocently explained that the women's was full and she really had to go. The man seemed to want to tuck himself away, but it was clear he was well into midstream and not able to stop the natural course of events his body had begun. With a last blatant glance toward his hands, where she could just make out some pinkness against the blue jeans he was wearing, Kate entered the small open stall.

This was the kind of cubicle she most liked – so small you'd have to be a contortionist to get down to business with any finesse. It would allow her to relieve herself in her most preferred manner, albeit at slightly greater risk, perhaps, but that was the way she liked it. Without bothering to close the door, Kate stood facing the toilet and began hiking her skirt up her thighs. Its length and snug fit meant she had to raise it right up over her bum, displaying her gartered legs and the tiny underpants she wore. Knowing the man had finished his business and was watching her reflection in the mirror in front of the stall, Kate leaned slightly forward to display more of her crevice as she wiggled her panties down her thighs. When they were low enough for her to take her pee, she turned around to the front of the stall. Sure enough, the stranger was barely keeping up the pretense of hand washing and was now just staring at her exposed flesh. She saw his eyes widen as she turned her uncovered pussy toward him and he visibly gulped when he noticed one of her hands was holding the uppermost part of her slit open. He was riveted as she sat down on the cold toilet seat and spread her legs open as far as they would go, limited by her panties pushed only to her thighs.

Kate smiled at the stranger while she put both hands at the top of her mons. She used them now to open her pussy so that she would be able to watch herself pee and hopefully delight the man watching her. It took only a moment of concentration for her flow to be coaxed free and she shivered visibly at the first touch of urine coming from between her thighs. Pulling the lips of her pussy as wide as she could get them within the restricted position she held, Kate looked up at the lucky man who was being given this wonderful gift of hers. Part of her mind was focused on the sensation of fluid running from her while another part was marveling at the rush of pleasure being watched by this stranger was causing. Evidently he too was finding it quite stimulating: Kate could see the evidence of that clearly bulging under his jeans.

When she had pushed the last little drop from her bladder, Kate reached for the toilet paper and carefully tore off five sheets. It was always only five sheets, unless it was the kind of dispenser where you had to rip off tissue on a jagged edge, then she estimated the least amount she would need. Why this mattered she had long since forgotten; it was just another necessary aspect of the game of erotica played out in public washrooms. She watched her hand as it moved between her thighs and reached back to her asshole and wiped slowly forward, rubbing over her clit as it finished the half-circle motion. Using one hand to hold her skirt out of the way, she then stood up and looked over her shoulder at the yellowed water in the bowl. With a small knowing smile touching her lips, Kate looked again at the man who'd just witnessed a story none of his friends were ever likely to believe. With her wares still exposed, she turned around and bent over much more than necessary to reach the handle for the flusher. As her urine swirled away down the mysterious hole, she held one leg of her panties and began tugging them up her large round hips. When her ass was covered by the skimpy material, Kate turned back to the quiet stranger now leaning heavily against the basin. This could sometimes prove to be the most difficult part of her game – convincing the man that the show was over and nothing more was going to come of it. This time, however, there was no problem as Kate brushed out the creases in her skirt and said simply, 'Boy, that feels better.'

The fellow showed a sense of humour as he walked to the door saying over his shoulder to her, 'You're not kidding.' Then he left.

Mike was waiting outside the door when Kate emerged from the men's washroom. He hardly needed to be told she had pushed the envelope way out there – he had seen the look on the man's face when he'd come out moments before. The guy had actually looked to Mike as if he'd wanted to share his secret but instead had shaken his head and with a clearly bemused smile on his face walked down the hall and re-entered the bustling mall. Mike knew his lovely wife had kept the door open. He could always tell: the average guy didn't get that particular look just because an unknown woman was peeing in the men's bathroom with him, unless, of course, the guy shared any one of the fetishes Mike and Kate embraced.

Knowing how raw her nerves would be after such a successful venture, Mike didn't immediately touch her. Instead, he nodded his head toward the opening to the mall and walked silently beside her until they came to the end of the hall. Even then he only took her by the elbow and began to steer her toward the food court, occasionally squeezing her elbow with his hand as he felt the shivers of pleasure her adventure had stirred through her body. She had been pretty hot going in after his first use of the facilities; now, knowing she had been blatant in her exposure and watched by a stranger, Mike figured she'd be ready for an orgasm if he stimulated her even just a little bit. He would, once they were sitting down drinking, but he wouldn't touch her for ages yet. He would get her primed with conversation and the two other sets of washrooms they had to visit.

After they got their drinks, the couple found a relatively secluded set of seats where they couldn't be overheard. When Mike looked closely at his wife he could easily note the evidence of her aroused body. Her face was shining, not with perspiration, but with that glow so often ascribed to pregnant women; she got it when she was horny. Her mouth was swollen, the lips full and almost pouty, her pupils all but obscured the blue of her eyes and the top two buttons holding her blouse closed across her breasts were tipping into the button holes, ready with little effort to pop open and let her swollen breasts have the freedom they seemed to be straining toward. Just looking at her when she was so voluptuous and aroused made Mike's cock give a little jerk in his pants, and knowing what had turned her on so much would have made his knees buckle if he'd been standing. God, he loved this woman!

Kate watched her husband watching her and knew, just as he had with her, what was going on in his mind. He was taking in all the signs of her arousal and feeding his own lusts from it, as was she. They were so perfect together, symbiotically able to find nourishment from each other's peculiar ideas of sexual arousal. There was no limit to the naughty things she would willingly do to turn Mike on. He could demand anything he wanted and she would do it even if it scared her. The public exposure and the inherent risks of getting caught had not been the original intent of their bathroom escapades, but had proven to be extremely juicy additions. They both actually had a fetish for the process involved in the act of peeing and had discovered it was a wicked turn-on just to watch each other in the beginning. Eventually that had grown to include peeing on each other, which was where all this morning's games would lead them once they got home. The possible participation of strangers in the washrooms was only something they could hope for, but never actually counted on, especially with the women. Too few ladies seemed willing to stand and watch Mike pee, and fewer still were ever willing to hold him or lick him while he did it. But, with Kate's ability to create stories for him at will, she could become all those strangers who really wanted to watch and touch but were just too shy to do so.

Getting as lucky as she had earlier with the man watching her in the toilet had pushed a lot of Kate's arousal buttons, but she suspected she was getting ready to get into some more intense experiments. After today's adventures it might be time for her and Mike to visit one of the large shops selling sex toys and look for ways to experiment with pain. She had begun to imagine having nipple chains, possibly linked to a piercing in her pussy, as the unknown men watched her pee. Just thinking about it now was enough to move her to suggest they finish their drinks and go to the next set of washrooms.

Mike wanted to fill himself with more fluids before he took his turn, so it was easy enough to decide that

Kate would go first at their second stop. This was a busier toilet than the other had been, as it was closer to the food court and took the bulk of the patrons. With all the men coming and going at such a steady pace, they decided Mike would go in and confirm the vacancy of the stall. It wasn't too difficult for the men at the urinals to believe that the women's facility was too busy for this ordinary-looking woman as she stepped in to do her thing.

Unfortunately, just as Kate was wondering whether or not she should close the door to the stall, a uniformed security officer from the mall came in. He nodded to the other men standing around and looked a question at Kate. With a brusque 'can't wait', she whisked herself into the small area and maneuvered the door shut.

The bit of anxiety she'd felt at the guard's initial entrance was quickly transformed into added excitement as she imagined him watching the open area at the bottom of the stall door. With experienced hands, she rolled her skirt above her relaxed and somewhat protruding belly, creating a spot for it to stay without necessitating she hold it up. With both hands free, she undid the garters holding up her stockings. She carefully pushed first one then the other now unhooked stocking leg down to bunch at her ankles, knowing the guard would be keeping an eye on the stall. Next she pushed her panties all the way down her legs until they too were bunched at her feet. Once she sat, she spread her feet as far apart as they would go and relaxed her bladder. The pleasure she got from letting her urine slowly drip from her insides and cover her cunt was strictly her own satisfaction. Whether the men in the john with her were excited didn't matter this time; she was more than willing just to enjoy the feel of her warm liquid as she slowly let it escape in small spurts. The image she had created with her underclothes lying disheveled on her shoes might or might not intrigue the guard. It really didn't matter to her.

She let her pee seep from her body slowly while keeping a keen ear for the sounds of the men at the urinals, easily hearing the contact of their liquids hitting the drains in the floor. The combination of her own fluid touching her, and the vision of all the unknown men holding their cocks and letting their pee arc out of them infused Kate with intense animal arousal. She wanted to throw open the stall door and have all the men there look at her beautiful pussy as her light yellow water cascaded out of and over her delicious lips. She imagined the mall guard using his club to push her cunt lips farther apart so all the men could have a good close-up look at her juicy, bright pink pussy. They would come close enough to smell her particular urine smell and smile at the delight of her.

As that last image faded, Kate realized she had been in the stall longer than was perhaps prudent, given the proximity of someone who just might want to take issue with a woman using the men's facilities. At the same time she saw a very familiar pair of expensive men's loafers passing by the bottom of the cubicle. That would be Mike letting her know he was there and perhaps telling her wordlessly it was time to get out. It was always possible that someone who had been the willing or unwilling recipient of their perversions earlier had told authorities and a warning might have been circulated to area malls. Kate didn't really care: no one was going to charge her with anything, and she could always stick to her argument of there being no room in the girls'. Women were another matter, and the partner of a man who did get to see Kate might always lay a complaint without knowing what Mike did in the ladies' room. No matter, she had gotten a lovely buzz from this scenario and was more than ready to let Mike have his turn.

Once outside the room, Mike filled Kate in on events after she had closed the stall door. He had come in moments behind the guard, also concerned that Kate's last conquest just might have complained or told someone from the mall. As it was, the guard appeared only curious at a woman's willingness to enter such a male domain until he saw what Kate was doing with her underwear. Mike watched his wife's breathing increase as he recounted the obvious arousal of the mall guard when he saw Kate lower her stockings to the floor. When her panties had followed, Mike had seen the guy's dick grow under his uniform pants. Not only that, but the fellow had nodded his head at the two other young men in the room and before long Mike had joined them in watching Kate's feet and ankles below the stall door as she squatted to take a pee. Mike suggested that there may have been more going on than even he suspected but without giving their game away he had thought he should not risk finding out just then.

Kate wanted more than anything to go back into the men's toilet and let her husband pee on her. She didn't think she could wait for him to visit two more women's facilities before she got a piece of him. The idea that he had shared her voiding with three other men was enough to make her legs weak. Her panties were thick with her juices and her nipples were desperate to be squeezed, hard. It frustrated her to know she could have had an avid audience if she hadn't been so scared of what the guard might have done if she'd left the cubicle door open. She could almost come on the spot at the thought of Mike sharing her display with these unknown men. As it was she settled for a quick press of her hand against his hard cock as they strolled over to the food area to replenish her empty bladder.

She knew Mike had unloaded himself while watching out for her and realized she didn't want to hold off her own needs for his turn at the game. She told him how much she really wanted to do it again with him in the room, something they didn't often do but were finding a lovely incitement today. Mike didn't mind, knowing he could always crowd himself into the stall with her and release his needs that way. In fact, after the last adventure he was just as happy to watch his wife being watched by other men while he peed in the same public room with her.

During the next twenty minutes Kate consumed two extra large cups of cola then walked around the mall for a time while all that liquid settled lower in her bladder. Arm in arm with Mike she strolled among the mass of harried shoppers, enjoying the secret only she and her husband knew about. She could feel her swollen vagina pulsing under her panties and whenever the crowds were thick enough she would snatch a feel of Mike's engorged penis. She would have loved to be able to walk through the mall with his member sticking out from his pants so she could touch it skin to skin at her leisure. Dismissing the notion as not an option, she contented herself with the occasional caress she could indulge in publicly. As they meandered, Mike was able to point out the two men who had been in the washroom with him and the guard. Both men had watched the couple walk past, and husband and wife realized they would now know Mike had been aware of what his wife had been doing in the cubicle. That too turned them both on to the point where Kate felt she just had to go into the last unvisited site.

This facility was probably the most isolated of the three the mall boasted, farthest away from the shops and food court. No one appeared to be heading toward it or coming from it when they first checked out the men's room. It didn't really matter to either of them not to have an audience. There were lots of things they could do together in this public place that would satisfy their aberrant desires. If someone came along and caught them in the act, they trusted their professional appearance would qualify them as newlyweds who just couldn't wait to get home. They'd found the average person might 'tut tut' but would generally forgive the indiscretion, with occasionally cautioning words about public lewdness laws.

Kate pushed Mike up against the sink and started to rub her body against his. She wanted to feel the friction of his jacket against her nipples and unwrap the hardness beneath his suit pants. She unbuttoned her blouse and pushed his head down to her erect nipple hidden beneath her bra. When he started to suckle her like a baby she felt a gush of wet soak her already damp panties. When he bit into her stimulated nipple her knees buckled and Mike's hand around her ample waist was all that kept her from sinking to the floor. As he bit into her breast, Kate reached a hand down to the front of his pants and squished his firm cock against his own thigh, causing his mouth to open involuntarily as he loosed his hold on her breast and gasped his excitement at her touch.

Kate had reached the point where she knew if she wasn't going to have an unfamiliar audience involved while she urinated in this men's washroom, she would be quite content to do it with Mike there, and then head for home. The things they could do in the car on the way would only make them crazy to get at it in the privacy of their apartment. Pulling gently away from her aroused husband, Kate left her blouse open and headed for the empty enclosure. While she stood within its confines, they both heard the heavy tread of feet coming from the corridor outside. Their eyes lit up as they imagined men approaching and Mike readied himself by one of the urinals to start his game of pretend as the man or men entered.

When she saw the three men who came into the washroom, Kate smiled somewhat smugly to herself. It was really not much of a surprise to see the mall security guard and the two others who had shared her visit earlier at the other set of facilities. Once they had seen her and Mike together afterward walking through the mall, it probably hadn't taken much imagination for them to realize there was something rather naughty going on with this couple. The guard might have had access to remote cameras and already noticed how Kate and her husband kept appearing at all the toilets. Heck, he might even have seen them both entering the 'wrong' facilities throughout the mall. In any case, the three unknown men were all in this toilet now and it looked as if they were quite ready for whatever game Mike and Kate might have in mind.

Kate nodded her head toward the door and the security officer walked over and turned the latch to lock position. While he was busy at that the other two men propped themselves on the sink counter, apparently content to wait for the event to unfold. When the lock had plainly latched, Kate began to take her skirt off. She pulled it down over her feet and stood in front of Mike and their three unknown companions. She folded it neatly and carefully hung it over the wall of the cubicle. Standing partially naked in this men's public washroom was causing Kate's eyes to close, making her appear to swoon as she reached for balance against the stall partition. With her free hand she began to unbutton the rest of her open blouse, keeping her eyes closed as wave after wave of lust and appetite crawled across her wanton body. Knowing she would still get to empty her full bladder in front of all these men later, Kate wallowed in the beguiling removal of her clothes.

Certain of their continued undivided attention, Kate easily dismissed from her mind any thoughts of the men's pleasure. Aspects of her own pleasure would surely come from knowing they watched, these three unknown men and her adoring husband, but what she did, how she touched herself, how she moved, would be done the way she would if alone and solely pleasing herself. She removed her suit jacket and laid it on top of her skirt. Standing now in only panties, garters, stockings and her half-opened blouse, Kate began to unbutton the blouse the rest of the way. When it was completely undone she took it off and put it with the other pieces of clothing hanging over the cubicle wall.

She felt decadent as she stood before the motley group of men, thinking of how naughty she was being taking off her clothes in a men's public washroom. The thought alone was a powerful aphrodisiac, but to be actually doing it, to peek from her closed eyes and see the urinals and the obvious mess of the facilities with her unfamiliar audience was making her desperate for more stimulation. She rubbed her palms across the material of her bra, her nipples sending bolts of desire to her cunt. With the picture of where she was and what she was doing in front of these strangers in her mind's eye, Kate was sure she could make herself come before she even got to the best part. It took more willpower than she thought she possessed to control herself and continue to the end she most desired.

She reached behind her back with one hand and unsnapped her bra, bending her torso slightly forward to take it off and allowing her abundant breasts to spill free. She imagined she could feel the heat of the men as they absorbed the sight of her large and lovely breasts and waited for the uncovering of her delicious pussy. But, before she had a chance to begin removing the few remaining bits of clothing, Kate felt a presence in front of her and could hear the rapid breathing of an unknown man. When cold hands filled themselves with her heavy tits she gasped with the contact and the thought that she didn't know whose hands they were, squeezing and rubbing her erect nipples. She opened her eyes just enough to see the uniform of the mall guard and his head as he bent to suckle the nipples he was pinching with both hands. Over his shoulder she had a brief glimpse of her loving husband and saw his lewd smile as he watched the stranger suckling her breasts. Seeing just how much Mike was getting turned on, it was easy for Kate to encourage more of this fondling from the man in front of her.

Even with the door to the stall left open, it was a tight squeeze for Kate and the guard, but when a second man stepped in to take one of her breasts in his mouth Kate was forced to have the two of them pressed up against her and found she could feel two hard bulges rubbing against her legs. As two unfamiliar men suckled and fondled her tits, Kate reached down between their bodies to grip the cocks hidden beneath their pants. When both her hands were full, shards of white light danced behind her eyelids as she pressed the engorged dicks against the men's own legs. The vision of them using these lovely rods to create the soft yellow arc only men could make caused Kate to gasp for breath and push both men away from her chest.

She opened her eyes to see the shining glow of lust coming from the two men she'd just disengaged from her nipples and the other two standing against the sink looking like little boys waiting for their turn. Motioning for the guard and the other man to move farther away, she ran her hand over her stomach and across the fabric of her panties. She slipped a finger into the side of one elasticized leg and pulled the panties to the side to expose her pubic area. She ran her finger through the manicured pattern of her pussy hair and shivered as she thought ahead to the moment when she could stand completely naked in the toilet stall.

With no particular intent to be seductive now, Kate unstrapped her stockings and quickly pulled them down and off her body. In moments she was standing in nothing but her panties and garter. The air touching her body felt like a million fingertips with tiny flames scorching her flesh with desire. This was exactly what she wanted; this was a dream come true. With her eyes still closed and one hand against the cubicle wall for balance, she turned her back on her rapt audience. When her shins bucked up against the toilet Kate used both her hands to pull off the last obstacle between her and complete public nudity. Standing naked with so many eyes raking across her voluptuous body was driving her to desires even more nasty than the ones she'd known she had. She bent forward over the bowl and ran her hands over her bare buttocks, spreading the cleft open between them. She felt so dirty, for a moment she imagined the men had paid to come sniff her very private parts and almost fell forward at the thought. Opening her eyes while she held her asshole and pussy open to the men, Kate looked into the toilet bowl beneath her and realized she could barely wait to pee in front of them all.

Straightening up fully, she turned to face the observing men. What she saw then thrilled her beyond description. Her adoring husband and his newfound friends were staring at her with their solid cocks in their hands. Four beautiful cocks, different in so many ways, but sharing the same desire to be more active participants in what she was doing. Kate moaned at the sight, relishing the images she created in her mind as she flitted ahead in her imagination to what might come next. She drank in the sight of these ensorceled observers, finding Mike looking somewhat dazed but still managing to convey his pleasure with her behaviour.

When their eyes met he nodded his head at her, silently telling her she should sit down on the toilet. As her bare bottom touched the seat she told herself again what a very dirty girl she was being, finding her thoughts alone enough to almost send her to orgasm. It seemed, however, that Mike had other plans to get her there. He stood in front of her to the side of the stall, not blocking the view of the other men. In a voice thick with lust held barely in check he told her to open her legs, wide. He entered the stall then and kneeled in front of her, reaching toward her very available pussy. Using his thumb he entered the very top of her crack and ran it through her cunt until he found her large opening. Looking up into her face he told her how wet she was as he pushed his thumb into her farther. Speaking still for her ears only, he told her only a slut would be so wet and as her husband he would have to do something very serious about that.

When Mike was standing again he motioned the other men forward around the entrance to the cubicle. Kate was going mad as she watched four grown men surround her with their oh so delicious cocks straining in their hands. With the audience of unknown men looking on, Mike stood directly in front of his wife and began to pee. With obviously experienced hand movements he directed his spray toward Kate's clitoris. She reached down to open herself to him and began a concentrated effort to force her own liquids to flow. The sound of the two streams of urine filled her to bursting, the touch of his fluid on her cunt making her gasp for each breath. She tried to spread her legs and pussy lips wider but they were already too far apart to be comfortable. Not that Kate thought about comfort: she would sit like this for ever to maintain the mind-shattering eroticism of the moment.

The wet assault on her swollen cunt stopped and Kate ground herself on to the wooden seat in a vain effort to stimulate herself. Frustrated by the absence of her husband's urine on her, she looked to him, intent on having him come back and finger-fuck her while she finished emptying her bladder. Instead, she saw him motion the guard to his recently vacated position in front of Kate and indicate the man should emulate him.

Looking every bit a man saturated by carnal thoughts, the guard wasted no time in letting loose his stream of urine. Less accurate than Mike, but in some ways more arousing, his wet arc was hitting her on her belly. Kate arced her hips forward to try to direct the cascading stream down through her pussy.

When another splash hit her, this time on a breast, Kate reached up to hold both breasts out for washing. In her mind she was telling herself she had been a bad girl for letting her cunt get so wet with desire, just like Mike told her. He was having his friends punish her by washing her in their pee. When she felt her knee jostled she realized her eyes had closed again and opened them to fill herself with the image of her public punishment. What she saw was one of the men squeezing into the very small space to the side of her seat and his cock coming to rest on her shoulder. She rubbed her cheek against the intruder and softly told him to pee on her. The man shuddered as he first spurted then streamed out his yellow fluid over her shoulder and down her breast.

Breathing in the smell of the liquid the men were covering her in, Kate knew she couldn't wait any longer. She started panting for them to pee on her, telling them what a bad girl she was and that she must be coated in their wet urine. Stringing together the filthiest thoughts she could come up with, Kate kept up a continuous flow of words, holding herself ready for the final act. Within moments of telling the men to please cover her with their come, Kate felt the shift from light warm liquid to hot thick sperm. She rubbed herself wherever she felt the contact of heavy come on her naked body. With her eyes wide open she watched as the three strangers covered her with their spunk.

She was aware that her mind was completely shattered at the glorious vision she was creating as she felt the ecstasy grip her stomach. She felt the relief building, burning through her womb to her vagina while she watched Mike move the now depleted audience out of his way. Standing as close to her face as space allowed, Mike jerked his hand and loosed his load of semen on to her face and into her mouth as she parted her lips to receive it. The noises coming from her throat escalated as her body was gripped by the satisfying wave of orgasm she had been waiting for. With her legs still wide and her body literally covered head to foot in four men's pee and semen, Kate exploded again and again until she had to calm herself or risk losing consciousness.

When she could unglue her heavy eyelids and open her eyes, Kate was thrilled by what she was seeing. The four men, with cocks still dangling from their pants, had torn the cloth from the hand-drying dispenser. Each of the men held a length of material and were wetting it in the sink. A smile began to play at Kate's lips as she sought to make eye contact with her husband. She made purring sounds deep in her throat as Mike looked at her with adoration in his eyes and told her, 'It's time we washed you, honey.'

Alien Sex Fiends

Dr Ann Magma

Alien Sex Fiends

❖ ❖

*T*he following excerpts are taken from a lecture delivered by Dr Ann Magma to Liberal Elders at the University of Axonite on 15 January 5007. The dissertation followed a ten-year study on propagation sponsored by the Centre of Cytoplasmic Studies. It is thought to be the definitive work on the methods of interplanetary procreation. *These are amended highlights only.* Dr Magma's complete dissertation is available through all branches of L. Ron. Lenin and affiliated orgs.

For the purposes of simplicity I have divided the reproductive cycles of galactic life-forms into the planets of origin.

Mars (animalian)

The discovery of life on Mars is, of course, universally attributed to David Bowie, but the definitive studies of Tharsian psycho-physiology were compiled by Dr Terence Trim and his team in the year 3020. Much is now known about the inhabitants of Mars, and, in particular the details of their galacto-erotic habits.

The Tharsian male can most simply be compared to the wild dog-like carnivores of the family Canidae. The giant Canis Maximus is the largest and wildest member of this group and inhabits the area known as Valles Marineris. The smaller Canis Minimus populate the dark hemisphere to the south. Canis Maximus is a powerful individual with a broad head, robust limbs, large feet, and deep but narrow chest. A northern male may be six foot long with a bushy tail of 50 centimeters and weigh some 170 pounds. The fur on the upper body is thick and soft and usually brown in color. The fur on the underside is lighter.

The Tharsian female, also known as Feminus Pneumaticus, bears no resemblance to her male counterpart. She looks as if she is a different species which, in many ways, she is. Geological research has shown that though he is originally from Mars, she is from Venus.

Feminus Pneumaticus resembles the human woman of pre-nuclear Earth, as we know it, through the study of techno-historical documentation and dated time capsules. She has no fur and is smaller at a weight of 115 pounds. This weight is thought to be optimum for reproduction purposes and, in the event that she gains weight, she will refuse to graze for two or three days.

Her teeth are less pointed than those of the male, her head hair is white or yellow, and her mammary glands are disproportionately large, swelling to an even greater size at the onset of the mating season.

Canis Maximus is an intelligent, social animal that was much admired by Dr Trim and other leading exobiologists. A family unit, or pack, consists of an adult pair and offspring of various ages. There is a clearly defined dominance hierarchy where only the lead male and female (the alpha pair) possess the right to mate. This sets up tension within the ranks of the younger members and the consequent friction usually results in groups splitting away from each other.

A pack's home range, or territory, typically amounts to several hundred square kilometers and is actively defended against neighboring packs. Once installed in a feeding ground the group howls in order to solidify its social structure and confirm territory.

The breeding seasons occur when Mars is in retrograde and Cancer is travelling through the third sector. The only exception to this are the packs living in the interior of the crater Stickney on Phobos where patterns of light and dark are irregular and set up abnormal hormonal rhythms which result in all-the-year-round mating.

The socio-sexual behaviour of Canis Maximus takes the form of forcible rape. The huge hairy male will push the smoother female down on to all fours so that her round pink buttocks are in the air and all the folds of her smooth genitalia are exposed.

The male will place his snout behind her posterior and lick the exterior flaps of her Mons with his long red tongue until her opening is lubricated with his saliva and her buttocks, stimulated by this attention, gyrate in front of his face, stimulating his optical nerves and his endocrine system.

The phallus pumps with blood and reaches a size of at least ten inches long. The tip turns purple and his sacs swell as the female's gyrations become more frenzied. At this point the male will force himself on the female from behind, grabbing her swollen breasts with his claws and hooking himself tightly on to her pelvis to ensure that maximum and deep penetration is achieved.

The nerve endings around the cervix of the female are sensitive and as they are pleasured by the tip of the penis, she groans deeply and then howls loudly. This response is thought to be designed to inform younger males of her activity and thus deflect any attempt to interfere with either the genes of the alpha male or the important gestation process.

The intercourse is rough, violent even, but studies of Feminus Pneumaticus, and in particular, her endocrinology, have revealed that high levels of post-coital endorphins remain in the brain for some time after the male has released her from his grip. A litter is born after 63 days. The young are reared in a den consisting of a natural hole or a burrow.

The appearance of many higher vertebrates changes with the onset of reproductive activity and this phenomenon is particularly pronounced amongst the creatures who live on Mars. The Tharsians have developed an ability to radically alter their behavioral patterns in order to accommodate changes in population or local environment.

This is particularly apparent when the pack has become large, meaning there is less food, or when more than an average number of females have died in childbirth or as a result of other natural causes. In these circumstances the young Tharsian male, on reaching puberty, will undergo a physiological transformation in which his body undergoes a feminisation process. That is, the wolverine creature will bite off his own fur until his body is smooth and he will then begin to dress in the leather apparel favored by the females. The internal organs change as he becomes more ladylike, therefore enabling him/her to become capable of reproduction.

When procreation has been achieved in this mode, the former male does not revert to type, but remains clad in the raiments of the female, becoming more colorful and exhibitionist as he/she grows older. Much attracted to olfactory stimuli (Chanel Number 5 and so on) and storing hordes of expensive shoes, the female/male cross-dressing wolf helps with the raising of any child that is the result of his/her domestic union. He will also indulge in such stereotypical pursuits as crochet, pie making and window shopping while still showing the ability to lead nocturnal hunts.

Jupiter (vegetalian)

The organisms of Jupiter (sometimes known as the tribe of Europa, after the icy moon on which they originated) have evolved in a climate of noxious gases, cyclonic winds and sub-zero temperatures. They are fungal in nature. The simplest breeds, found on Io, live in an area of volcanic eruptions and resemble a sooty mould, while a squamulous lichen has been observed on the so-called Trojan asteroids. The most complex hybrids bear comparison to more specialised structures such as the puffball and stinkhorn.

Propagation is vegetative and most meaningful intercourse occurs when the moist mulch on which most of the organisms live achieves a warm temperature that allows the stems (or body) of an individual to attain a certain stage of growth. Fruiting polyps, engorged with fluids, are capable of producing dust-like spores, but this form of asexual reproduction is only used in the event of an environmental emergency – in particular on the aforementioned Io, where tectonic activity is very severe and the casting of spore settlements is the only means of successful dispersal.

The tribe of Europa, or Jovians, favour sexual reproduction as an important source of genetic variability. The methods are efficient and have allowed the species not only to proliferate all over the planet, but to adapt to the many different environments that exist upon it.

The Jovian growths are of particular interest to the student of biosexology because they possess the ability to produce the most powerful pheromone in the known universe. These chemical stimulants are produced by one partner to elicit a sexual response in another. The odorous substances secreted on Jupiter are so potent that they are said to be able to travel through space and time.

The sensory chemicals produced by the tribes of Europa produce a wide range of neural responses whose effects are not confined to the species from which they originated. The attractants produced by the organs of the Jovian symbionts serve to lure all forms of life towards them. A scented cloud produced by a unicellular conjugation sprouting underneath the infrared aurora can stimulate the nasal linings and gustatory responses of any extra-terrestrial whose receptors come into contact with it. They are responsible for the sophisticated biochemical interactions which cause the sexes to grow towards each other rather than remain in the mutually repelled state that is natural.

In 4028 Dr Dothpax and a team of ethologists conducted a series of experiments from the satellite ship *Ziggy Stardust 111*. Orbiting Jupiter for a period of six months, the team of specialists collected the sterol chemicals found in the attractants sent out by the symbionts of this planet. These studies proved conclusively that, unless carefully contained, the sexual scents of the tribes of Europa can prove to be extremely hazardous. Some may recall the so-called Priapus Incident where a test-tube tipped over in a lab on *Stardust 111*, allowing the collected pheromones of a giant Jovian fungal cluster to release chemical attractants into the atmosphere of the ship. The sensory stimulators wafted into the air ducts and spread all over the craft causing dangerous chaos.

The mass inter-species mating was filmed by surveillance cameras and, although this tape was subsequently of use to serious research, highlights were pirated and edited for the best-selling adult entertainment video, *Space Orgy 2*. The leakage of Tharsian attractants caused a frenzy of satyriasis and nymphomania amongst the crew of the *Stardust* as all members left their stations to engage in sexual activity. This resulted not only in inter-species sex, but also some incestuous activity amongst the swamp things of the lower ranks who fused in familial conjugation.

The Blobs of Beta Persei attached themselves to parent slime-balls and immersed themselves in a shuddering jelly of moist lubrication which eventually spawned a series of space oddities that are still living in the galaxy today.

The footage from *Stardust 111* shows female endoplasms fusing with Venusian zygotes as various Lepidoptera perform oral sex on the stiff white proboscces of Saturnine entities while, all around them, organelles from the Pleiades wind spindly limbs around avian throwbacks.

A Miss Golfar from the planet Earth, deranged by the aforementioned stimuli, jumped into the study tank and engaged in full coitus with a male dolphin, performing a long series of aquatic foreplays from which the dolphin never fully recovered.

Dr Dothpax was the most affected by this spillage. Being a humanoid phenotype he carries the traditional penis and this rose to a great size as all the nerve centres became stimulated. Deranged by sexual excitement, Dr Dothpax (who later informed a court that his groin felt as if it was on fire) pushed various supernubiles on to the floor and indulged in fierce coition with them.

The supernubiles are lissome, womanly creatures from the Andromeda Galaxy. They are known for their physical beauty and Amazonian appearance, being tall, full breasted and wasp waisted. The film shows two supernubiles fiercely sucking on the cock of Dr Dothpax while a third sits on his face and allows his tongue to stimulate her clitoris.

The supernubile has a particularly sensitive and exposed clitoris meaning that she climaxes often. As one of the sisters lowered the smooth lips of her sex organs on to his mouth, two others took turns to slide the opening of their wet genitalia up and down on the tip of Dr Dothpax's erect penis, enjoying multiple climaxes as they did so.

Finally, as Dr Dothpax climaxed for the seventh time, the supernubiles entwined with each other, forcing their hands into the other women's excited openings and stretching their buttocks apart to allow the doctor to commit hard anal sex. This episode only ended after three days when the pheromones in the air had ebbed away and the particles that had entered the entities living on *Stardust 111* had dissolved into the circulation of the blood and were eventually expelled.

The Supreme Court of Canis Major may have merely suspended Dr Dothpax as being the victim of an accident had it not been for the series of hybrids that were the result of this orgy. As it was he was struck from the Register of Outer Planetary Practitioners and prevented from pursuing any form of cosmic medicine.

Inter-species procreation is, by and large, illegal, and the Supreme Judges felt that the doctor should take legal responsibility for the mutoids that were the result of the incident that had occurred on his ship.

Several slime-balls, for instance, were born with legs which were of little use on their home planet as it is composed entirely of water, while the son of a liaison between a Man in Black and a Dalek was born with a torch sticking out of the centre of his forehead and a severe personality disorder.

Saturn (humanoid)

The droids of Saturn are dispossessed isolates with sado-masochistic tendencies. Tall and lean with attractive oriental features, the men are equipped with a uniform nine-inch penis while the women, slim waisted, full bottomed and large breasted, are blessed with unblemished skin, thick black hair, and brown eyes.

The Saturnines are technically advanced in the arena of sexual techniques and the manufacture of auto-erotic equipment. They have combined advanced animatronic engineering with assorted mechanical devices in order to equip themselves with the most sophisticated sexual machinery in the solar system.

The Climacteron is now considered to be a design classic. Manufactured by the company Charon Inc. and exported to planets all over the galaxy, the Climacteron has spawned many imitators but none with the faultless proportions and excellent quality of the original machines produced in the factories on Mimas. An antique Climacteron has been known to fetch as many as eight zillion squids.

The more modern examples (designed by Alimetry Jesus, inventor of a successful range of home-gym equipment) are based on ideas found in the devices on exhibition at the Museum of the Spanish Inquisition. They are already highly rated as valuable collectibles.

The Climacteron is, essentially, a rack made of polished wood and stainless steel and equipped with specialised mechanisms depending on the price and the model. The least expensive Climacto-Junior is also the simplest. It is flat-packed for home reconstruction and consists of a wooden bench, two planks of wood and an iron bar.

The recipient is placed with his or her back on the bench. Legs are spread akimbo and tied on to the planks with chain or rope. The head falls back on to the floor, the breasts thrust up into the air, and the arms may be restrained according to taste.

The effect is to splay the legs upwards (both feet are pointing towards the ceiling) so that the flesh of the inner thighs is pushed apart and the genitalia, fully exposed, provides an easy target for the ministrations

71

of the partner or partners. The subsequent act may involve oral sex whereby the imprisoned submissive can reach whatever portion of the partner that is offered (the slave is usually gagged by the fully erect cock of the master as it is pushed down into the mouth and throat). The master, meanwhile, can gain access to the folds of the labia with his tongue and, by slick licking, causes the gagged mouth to emit muffled shrieks and moans as tears of pain, pleasure and frustration pour down the face.

The Climacteron is effective. The bottom that is bonded to the wooden bench will stay pinned down and unable to move and will be forced to receive any punishment that the Saturnine master chooses to enforce. The flesh of the inner thighs may receive light flagellation, turning the skin into a pink blush, or the harsher measure of rectal insertions and vaginal pump from Charon Inc.'s unique Phallo-Bob, a stainless steel dildo device powered by a Van der Graaf generator.

Climacteron 2 consists of a criss-cross of wooden bars, wheels and pulleys that can be raised and lowered according to the position required. The naked body may be placed face down or face up on the rack, depending on whether the dominant aims to accomplish anal sex or full frontal penetration. In both events ankles and wrists are padlocked to wooden bars and the pelvis is pushed up and out by a leather cushion nailed to the middle of the rack.

A control console with multi-speed dials measures the levels of climax achieved and tests blood pressure. Orgasms may be controlled from this console with a series of wires, one end of which is attached to an electronic device and the other suckered to the inner thighs, buttocks or nipples. The attached pads release a pleasuring vibratory current which ensures maximum stimulation of the erogenous zones.

The Climacteron De-Luxe (Bunny FX) arrives with a

series of luxury accessories. A system of pulleys may be attached to the ceiling or floor allowing a more complex form of bondage whereby the submissive may be bound and trussed in any position required. A rotating wheel, or Flagellator, powered either by an electric motor or by hand, is placed near the exposed buttocks of the submissive and slaps down on the trembling flesh with a series of detachable implements such as hairbrushes and leather paddles, thus delivering harsh punishment to the posterior of the bound supplicant with the least effort on the part of the dominant.

The Climacteron then offers a full range of deviant devices for any Saturnine pleasure seeker. The bound body of the submissive, trussed with leather belts, or rope, often masked, always naked, may receive a soft stimulating whipping from a calf-skin cat-o'-nine tails. A more severe cropping may be administered with bamboo, that causes purple lines to streak the exposed areas and stain the flesh for some time afterwards.

The submissive man or woman may then be anally humiliated with any number of phalli that arrive with all models. There is also a wide choice of other accessories such as nappies, schoolgirl panties, rubber bras, rubber sheath dresses, tattooing needles, wire and more than 40 thicknesses of rope.

The most popular accessory, though, is the thigh-high patent leather unaboot which has two feet and two high stiletto heels but is joined together as a hollow tube at the calf so that the slave puts both legs into one boot. This ensures complete submission and total servitude as she will not be able to move unless lifted by the master or transported on the special trolley provided with the equipment.

The habits of the Saturnine humanoids present a basic conundrum to the student of eroto-galactic misbehavioral patterns. They are advanced sexually but they do not breed. Saturnine women are all infertile. There is no offspring. The mother is not part of the culture. The population, as a result, is dying out.

The socio-sexologist must conclude that, on Saturn, at least, recreational perversions are part of the natural mode of life and are unrelated to the primordial instincts of genetic replication.

Pluto (robotic)

Robot sex, or Borg Amalgamation, as it is more correctly known, tends to be an efficient mechanistic coupling where two thoracic carburettors are fused together with jump leads. This leads to the exchange of motor oils and a mutual recognition of integrated circuits.

Technicians from Achondrite and Co. have endowed the robotoids of Pluto with a sophisticated technological status that sets them apart from other mechanised systems in the universe. Most galactic citizens are familiar with Pluto through digital advertising. The original autotypes, sold as household aids and domestic appliances, were top-range vacuum cleaners, electric cocktail shakers and microwave units.

In 4010 the Plutonians abandoned the crude systems of piston cylinders and valves that characterised their primary genesis. Now built with enlarged cortexes, flexi digits and optical apparati, they are more advanced than any other mono-automation or mechanised polymer composite.

Achondrite and Co., run by the solid-phase philanthropist Dr Zed, are known primarily for their work with advanced sensory technology and proto-prosthetics. Achondrite and Co. developed what became known as the Perfect Penis, a best-selling product that enabled the company to go public to the tune of a billion billion squids.

The Perfect Penis, or the Space Stick, was developed at the Achondrite Lab on the Kuiper Belt. The specifics took several years to perfect as the neurology required by the pump device was complex. Finally they emerged with an organ of synthetic polychrose whose nerve endings could be connected, with wires, to the nervous system of the host. Thus tied to cortical and spinal centres, the polychrose phallus rose at the command of the thought processes.

The Perfect Penis could be as large or as small as the controlling mind required, swelling, as it were, to individual specifications. Its tip was covered with electronic micro-sensors that returned data to the central brain and informed it of the length and width of the cervix. This allowed the member to automatically alter to the size required of maximum penetration and progressive physiological satisfaction.

Achondrite technicians turned their attentions to the robotoids of Pluto some 50 years ago. Having rebuilt and developed the main organisms, they supplied both sexes with a bimetallic strip which was welded to artificial erogenous zones between the metaloid limbs and linked by sensory circuits to the logic functions and bubble memory.

The bimetallic strip, or system actuator, is activated by a rise in temperature. When the local environment achieves the required degree, the bimetallic strip, a tiny tongue concealed by the metal casing between the limbs of the main automation, grows red and swells. This triggers a thermostat and a heater warms the automation, giving it the energy required to achieve synthesis.

The consequent links to the sensory mechanisms of another robotoid results in a surge of electricity to the 'brain' patterns of the helmet where there is a rise of pseudo-neuron activity. The main body closes down, the vents open, and there is the automatic discharge of ejectile lubricants.

Three hours or so later the inner software of both

automatons, having reprogrammed themselves to post-natal planning, utilise the functioning motor and cranial facilities to build a new organism which combines the most efficient operational systems from both bodies. The baby robotoid cannot fail to be an improvement on both its parental facilities and an artificial evolutionary process has been implemented.

Pluto (Reptoid)

The seventh planet is worth mentioning as hosting the successful asexual-symbiotic relationship between the giant godzillas of Epsilon and the pioneers of Japan. Acclaimed cryptozoologists such as Itchynosey, Waga-mama and Yamomoto collected data on the giant liz-ards and then fed them with formula health foods which boosted their development. These polymorphous reptoids are now sophisticated beings with huge neu-rotransmitting capacities.

Artificially boosted brain cells enable them to negoti-ate their own foreign rights in licensing contracts. Mech-agodzilla and Titanozilla are two of the richest beings in the cosmos and, as a result, are allowed to live above the usual interplanetary laws. They enjoy sexual rela-tions with whomever and whatever they please and, recently, the unusual penetration of a spider-geisha from Panang won a coveted place in the Inter-Galactic Kama Sutra (reference pp 526 and accompanying col-ored plates).

The researcher will note that the spider-geisha has chosen to spread her eight legs and sit astride the zilla in order to receive its hard and horny phallus as she propels herself up and down its long shaft.

The Moon (humanoid)

After *Star Wars* (Episode 3) resulted in the final annihilation of Earth, the Moon was colonised by a capsule of escapees whose random demographic gives this population its current characteristics. There are now five men to every one woman living on the Moon and this gives new meaning to the phrase Big Bang.

The sexual tension and violence that was the result of this imbalance came under the auspices of several governmental edicts to ensure that the minority females did not commit themselves to any one man. They are legally bound to see a different man every night and have learned advanced Tao-based love-making techniques to please all types and age groups.

Monogamy was made illegal and Valentine's Day is still a public holiday, although romance, as it was transmitted in the history of the human race, is banned completely as being both time-wasting and obsolete. There is a thriving black market in foil-wrapped chocolates and the poetry of Coleridge exists as an outlawed sub-culture, but this is inevitable in a species with a history of personal freedom within the liberal arts.

Campaigns were conducted to persuade females from other event horizons to migrate to the Moon and aid the balancing of the demographic. The campaign ('Come to Heathcliff Country') succeeded admirably, promoted as it was by the sexually magnetic cyber warrior Jonathan Creek. These advertisements were only abandoned when word went out on the digital nodes that the women of Letronne and Gassendi were dying of sexual exhaustion. There are now 20,000 or so humanoids living on the Moon, mostly inhabiting the areas of De La Rue and Mare Nubium. The women, or Queens, are righteously pampered from the time they are born; worshipped throughout their lives they are still regarded with awe when they are in their 70s and 80s.

There is no culture of youth on these lunar cities. All femmes are seen as love machines and admired for who they are not what they look like. Their relative rarity provides them with spectacular attributes that might be less admired if numbers were greater. It is common for even very senior women to enjoy rigorous sexual intercourse to the end of their dying days and, in specially permitted cases, to become surrogate mothers.

There is little pressure on women to succumb to any of the painful or dangerous beautifying techniques normally abundant in humanoid populations. They dictate the culture of aesthetics by their rare presences and do not have to conform to any norms promoted by the traditional commercial concerns.

They do as they wish, wear what they like, and are still noticed and admired. Huge breasts are as good as deflated teats; blonde hair is seen in as many photographs as a bald pate adorned with tattoos. Legs can be any shape or width; there is no ostracisation of cellulose and puppy fat. No-one is on a diet.

Promiscuity, however, is demanded as a municipal protocol rather than a personal choice. This means that the private parts of the women living in lunar areas are largely regarded as public possessions. They must expect to have serious sexual intercourse about five times a day. They will do it any time and anywhere, surrendering to the basic animal demands of the local male population. Sex is promiscuous and casual, skirts are lifted in public bars as a man will pull down the panties, place his face in her groin, and lick her to shuddering arousal before banging her vigorously in front of the watching crowd.

In the same way women are casually bent over tables in office buildings or cafeterias, their dresses pulled up to expose fleshy buttocks, and taken dog-style from the back by any casual passer-by who feels like a good fuck.

Sex is allowed on the sides of the public highways, in cinemas, in car parks, in country lanes, in alleyways, in museums and art galleries, and in DIY stores on Sundays. Thus it is a common sight to see pleasured coupling and maximum penetration in all places at any times of the day, quite often between men and women who do not know each other but have submitted to the brief passion of intercourse.

A woman will lie down in the middle of the road, or on the back of any bus, spread her legs, and receive any number of men into her vaginal and anal openings. She will shriek with ecstasy as orgasm after orgasm is the consequence of her lucky position, to be fucked at any time by any man whenever anyone feels like it.

Full coitus is a common sight. As young humanoids would once indulge in french kissing in public places, the phrase and act is now known as french fucking. It is done anywhere at any time and in any way.

(Editor's Note: Dr Magma read protean psychoid phenomena at the Orthon Institute before choosing to specialise in interdimensional sexual techniques. She sporadically combines with a plasma vortex from Io and is the progenitor of two foo fighters, Alexis, 2, and Spokane, 67.)

The Shape of Venus

Fransiska Sherwood

The Shape of Venus

❖ ❖

Sherry stood by the window, looking out at the brown earth in the garden. The ground was frozen; there was no point going out and trying to do anything. She picked up the little effigy Nathan had made for her. She'd kept it, all the years, in fond memory of the shy fifteen-year-old who'd come to her to learn how to pot. He'd given it to her when he left for art college, had come over specially. She hadn't known what to think at the time; had been thrilled and bewildered and perhaps even a little insulted.

The figure resembled the fertility goddesses of Stone Age finds: the Venus of Willendorf and the like. Portrayals of the Earth Mother (or was this perhaps supposed to be the Michelin man?) Thunderous breasts, a great sagging stomach, thighs like two tree trunks. Is that how he saw her?

Perhaps now. But in those days she'd still been in her twenties – amply curvaceous, but not grossly overweight. The kind of body Rubens would have delighted in – bouncing, buxom, baroque. Sadly, the look hadn't been fashionable in the early 1990s. Now, in her thirties, her female attributes had become somewhat plumper –

and they still weren't fashionable. But nevertheless that seemed to be what he liked.

She shivered from the frost coming off the window-pane and the delicious thrill the memory of his visit gave her. It had been so unexpected, unreal – yet somehow the logical conclusion to everything that had gone before.

When he knocked at the door she'd been sticking handles on mugs. A whole series in sets of six. They sold well. If people didn't have the money for bowls and vases, great terracotta planters, or her more bizarre creations, they usually went away with a set of mugs. Blue polka dots on white glaze seemed to be particularly popular – she didn't know why. They did so well she could almost go into mass production. But that defeated the object.

She'd gone to the door with clay caked round her fingernails, her fingers sticky with slips, the palms of her hands dry and cracking and powder-grey. She hadn't recognised him, not even when he'd grinned and said, 'Hello, Sherry, remember me?'

Oh yes, the voice had been familiar, but it just didn't tally with the data she had stored in her brain. Surely she didn't know anyone like this? A young man in his early twenties, a cocky smile on his face, and so embarrassingly good-looking she hardly dared look him in the eye. But those eyes certainly were familiar: blue-grey, the colour of fired clay. And the way the brown tufty curls fell over his forehead, now slicked with gel and the sides razor-short. The ear-ring was new too.

'Nat?' she asked, hardly able to believe who was standing before her.

'Yeah,' he laughed. '*You* haven't changed a bit.'

'Oh, go on!' she said and planted an exuberant kiss on his cheek in welcome.

He smelled unfamiliarly masculine; used an after-shave she'd never smelled on him before. Something sporty, fresh. Her lips lightly detected the bristles of a beard hardly apparent the last time she saw him. He was taller, stronger, altogether different, and yet the same person.

'My, you've grown,' she exclaimed, immediately feeling foolish for talking to him like a child. But in those days he'd almost still been a child and she'd always been careful to treat him as such. Careful because she was attracted by his boyish charm – all the more dangerous because she suspected in his quiet way he fancied her. Even then his face had held the promise of what was to come. And, boy, had he blossomed!

Automatically they went into the pottery, Sherry's heart aflutter in the anticipation of showing him round and the things she was making. Nat glanced at the trestle tables lined up with dark grey mugs ready for firing.

'Mugs,' said Sherry.

'Aha, that's what they are,' said Nat, pretending to be enlightened, and he flashed her a wide grin. She'd never noticed what even, white teeth he had. Had she ever seen him smile like that?

His new self-assuredness made Sherry blush. There she was blabbering rubbish, just because she was excited at having a visitor, and he was full of confidence and in control. He must think her a bit of a fool.

But he was no ordinary visitor. His face awakened memories from the past, and hopes for the future. She couldn't get over the way he'd changed, how he'd grown up, in just five or six years. Had it really been that long?

A tinge of jealousy flashed through her because she'd not seen it happen and there might have been other women who had. She yearned to know what he'd been doing, and with whom; what had engendered such a metamorphosis.

He'd been such a shy, withdrawn boy, even up to

being nearly eighteen; had hardly ever said a thing unless he'd had a question about pottery. That day he brought the figurine he'd been so awkward and tongue-tied. And now he was as bold as brass, and she was the one feeling awkward with nothing sensible to say.

'So tell me what you've been up to all this time.' She tried to sound casual. 'Surely you've not moved back to town?'

'No,' said Nat. 'I just wanted to drop in and see you again before I go to America – to say thank you.'

'America?' she asked, panic-stricken at the thought of losing him again so soon.

'I've been awarded a grant for a year in Boston.'

'Boston?' squeaked Sherry. She realised he probably expected her to be pleased, was waiting for her to congratulate him, but the words just wouldn't come out. She felt her throat had been taken in a stranglehold.

'Yeah, I know it's not exactly the centre of the artistic universe, but I've got the chance to work on a project with some up-and-coming American ceramic artists,' he replied, saying more than she'd ever heard him utter in the three years he'd come to her for lessons.

'Marvellous!' said Sherry, her attempt at pleasure hideously unconvincing.

'Yeah,' he said, without sounding enthusiastic.

She desperately wished she could think of something to say now to save the situation, before it disintegrated into embarrassment and he said 'nice seeing you again' and made to leave, probably regretting he'd ever come.

But it was Nat who broke the silence. 'So what have you been doing, apart from making mugs?'

'Me? Oh, nothing exciting.'

'Do you still take on pupils?'

'No, you were my one and only.'

Nat blushed, now reminding her more and more of the boy she'd known.

'You didn't marry?' he suddenly asked.

Sherry laughed breezily, concealing her embarrassment. 'Never found one I liked, I suppose. Always had my nose stuck to the wheel and streaks of clay across my forehead.' She'd a way of trying to talk herself out of uneasy corners, seldom though it worked. 'No use crying over spilt milk – oh, you know what I mean! What wasn't to be, wasn't to be,' she sang with feigned merriment. 'No one was ever interested.'

'I was,' said Nat, coming unnervingly close. He was looking at her intently, his grey eyes reaching into hers. 'You can't say you never noticed.'

No, she couldn't. But what good had it ever done her? She wanted him then just as desperately as she wanted him now, but all those years ago she'd kept a tight rein on her desires out of some vague scruple about the ten-year age difference, and this time round she didn't think she could still be in the running. He was far too attractive to be interested in her, probably had girls queuing to go out with him.

Nat blew a wisp of hair out of her face, his breath tickling her forehead and sending a ripple of goose pimples through her body. His breath held the faint scent of a good meal – wine and garlic, over-laced with the peppermint freshness of chewing-gum.

When he'd first known her, she remembered, she'd had a mane of coppery curls so long it reached down to her bottom. If she tipped back her head, she could sit on the ends of it. She wore her hair much shorter now, but the curls were still lusciously thick and the henna she used had given them a radiance like burnished gold.

She closed her eyes, breathed in the smell of him, tried to drink her fill of the sporty aftershave and the musky fragrance of his skin, commit its perfume to memory before, inevitably, he left her again. She could only guess how near to each other they were now standing from the warmth emitted by his body – like the glow from the kiln on the outside, when inside it was afire with molten heat.

Then she felt how one hand reached through her thick curls and tilted her head so that he could reach her lips with his mouth. He kissed her with a fervour she'd never experienced before, or all those years ago would have dreamed this boy capable of. But a boy he was no more. He'd crossed that borderline long ago. Time now for Sherry, too, to let go of the memories and live for the present.

'I always wanted to do that,' Nat said. 'You're not angry, are you?'

'No,' she said. 'I always wanted you to.'

A slow smile crept across his face. He was probably divining what else she'd secretly wanted him to do.

She felt the heat inside her rising, her heartbeat quickening, her flesh trembling. Never before had he looked her in the eyes for so long and she almost couldn't return his gaze, so intense was the feeling those smoke-coloured irises generated in her.

'The girls at college were all so thin,' he said. 'There was no one with a body anywhere near like yours. No one who could really give me what for years I'd craved for.' And he slipped a hand inside the shirt she wore when potting and gave her breast a little squeeze. Sherry let out a gasp of surprise – at it happening at all and the unexpected pleasure it gave her. 'I like to have something I can get hold of,' he said.

Her head was reeling, and her usually sturdy legs had turned to jelly. Something like a giant fireball was rolling up through her stomach, rapidly gaining momentum, until it broke loose and she felt herself come out in a sweat.

She whisked off the clay-streaked shirt and Nathan, visibly hotting up, took off the long black coat in which his body had been concealed and draped it over the back of a chair. Underneath he was wearing black and grey – designer chic. So was this the art-college garb these days? Gone the floppy jumpers, jeans and scarves? Dressed like this, he looked infinitely sexier, that was for sure. So well groomed, in fact, she was afraid to ruffle his hair.

Beneath his black V-neck sweater she could see a black T-shirt of some shimmering modern fibre. His trousers were of a grey, slightly stretchy material that clasped his strong thighs, clearly defining their outline and the sleek muscles. The trouser fronts were smooth and close-fitting, revealing the neatness of his hips, his well-hung crotch. Tiny pockets slit into the waistband, too small and tight to hold anything but a credit card. The legs were overlong and hung down at his heels over black boots. Even clothed, Sherry could tell he had a well-proportioned, athletic figure.

Then she realised the scrambling about her waist she'd at first hardly noticed was his hand as he tried to come up under her smock. She looked down at the pale material caked in powdering flakes of clay to see what he was doing. But already he was plucking at the buttons of her blouse, and then his hand slid inside her bra and she felt the hot sting of his palm on her flesh. It clasped the nipple like a snugly fitting cap, squeezed and then pushed against the rounded form as if testing its resistance. All of this with a speed and urgency she could barely keep pace with.

She let out a little cry, almost breathless. Nat brushed his lips over hers. His face was contorted with immediate desire, as if he had to do this now or the moment would be gone.

A place deep within her stomach contracted as he squeezed and a strange little spasm shot through the neck of her womb. She felt as though her breasts were connected to her sex, and everything he did to them he did to the trembling ring of muscle that was now pulsating with such longing.

He began to whisper urgent, inaudible things in her ear, but she was no longer comprehending, only surrendering to the kind of love she'd always yearned for but never found, and at this point in her life had no longer expected to find.

As if time had suddenly become a scarce commodity, the smock was lifted over her head and the remaining buttons were popped undone to reveal the expanse of her midriff and the excitingly large cups of her lacy, double-D bra. Nat's nostrils flared as he caught sight of the padded fabric and what it contained. For a second or two he checked his haste, then the tails of her blouse were snatched out of the trouser waistband into which they'd been so neatly tucked, and he slipped the blouse off the smooth fleshy orbs of her shoulders.

Fervently Nat began to plant kisses on the soft peachy skin until she seemed to melt in a fury of kisses and caresses. Her head was strangely light, her pulse racing, and then her legs folded under her and Sherry dragged Nat down to the ground with her, underneath the trestle with all the mugs.

'OK?' asked Nat, laughing and concerned at the same time.

'Yes, yes,' she breathed. Just don't stop, she thought, pulling him closer to her. His foot caught one of the legs of the trestle and the structure jarred shakily for a moment. He looked up, all set to steady the table if necessary. She clasped his head, bringing it back down to her. 'Don't bother about the mugs,' she said. Her words were urgent and compulsive, and soon they were lost in the depths of a kiss that obliterated everything around them.

Then she felt his strong arms lift her so that he could slip a hand beneath her back and pinch open the hooks to her bra. His fingers teased the straps from her shoulders and he pulled the lacy padding away from her body by the little bow positioned at the centre. A sweep of his hand and it fell to the floor.

Now she lay before him revealed in all her glory and he seemed to delight in the sight. The smouldering glimmer in his eyes had become a bright glow of desire; his breathing was getting heavier and his nostrils flared as if at full canter.

'I used to sit at the wheel hardly able to breathe when you sat next to me and put your hands over mine. I thought my heart would burst with the pumping. I was sure you must be able to hear it. And when your breasts pressed against my arm I thought I'd die from wanting to touch them.'

He bent his head and his lips closed round the large reddish teat and he began to suck. His sucking produced the strongest pull on her womb she'd ever experienced. It seemed to draw up and swell inside her with every tug from his mouth. A feeling that went right through her and throbbed into her cervix. She didn't think she could bear much more of it.

And then Nat sat back on his heels and ducked out from under the trestle. Immediately he stood up she saw his erection straining at the grey material of his cargo pants. He slipped off the black ribbed sweater, revealing the shimmering black T-shirt that clung to him like a second skin with an iridescent sheen.

He'd been working out: his biceps were well developed, his pectoral muscles steely hard. His shoulders were wide, his torso tapering off to his narrow hips.

He pulled off the T-shirt and Sherry gasped at the silky threads of brown hair that covered his chest. How would it feel to have them brush against her breasts? She could barely wait for him to return to her level and feel their bristly caress tickling her skin.

Then he unzipped his trousers, prising himself out of their unrelenting grip. Beneath he wore snow-white briefs with the name Calvin Klein woven into the elasticated waistband. Proud and defiant, his penis stretched the ribbed material that hugged him so closely. Now Sherry knew she was to be denied nothing. They were heading for the home straight.

Sherry now unzipped her own trousers and was trying to wriggle out of them. Nat bent down and pulled them from her legs. Her thighs had power; her hips were broad and strong. For what seemed like ages, Nat lingered over the mound of her stomach, gently stroking over its generous proportions. As much as she enjoyed it, she ached for something more.

Then his hand travelled down over the soft cotton material of her panties and came to rest on the bump of springy curls adorning Venus's mount. Clearly sensing Sherry's consent and eager anticipation, Nat gently stroked over the material until he found the place that made her sharply take in her breath when he touched it – the bud of her clitoris, seat of her pleasure. With circular motions he began to caress it through the already damp material.

The spasms that had gently pulsated through her now shot through her cervix with ever greater intensity. The muscles contracted, her womb seemed to be caught in a cramp and she knew that surely any moment now she must come. And then, like the breaking of a dam, a flood-like ripple washed through her.

She threw back her arms with a low moan of pleasure, knocking over the bucket of slips that stood by the trestle table. The cool grey mixture spilled over the floor, already seeping into her hair and wetting her shoulders before she could gather her wits enough to move.

Frantically she tried to scoop it back into the bucket, but the pool had spread all about her. Nat, splashed as the bucket went down, instead of helping, was plastering streaks across his chest like a Pictish chieftain painting himself with woad before entering the foray. He appeared to like the feel of it on his skin, its clammy caress cooling its sweat-streaked surface. But rather than dampening his ardour, the chilly poultice only seemed to heighten the fever burning inside him. Dipping his hands in the liquid clay still covering the floor, he began to smear his body with the grey paste.

As Nat was obviously enjoying himself so much, Sherry decided to test its texture herself, and wiped her wet hands the length of her arms. She laughed at the coolness of it, its heavy embrace. Little rivulets were now trickling out of her hair and running down her back. She arched her spine, and her laughter tinkled as the slow streams of clay tickled her skin. She dipped her hands in the pool lapping her thigh and with visible pleasure coated both nipples with slips, slowly stroking over them in circles with her palms. The immediate coldness and gentle stimulation made the points harden and soon her breasts began to swell beneath the motion of her hands and the friction soon generated as the clay became sticky. It was a pleasure akin to Nat's sucking at the teats, and again she felt the plucking spasms deep inside her.

Nat watched transfixed as she stimulated her own breasts. It seemed to excite and arouse him, and manically encouraged he began to scoop up clay in handfuls and smother her breasts in the mud-like paste. Sherry didn't protest – his cool moist fingers slipping about on her skin sent a delicious tingle right through her. These were very particular sensations they were now enjoying. There was nothing either liked better than playing about with clay and plastering each other's body was just taking their favourite activity to its zenith. Before long the pair of them were grey all over except for their clay-streaked underpants.

It wasn't long until the heat from their bodies began to dry the veneer of clay. Sherry felt her skin tighten as it did so. She imagined that must be what it felt like to be shrink-dried, an extraordinary slimming and toning process, faster than any wonder-diet, and one that left the skin supple and taut. As it dried out, the surface started to crackle, looking like raku glaze. But there was no need to heat her up to 1000°C; she was already red-hot, near molten with desire.

Nat, too, had had enough of games. Sherry could see his cock, now fully erect, straining to free itself of the cloth of his underpants. She kneeled beside him and eased the material over his penis, careful not to disturb its rigidness. She wondered at his dimpled buttocks, the narrowness of his hips, and couldn't resist grasping the firm, rounded flesh with her crackling hands. Short stubby bristles tickled her fingertips as she stroked over the skin at his anus.

Urgently Nat slipped her out of her panties, so that now both were naked, painted powder-grey like some primeval tribespeople, a band of pink flesh highlighting their genitals, the sacred area of worship.

Nat clasped her clay-parched hands and lowered himself on to her. His cock slid easily into the moist cavity of her sex and Sherry knew her pent-up longing was about to be fulfilled.

Slowly at first, Nat rocked over the mound of her stomach, dipping inside and sliding back out of her like a well-oiled piston just picking up steam. Gently to start with, the shaft of his penis rubbed against her inner walls, stimulating them to produce yet more lubrication, exciting them to contract and pulsate. Sherry felt how the muscles of her cervix tried to grip his cock and hold him within her for evermore, but he was deliciously slippery and kept easing out of her grasp – a feeling that reminded her of pulling clay to form a handle. And the stronger she held on to him, the faster the motion of his hips became, as if standstill might really cement him inside her. Soon their powder-dry skin became streaked with sweat as Nat heaved and thrust, and the increasing stickiness seemed to glue them together on the outside instead.

The faster the motion, the greater the friction, and the spasms, which before the mud-bath had shot through her cervix and caused a flood of pleasure to wash over her, now recommenced with even greater vehemence. All she'd felt before was a pale reflection of the pulsating contractions that now shook her body. The throbbing in her womb was so strong it almost hurt. It reminded her of the cramps she suffered during her monthly discomfort, but this was a spasm so eclectic it held her halfway between pleasure and pain. It seemed to hold her in its grip. All the muscles in her cervix tensed, until, as if a clenched hand around her womb had suddenly let go, it granted her her freedom, bringing release in a spate of rippling waves that broke over her one after the other.

The climax of their love-making was everything Sherry had ever dreamed it would be. It completely filled her consciousness, transported her to another sphere. She felt as if her head were swimming off in a completely different direction to her body. And the presence of her body, as big as it was, had never before seemed to be of such magnitude.

And as she came, Nat gave a moan, his hips momentarily suspended as he ejaculated. They climaxed together, Sherry's body awash with waves of pleasure. It was a feeling she hoped would never end.

As Nat withdrew from her there were one or two last tantalising echoes before it at last subsided, an ebbing away of the tides that had flooded over her. Carefully Nat extricated himself, unlocking their fingers and genitals from each other's hold. Sherry's fingers were ablaze from the warmth of his hands. Her skin was on fire.

As their heartbeats slowly returned to normal they lay in the slippery pool for several minutes looking up at the underneath side of the trestle, trying to comprehend the enormity of what had happened. When lying on the studio floor started to become chilly, they went upstairs to shower.

The first drops of water splashed down on to the flaky surface of their skin like rain in the desert after a drought. The shrinking grey embrace turned into a river of mud-coloured water, a lightening flood after the sudden deluge. Sherry revelled in the heavy downpour that pattered on her skin like the drumming of hundreds of fingertips, and the cleansing and rejuvenating powers it held.

Squeezed into the cubicle together, warm water running over them from above, the heat soon started to radiate through their bodies again, and Sherry felt her skin begin to tingle with her rising temperature and upsurging desire. Nat's wet body had an unusual, velvety texture to it, like chamois leather, and Sherry couldn't help wanting to kiss him all over and run her tongue over his skin. Her lips soon found his and, enveloped in steam, they became oblivious to anything else but themselves and each other.

After the last of their fervent kisses, they washed the remaining clay off each other's body, lingering over every secret place, venerating every curve and mound, every muscle and sinew. When at length she was completely clean again, Nat rubbed Sherry dry with a towel. Her skin now had a peachy glow to it, silky soft for having been coated in clay.

'When do you leave for America?' asked Sherry.

'Tonight,' Nat replied, despondency in his voice. 'Will you still be here when I get back?'

'I'll still be here – *if* you come back,' she replied. She had no illusions. She knew how big some of those American girls were. But she had her hopes. What they had experienced was something very special, grounded in a mutual past that no one else shared.

And now, a few days later, Sherry stood looking at

the plump little figurine, thinking that no matter how fashions came and went, deep down the primordial instinct was always there. Those Stone Age craftsmen knew very well the shape of Venus.

I Like Boys

Marilyn Jaye Lewis

I Like Boys

❖ ❖

I like boys who are decidedly youthful-looking, who don't have a lot of body hair. Preferably, boys who maybe just dropped out of college. Boys who wish they knew a lot but who know they haven't got a clue yet; and who, regardless of the variety of their sexual experiences, still feel overwhelmed by me because they know I'm so much older.

I like boys who consider themselves to be straight but who, after spending a long time talking with me in my bed in the dark, eventually admit that they might be bi – that sometimes they've even wondered if they're actually gay.

I love to hear the stories that a boy has never told another living soul: the ones about the stretch of backyard that extended beyond the trees back home, where he may have gone with a friend, a buddy, an overly attentive pal; the stretch of yard that was hidden from the world, the place where he'd finally acquiesced, where he'd let his pal sink down to his knees in the grass, get between his legs, and suck his dick. The story usually involves the boy's surprise over getting so hard so fast, and the emotional mixture of desire and loathing he'd felt as he'd watched his dick growing stiffer, thicker, as it moved in and out of his buddy's mouth. Usually there's a part about the pal being too eager – a thing that unnerves the boy still, even in the retelling of the secret tale. An eagerness that compelled him to grab on to his pal's head and pump into his mouth hard, even though he didn't think he'd wanted to do it, until the jizz shot out hot and with such uncontrollable force that the pal had to hold tight to the boy's thighs to keep his balance while the jism went down his throat.

You can't beat hearing a story like that – it's a sign that a boy trusts you.

I like it when a boy trusts me. It means we're likely to go places together. I don't mean to cafes or bars or nightclubs; I'm talking about those less tangible places, which usually involve taking off all our clothes and not being in a hurry to leave the apartment for a few days. When take-out food deliveries are our only meals and even the wine is ordered in.

I like going places with a boy that involve changing into different outfits, different shoes, and then leaving them strewn all over the apartment, and wearing down my favorite tube of lipstick, because it keeps smudging off on the wine glass, the cigarette filters, the boy's slightly rough unshaved face, and his thick, stiff cock. Sometimes the lipstick smudges off on to the pillow cases if I happen to have my face buried there; or if maybe I'm biting on the pillow because I'm getting that thick cock stuffed into me hard from behind.

That's when the boy seems most like a man, though. That's when the subtle aroma of the wine, as it's poured into the wine glasses just in reach on the night table when you're taking a break from fucking, only serves to remind you of how elusively time passes. It helps if it's twilight, too, and through the open window you can see the lights coming on in the apartments across the Hudson River.

I like boys who watch me very intently as I start to tie them up; they're not in a hurry to protest, but they're young enough to be unsure of how far I'm likely to go. I like it when a boy feels like he doesn't have to be in control, though. Maybe I've tied him down, spread-eagled to the bed, and he's watching intently as I kneel between his spread legs, and then his erect cock moves in and out of my lipsticked mouth, and when he feels my finger slip up his ass, he doesn't complain. Or how a boy surrenders when you slip the blindfold over his beautiful eyes – I like that, blindfolding a boy who's tied down. I can plant my soaking pussy right on his mouth then, and he acts like he's never wanted a pussy more in all his life; he devours my swollen lips with a lot of passion, as if not having a choice in the matter is what's really turning him on.

Sometimes it's fun to turn around, then; to keep my pussy planted on his mouth, but lean down and let my tongue lick lightly at his piss slit, and run up and down his aching shaft. Maybe lick determinedly at the spot just under the swollen crown – or maybe down under his balls – but not take his whole dick in my mouth again for a while.

A boy can get really excitable when my mouth is doing stuff like that. He'll moan distractedly, or go at my clit with such enthusiasm that I start wondering, How can he even breathe? His nose is practically buried in my soaking hole . . .

But here's what I really like: a boy who isn't afraid to show me his asshole, who might even like to lay belly down and spread his legs for me while I admire him. I like it best if he doesn't want to be tied then, because it indicates to me that he's really wanting it, and I like it when a boy is really wanting it – the analingus part. I do that first. I try to be really thorough and patient with the analingus – push his cheeks apart and hold them spread, while my tongue licks slowly at his hole, or around his hole, or up and down his crack – because it really helps a boy relax. And a boy needs to feel relaxed, he needs to feel he can trust me, because soon I'm going to strap on a silicone tool and slide it up his ass, and he knows it. He's agreed to it beforehand; sometimes he's even been the one to suggest it, to ask for it.

And if he's liking it enough, if he's into it and his hole is opening up easily for me, I'll probably fuck him hard, hold on to his arched ass while I fuck him and tell him how beautiful he looks, how incredible his ass is, taking the tool in deep as I fuck him. Maybe I'll even have him pull up his knees under himself so he can jerk off while he's getting reamed. And then the noises he'll start to make – the grunting. I love to listen to the lusty sounds a boy getting fucked is likely to make.

But it won't happen at all if a boy's not willing to turn over for me.

Which doesn't mean that I don't like boys who won't turn over.

I even like those boys who like it best when I'm flat on my back, who hike my long legs up over their shoulders, who maybe keep my wrists pinned down to the mattress with their large, substantial hands, and who shove their hard dicks into me deep, over and over. Maybe getting in too deep, and maybe liking the fact that I'm grunting like an animal, even while my mouth is being kissed – devoured, almost – a tongue shoving in and filling my mouth while I whimper.

I like a boy who knows enough to keep fucking me even if it sounds like I'm in pain.

I like it when a boy lights up a cigarette in the dark – after we've finished fucking, maybe, and there's a jism-filled condom lying somewhere on the bed but no one wants to turn on the light yet and find it. So we lie there instead, naked and entwined, and share a cigarette – pass it back and forth, even though we've heard all the stories about how smoking is no good for us.

As we share that cigarette, I like a worn-out boy to lay his head against my bare breasts in the tangle of sheets and pillows while I hold him in the crook of my arm. There's something about that fiery glow, as we drag on the cigarette in the darkness, that makes confessions seem simple. Boys will tell you the oddest things, if the room's really dark and they're sure no one but you can hear them. I'm not big on confiding, myself, but I love to listen to a boy's dreams.

The Good Girl

Marilyn Jaye Lewis

The Good Girl

❖ ❖

*F*riday night I went home with some married people.
I wish I could tell you they were vibrantly tan,
Hollywood fast-lane types, but they weren't. They were
just married people. Intellectuals. Two married couples
clearly pushing something like their mid-fifties. I have
to say that they weren't even very attractive. They
certainly weren't fans of cosmetic surgery or fad diets.
You're probably wondering why I went home with
them. I'll tell you why: they asked me to.

I was hanging out in one of those book bars – small
and stuffy, with the built-in-bookcases lining the walls,
a tiny fire in the equally microscopic hearth. I was there
being stood up. Nothing serious, though, no *tragédie de
l'amour*. It was just my intensely hyper girlfriend who
had stood me up. She'd obviously gotten snagged into
working more overtime.

So I was alone in a surprisingly comfy chair, tentatively nursing a glass of red wine since I wasn't sure if
I was just going to turn around and go home. That's
when they walked in. Two unattractive married couples
in their mid-fifties. They made an instant commotion,
dragging around a tiny table and scooting together a

109

bunch of comfy chairs so they could all sit down, practically on top of me, and proceed to order an incredibly expensive bottle of wine. I loved watching that: the waiter trying to find a spot to stand in that was anywhere near them while they ordered, and then having to set up an elaborate pedestaled wine bucket somewhere in reach of them, too. Thank God they smoked. They really needed some more stuff on that tiny table.

They couldn't help but notice me since they were pratically sitting in my lap, and they kept trying to engage me in small talk. I resisted their stabs at friend-liness until they offered to share their wine, which necessitated their ordering another bottle. The waiter was really glad to see a fifth party, me, push into the already unmaneuverable fray. So physically we got close in a hurry. We couldn't help it. Still, one of the women, Fran, seemed to impinge on more of my personal space than I thought was really necessary. Right away I figured she was hitting on me. After a couple of glasses of that expensive wine, I realized they were all hitting on me.

I went home with them mostly because I couldn't believe they'd had the balls to ask me. They were so matter of fact about it, too, as if they always came on to younger, much more attractive single women and got affirmative results. I was swept off my feet by their sheer blind optimism. Well, no. Actually I was swept off my feet by them, literally. I think they wanted to rush me into the nearest cab before I could change my mind.

We wound up at Cy and Ruthie's, the home of the couple who lived closest to the bar. It was a really nice apartment. Cy and Ruthie had never had any kids. Every extra penny had been available for them to spend on themselves. They favored upholstery. Everything was upholstered, in every conceivable pattern. I could tell an interior decorator had been paid handsomely to have his or her way with Cy and Ruthie. But I ceased noticing the decor when Fran started to undress me.

At first I felt alarmingly uncomfortable because no one else was undressing. I shy away from being the only one naked in a crowd of strangers and I was wondering what I'd gotten myself into. But after she'd stripped me naked, Fran gently pushed me down on the sofa and started to massage my feet. I began to relax. I sank deep into the upholstered sofa while Fran sat on the coffee table in front of me with both of my feet in her considerable lap. Her hands were unexpectedly soft and steady. She worked each and every one of my toes and the balls of my feet with just the right amount of pressure.

She smiled encouragingly at me while the others just watched. I wondered if I was being lured into some exhibitionistic *pas de deux* with Fran. As I sunk deeper into the couch in a state of increasing bliss, I wondered how a group of people arrived at that sort of arrangement. 'Hey, I know,' I imagined them saying. 'Let's all go out together, find a girl half our age and watch her get frisky with Fran.' There would be general agreement all around.

Then Fran broke my reverie. She lifted my foot to her mouth and sucked in my big toe. I was ready for it. Fran's mouth was so warm and wet, I moaned. And slowly but surely things started to move around me.

Cy got out of his chair. He came over and stood by Fran, his crotch level with her face. He unzipped his fly, but when he took out his dick it was flaccid. Completely limp. Fran didn't seem at all perturbed, but I felt a little indignant. I was thinking, Hey, I'm naked here! The least you could do is have a raging hard-on! But alas, Cy was no longer nineteen and Fran appeared to be used to it. She went right to work with her mouth, alternating between my big toe and Cy's flaccid dick

until remarkable things began to happen. It turned out
Cy was hung.

Ruthie came over to join us. She completely undid
her husband's trousers, letting them fall rather dramti-
cally to his ankles. Then while Cy went to work on
Fran's mouth with his stiff dick, Ruthie kneeled behind
Cy and started tonguing his ass. Her face was way in
there and I figured if I were Cy, as I watched his huge
erection pumping in and out of Fran's mouth while his
wife, fully dressed and on her knees, tongued his
asshole . . . Well, I figured I'd probably be liking that an
awful lot. I got wet between my legs watching those
three carry on like that.

Kenneth, Fran's husband, was the last to take the
plunge, but suddenly he was naked and sitting on the
couch next to me. He had a lot of hair, a touch more
than I would have preferred. He didn't seem to notice
that he didn't appeal to me, though. He lifted my arms
and held my wrists together behind my head, then
proceeded to lick my armpits. It was an unusual move,
but it made me shiver and my nipples got erect. Kenneth licked his way down to my breasts, and when his
mouth closed around my erect nipple, I moaned again.
Hairy or not, he was good with his mouth. My nipple
swelled from the perfect pressure of Kenneth's sucking
and I decided, at that moment, that I ought to have sex
with older people more often. They understood the
nuances of pressure.

The coffee-table gang was starting to get rambunc-
tious. Fran was flat on her back as Cy straddled her on
the low table, completely humping her face. She was
making eager but smothered little sounds. Ruthie had
removed Fran's panties. She'd pushed apart Fran's legs
and buried her face between her fleshy thighs.

Kenneth's mouth was still working expertly on my
nipples, moving from one to the other, tugging tugging

tugging, but now one of his hands was between my legs, rubbing my slippery clit.

I didn't think I'd be able to take much more of it, the free show on the coffee table and the perfect pressure on each of my three most responsive spots. I thought I was going to come.

That's when Cy startled all of us. He stopped humping Fran's face and went for her hole in a hurry. Ruthie had to get out of the way fast. She plopped down next to me on the sofa. She was the only one still dressed. She began to unbutton her blouse while Kenneth was rolling a rubber on to his erection. I felt a little overwhelmed. I didn't know who to focus on. It was obvious Ruthie wanted me to suck her fat little tits, but I was kind of hoping Kenneth was wanting his dick in me because I was definitely ready for it. That's when it occurred to me to quit sitting like a blob on the sofa and get a little assertive, get into the rhythm of being a swinger. Nothing was preventing me from having them both.

I turned over and raised my ass in Kenneth's direction while I let Ruthie guide my mouth to one of her jiggly tits. 'Would you look at that tight tush,' Kenneth declared as he slapped my ass hard. 'Fran had a tush like that when I married her. Thirty years ago.'

Then he mounted me. He slid his substantial hard-on into my soaking hole without needing any help from me. He slammed into my hole hard, making me cry out right away. He had a firm grip on my tush and was going to town.

Ruthie lifted my face from her breasts and started kissing me. Her tongue was crammed deep into my mouth while I grunted from the force of Kenneth's cock pounding into my pussy from behind.

I had never been with more than one person at a time before. It was kind of a scary feeling. I felt myself becoming insatiable. It wasn't long before I was flat on

my back on the carpeting. Ruthie had stripped completely and was straddling my face. She had a tight
grasp on me and I kept my legs spread wide, giving
Kenneth's hard cock free rein on my helpless hole,
pound pound pound.

Ruthie's snatch was completely shaved. Her mound
was smooth from the tip of her clit to the cleft in her
ass. It had to be a wax job, I thought, she was that
smooth. And I wondered: Why would a woman in her
fifties wax her pussy completely bald? I figured her
husband, Cy, had something to do with it.

Cy was sitting in a chair, sucking on a cigar and
taking a breather, but his dick was still rock hard. It
was poking straight up like the Chrysler Building. Not
that I could see him too well with Ruthie's ass in my
face, but I could tell that Cy was watching me get
nailed. I was curious what he was thinking.

'I have to pee!' I suddenly announced as the urge
came unmistakably over me. Rather than cause a chorus
of disappointment and regret among my fellow swing-
ers, the news didn't cause them to miss a beat. They'd
switched partners before I'd even stood up.

When I came back into the living room (and I hadn't
been gone long, mind you), Fran was down on all fours
with Kenneth's hard-on seriously down her throat and
Cy was fucking her ass. The incessant pounding she
was getting at both ends was making Fran's boobs
bounce around like crazy. The sight was mesmerizing:
what the men were doing to her and the way Fran
seemed to be wildly into it.

Ruthie came in from the kitchen with a tray of decaf
espressos. She had that look on her face, like she'd had
her orgasm and was feeling completely contented. She
sat down next to me and we both watched Fran go the
distance with Cy and Kenneth. Right when Fran started
to jerk around and squeal, an indication that Fran was

probably coming, Kenneth pulled his dick out of her mouth and shot his load in her face.

She seemed a little peeved by that, but she didn't do much about it because Cy was still going hog wild on her ass. I wondered if Kenneth was going to hear about it later, though, when he and Fran were home alone: 'How could you come in my face like that?' I could hear Fran saying. I knew she'd be capable of some serious chiding. 'In front of everybody!' she'd probably continue. 'You know I hate it when you do that.'

But for now everyone was amicable; everyone was drinking decaf espresso except me. I hadn't come yet. I felt fidgety and distracted. Since I'd never been a swinger before, I didn't know the proper etiquette. Was it up to me to let everyone know I wasn't through yet, that I hadn't come?

I felt so ignorant, so ill equipped to swing. I toyed with the idea of slipping off to the bathroom again to take care of myself alone. No one had to know what I'd been doing in there. I could come quickly, I felt certain of that. Still, I felt a little let down. I'd been having too much fun with everybody to suddenly resort to climaxing alone in a stranger's bathroom.

After only a few moments, it seemed as though coming alone in Cy and Ruthie's bathroom wasn't even going to pan out. Fran and Kenneth were dressing. It was late, they said. They had a baby-sitter running up a fortune.

Then I wondered how old Fran really was if she had a child at home still young enough to need a sitter.

I figured I'd better get dressed, too. I didn't want to overstay my welcome. I helped Ruthie clear up the remnants of the espressos while Fran and Kenneth left.

'I'll get your coat,' Cy said to me. 'I'll walk you down to the street.'

'That's OK,' I protested half-heartedly. My head was

pounding. This swinging business had left my now-sober nerves a little raw.

'Nonsense. It's late. I'll walk you down.'

Cy helped me into my coat and we got on the elevator. He pressed the button for the basement. I saw him do it. Maybe he was going to show me out the back way.

When the elevator doors opened, Cy led me down a narrow hallway and then out a door that led to the tenants' parking garage. It was dimly lit, with only a couple of naked bulbs burning.

'Look, you don't have to drive me,' I insisted uncomfortably. 'I don't live far. I'll get a cab.'

'Why don't we get in my car anyway? I didn't come yet either.'

I couldn't believe I'd heard him correctly. 'What did you say?'

He looked at me and smiled engagingly. 'I didn't come yet, either. I thought maybe I could persuade you to fuck around with me in my car.'

I was stunned. I tried to feel affronted, but actually it kind of appealed to me. The parking garage was deserted.

Cy unlocked his car door and we slipped into the back seat. 'We'd better not undress all the way,' he said, 'just in case anybody sees us.'

I agreed.

I climbed on to his lap and started kissing him. On the mouth. My tongue was shoving in deep. Cy's breath tasted like wine and espresso and cigars, and he suddenly seemed like he was seriously grown up. I felt incredibly attracted to him. 'How old are you?' I challenged him. 'Are you old enough to be my father?'

'Probably. Why? Did you want to do a little role-playing?'

'Excuse me?' I didn't know what he was talking about.

'You know, I could pretend to be your irate father and slap your fanny really hard until we're both really hot. Then we could cross over that line together.'

I didn't reply. I felt a little overwhelmed by how instantly appealing his idea sounded.

I let him maneuver me until I was across his lap. He methodically raised my coat, lifted my dress and, with minimal effort but a nice long lecture, tugged down my tights and panties and left them halfway down my thighs.

When my ass was completely bare and smack dab over his knee, he let loose with a good old-fashioned spanking. The stinging, smarting kind.

'Shit!' I cried, trying to shield my ass.

But he wasn't at all deterred by my screams. He lectured me sternly on the perils of going home with perfect strangers, and behaving rather wantonly, to boot.

I squirmed around in Cy's lap as my bottom heated up and tried to dodge the steady, stinging slaps, but Cy kept them coming. He clamped my waist tight against his thigh and aimed directly for my helpless behind.

I could feel Cy's erection growing underneath me. He was really laying into me, spanking me hard, making me squeal promises that I'd never do it again.

When my ass was completely on fire and I didn't think I could stand any more, Cy released me. He turned me over in his lap and unbuttoned the top of my dress. Slipping his hand inside, he worked my bra up over my tits and fondled my nipples. They were instantly erect.

I was still naked from my waist to my knees. The feeling of being so awkwardly exposed, my bare ass burning, while Cy fondled my breasts and tugged on my nipples made me want to get irredeemably dirty with him. But that was going to be difficult to do while keeping our clothes on.

117

I turned over and undid Cy's trousers. I unbuckled his belt and unzipped his fly and his dick sprang out. I was happy to see it looking so lively. I buried my face in his lap, taking as much of his shaft down my throat as I could. I kneeled on the back seat with my naked ass in the air and I didn't care if anyone could see me. I was feeling unabashedly aroused. As I sucked Cy's dick more fervently, I heard him begin to gasp and moan.

'Lie down on your belly,' he said insistently. My bra was still up over my tits and the leather seat was icy cold against my nipples. It felt great.

Cy unrolled a rubber on to his erection and told me to raise my ass up a little.

I did.

He mounted me with my tights and panties still around my thighs. I felt his dick poking into my asshole. At first I thought he didn't realize he had the wrong hole, but he knew what he was doing.

The lubricated condom slid into my ass without too much effort but the pressure was intense.

'God,' I groaned. Then I cried out uncontrollably while his huge tool went to work with my pitiful little hole.

'I hate to have to do this,' he grunted, 'you know that. But maybe this'll teach you not to go home with people you don't know.'

'God,' I was panting as he pounded into my stretching hole. 'Jesus, God.'

'Are you going to be a good girl now?' he continued, lifting my hips off the back seat and deftly sliding his hand down to my swollen clit.

'Yes,' I whimpered, while he rubbed my hard clit.

'Yes what?'

'I'm going to be a good girl,' I cried, as his cock seemed to swell in me even more, filling me to capacity with every thrust.

'And what happens if you're naughty again? What is Daddy going to do?'

'Spank me,' I sputtered. 'Daddy's going to spank me!'

'And what else?'

'Fuck my ass!'

'That's right,' he concluded. 'Daddy is going to fuck your ass.'

These last words he enunciated slowly and carefully because he was coming at the sound of his own words. He slammed deep into my hole then and mashed me down on the seat. 'Jesus!' he exclaimed with one last powerful thrust. 'Jesus!'

And I was saying it, too: 'Jesus!' Partly because I was coming underneath him, shuddering and squirming against the leather seat, but mostly because I was testifying. I wanted my joy to be heard.

The Bad Gal

LaToya Thomas

The Bad Gal

❧ ❧

*T*hey've been trying to get me to say that I hadn't known what I was doing; that I hadn't been of sound mind; that there's a man somewhere who forces me to dress like this and keeps me on drugs so I can earn the cash to buy more. That sometimes this man makes me go out and pick up young men and bring them back to my apartment so he can watch. Is he my pimp? A ponce? Some kind of sicko that has got me involved in all this against my will? 'No,' I insist, but still they refuse to believe I'm telling the truth. They've read so many stories in the local paper they think I'm a victim. They can't believe I gave my consent.

I've had plenty of opportunity to give in and humour them; to say that this pimp mostly makes me go with older married men, 'cos they've got more cash and they want a bit of exotic black ass. I could get away with saying that teenage boys aren't really my thing 'cos sixteen- and seventeen-year-olds don't have the cash for it and they wouldn't dare touch what they can't afford.

But I've said nothing of the sort. So now I've been sat banged up for hours saying nothing while the social workers try to get an inner-city sob story out of me. The thing is, I hardly look like a victim. The cops have already tried to slam a drugs charge on me but I'm as clean as a baby. No evidence of dirtiness on my perfect skin. I even wiggled my butt at them earlier in case they wanted to check if I was packing rocks up there. The scrubbed-faced blonde one who brought me in declined my offer. Just as well, man. I didn't fancy her rubbing round my minus-plus. She's one of those types who have that lame goody-goody appearance. Bad, 'barely there so why bother' jewellery, you know, like small pearl earstuds and stuff, and an overneat, short layered hairstyle. It's the look of no imagination – and it makes me glad to my soul that I have what I have. I love my weave-on four-tone hair and body jewellery. I got two belly-button piercings, both nipples, a small gold eyebrow bar, as well as my diamond nose stud. My body is cared-for and toned. My caramel skin shines with health, and I glow with loving myself and being worshipped. I can make a boy come in his pants just by licking my lips. My friend Carol is always telling me I could give the bus driver a hard-on just by asking for my fare.

I bet that cop has never given anyone pleasure. I bet she doesn't even know what pleasure is. Her pussy is frozen, man. A guy could get himself a frostbitten cock in there, boy. I laugh for a couple of seconds. The bastards can't take my humour away from me but they have taken my mobile. God knows what messages they're picking up. The cops are probably wanking off to it. I could tell in their eyes when they brought me in that they wanted to fuck me. I know that for a fact. All men do. And wearing what I'm wearing makes it more so. I stand tall enough to be at eye-level with most of them. I never give them the sweet stuff – the coquette look – and that kinda threatens hard men. They see me as a challenge. They don't want to love and protect me; to make love or have the kind of sex with me that you see on those Lovers' Guides. They want to chase me and hunt me down; get me by the neck and have it rough. They can't stand that my spirit might be stronger than theirs. But they can't ignore me 'cos they can smell my sexy stuff. It gets their cocks hard and makes them want to fuck me and hurt me. They want to slap me and dominate me. You know, I've never known a hard white man that wasn't a brute inside. And that bitch who got me busted, I swear she's gonna regret it. Still, it was quite a laugh seeing the look on her face as her precious little boy was losing it in my sweet pussy.

My brief's got to show up soon. Fucking Sunday afternoon, man. Trust me to get pulled in on a Sunday. If I hadn't made so much noise, it would probably have been all right. How was I to know that one of them lived on the same level as me? That his mother was that fucking freak-out who always gives me filthy looks in the walkway along our estate. If only I hadn't gone to the shop in my fineries, and *they* hadn't been standing around outside, looking so bored. If only I hadn't started sparring with them. Yeah, well, we all know how easy it is to look back and regret things. Well, fuck that, man, 'cos I enjoyed what I did, and it ain't so serious really. I'm such a pushover for a new experience. I'd not tried it fives-up before. And all of them were so hard and young and nice-looking. I swear boys nowadays are better at keeping themselves clean and nice, you know. When I was a young girl, boys my own age were rough, man. They always had stinkfoot trainers and bad underwear and stuff. Now, them all got Calvins and body lotions for men and that. And, I tell you, I'd been feeling horny all morning. I wanted stiff cocks in me; to suck on 'em and watch 'em being rubbed up. Mmmm. So there I was coming out the shop, and this big, cold gust of wind caught my full-length fun-fur coat and blew it right up and showed all the boys what I had underneath – like, not much.

You can imagine. Nuff noise. The feistiest one comes up to me and he says: 'You is fit, man. I wanna . . . you know,' and grabs his crotch and his mates start squealing with laughter and dancing around. He stands there jiggling his young slim hips around while his pals slide their butts off the wall and start dancing around him. The cheek, man. I was vex. I was about to shout for them to watch their manners, but something wicked got a hold of me and I couldn't be mad with them. So I calmly put down the shopping bags and walked up closer to the feisty one and opened my coat and showed him everything. And I said to him: 'So you want a little bit of China Blue, then?' I always use that name. It was the name of a ho' in a sleazy movie I'd seen years ago. It sounded so good I kept it. I like those hooker names like Roxette and Chelsey and stuff. I didn't want no corny thing like Coffee and all those other cheesy black-gal names. Yeah, China Blue was my favourite. These days I always keep the front bit of my hair bright blue and oiled down. I look bad gal 'cos I is bad gal. And if you have a problem with that, I feel no way about it.

So the others now get bold enough to start asking me questions like, 'So, who are you, China Blue?' and 'China Blue . . . is you a ho?' Then peals of laughter as I stand there looking as if I'm waiting for them to impress me. Then one grabs my tits and he can see through the slinky material that they're high and firm and the nipples are hard – partly from the cold and partly from me being really ready for sex. Then the feisty one grabs at my ass. I'm wearing a skirt that's shiny and a two-tone apricot/pink colour. I don't know what the material is, but it feels like some sort of plastic. It's dancehall wear, really. And my shoes are black patent with high heels with the backs cut out of the foot and ankle. They look like hooker shoes, I suppose.

So there I am at eleven in the morning looking like I'm fresh from a dance. Full make-up, no knickers and

smelling sweet and musky. And those boys were capti-
vated. Their pupils were dilating and they were all
getting stiff. I could see it. Two or three of them had
their hands in their pants, adjusting stuff. And it was
making me wet, and I was so excited, man. It was their
enthusiasm that did it for me; and their total inability to
control themselves.

'So what are you doing?' I ask. 'Is this all you have to
do? Hang around outside the Spar?'

'Yeah, man, it's dry round here. There's nothing, guy,
nothing.'

And just at that moment I felt really sorry for them. I
wanted to brighten up their day. Give them something
to talk about for months. So I invited them back to
mine. I know I shouldn't have, and that I'd probably
regret it and have them following me around and
calling at my door for the rest of the time I'd be living
there but, well, it was a snap decision. I wanted to play
a part. And get my pussy rammed by all that young
cock.

Straight to my flat, then, and at first things felt like they
could get a bit tense. I hadn't expected them to be quite
as nervous as they were, but I guess it had been quite a
while since I'd had anything to do with sixteen-year-
olds. Even the feisty one kept going to the bathroom,
and they were all rushing about the flat getting drinks
and looking at my pictures and CDs and stuff and
avoiding the issue, basically – the reason why they were
there in the first place. When one of them started asking
me about music and what clubs I went to, it was time
to regain control. It was all getting too much like a
youth club and, believe me, I had no intention of being
their social worker. I didn't want to be friends with
them; I wanted to fuck them. So I had them all sit down
on the sofas while I told them how it was gonna be.

I stood up and told them, 'We'll go into the bedroom

'cos there's more room there. You might think you're all going to get a turn with me separately but I want you all at the same time.'

Well, my God, that made them look fear. Then two start giggling. One of them said in a serious voice, 'Tony, man, no looking at my cock, right?' The one called Tony looked back at his mate in horror.

'What you thinking, Darren, man. That I is batty boy or something?' Then much sucking of teeth and 'Get off, man', 'No, you get off, man.' Foolie boys. Then it dawned on them that one had to be last, and a muddled wailing started of, 'I'm gonna be first.' They were looking at things in a typically male way – start to finish, one after the other.

'If you're gonna argue, no one's getting any,' I shouted. I felt like a teacher in a primary school, dishing out birthday cake or something. 'If you want my pussy, you wear Jimmy hats, right. I got them, don't worry. If you wanna ride bareback I can suck you.' None of them were looking me in the eye, even though I was rubbing my thighs slowly and walking up and down past them. They wanted the action, but they knew they were being told righteously that they had to do things the way I wanted. I was so in control. And they were all so scared of fucking up, even if one or two were still looking cocky. Then things were quiet for a bit while they sucked on bottles of drink and reached out to touch me. I kneeled in front of them and let them all have a turn of feeling my tits and ass.

When the time was right I got up and slowly walked towards the door. I was almost out of the room before I realised not one of them was following me. 'So, are any of you up for it, then? Or shall I put the TV on instead?' I asked sarcastically. Then, finally, movement. The boys were looking at each other and in a state of excitement so great that they couldn't even speak.

* * *

My room was immaculately tidy and the huge bed was made. There was room enough on that bed for six people – just. So I lay on the bed and rucked my tight plastic skirt up so that when they started trooping into the room they could all see there was nothing underneath that skirt except my sweet wet pussy. Then I rolled over on to my knees and bared my backside at them and rubbed it. And I did all the porno moves. The tongue came out and the fingers went in. And I told them I was so horny, and I was wanting them to fuck me. I was loving it. They were all rubbing their crotches. Then one by one they were unbuttoning and unzipping themselves and pulling out their wood.

'Ah, man, I'm so ready,' said Tony. 'I'm gonna shoot my fucking load in this sweet pussy, man. I want to do it really bad. Really gonna come hard. I'm gonna rump her, and fucking soon, I can't hold it.' Darren may have been worried about Tony looking at his cock, but Tony's concentration was most definitely fixed on what was between my legs. Sweet things.

Then he grabbed me and forced me down on the bed and pushed his young hard white cock in my face, and rubbed it across my maroon-coloured lip-glossed mouth. It smelled of musk and man, and it was so, so hard.

Well, by this time I could barely stand it myself. I snaked my hand down between my legs and started curling my fingers over my wet clit. I have to be careful with this business 'cos my nails are, like, three centimetres long or something.

'God, man, I've never seen a woman play with herself before!' one of them shouted in total shock.

'Well, you can get real close up to it if you like,' I invited. 'What's your name anyway?' I asked. I weren't gonna have no boy watch me rub myself up without me knowing his name. That would feel well strange.

'I'm Linton, China Blue. You see me, I check for you.

I got wood in a brief and I is hot for you.' And we all start laughing at his little rap. And I'm laughing really loud until Tony forces that cock of his in my face and I has to shut up. Then Linton climbs on the bed and he's unzipped himself. Out the corner of my eye I can see he's rubbering up, so I'm relaxed that they're having respect for me in that way. As he bounces on the bed my head shakes a bit and it makes me swallow about two centimetres more cock than I'd anticipated. And that's it. Tony is hissing words I can't make out through his gritted teeth. I open my eyes again and I see he's losing it, and then suddenly a warm gush at the speed of a bullet shoots from his cock and down my throat.

At the other end Linton is nudging himself into me and boy it's big!

'Get the fuck out the way, Tony, man,' he orders, and Tony gets off me and the bed, looking satisfied.

'I'm gonna put a tune on, man,' he says, all calm.

Then, just for a few seconds it's me and Linton: the experienced woman and the feisty boy. The three others are standing there hard and expectant, rubbing themselves slowly with excitement in their eyes. The bass starts coming from next door as Linton's ramming himself up into me. I swear I've never heard it that loud before. The fool's gonna blow my speakers if he ain't careful. But the thud goes on and I'm carefully circling the flat of my finger around my clit, just drawing out the pleasure as long as I can, 'cos I would go off like a rocket if I didn't exercise a little self-control. But he's good, that Linton; he's really good, and then suddenly another boy is coming towards my face with his stiff load in his briefs. And he tugs it out and just starts jerking furiously. I look him in the eye and say it's OK, that he should wait his turn, but he can't, and before I can get the message through to his young eager brain, he's shooting it all over my smiling face, pulling on his balls as he milks the last couple of drops of sweet boycum.

I'm sorry, but that was too much for me. I start coming and, I tell you, I was loud. I was louder than I had ever been. I look up at Linton and he's going, 'Oh, oh, yeah,' and the both of us are making so much noise, man.

I don't know how many minutes pass before I bring myself to my senses. Then I start to notice the bedroom door opening slowly. Expecting to see Tony back for seconds I look up and straight into the eyes of a woman – a furious-looking woman – and, before I know it, she's got her hands around sweet lover-boy's neck and is pulling him off me and out of me. My pussy is still throbbing and I'm in the most compromising position.

'You fucking twisted bitch,' she screams at me. 'What do you think you're doing? That is my only son and you've ruined him! I've never seen such slackness in all my days!'

'He don't look ruined to me,' I says. 'And if you can't figure out what is going on, I'll spell it out for you. I was having a fives-up with my little gang and –'

And I get cut off in my speech. She starts flying at me. I'm screaming and fighting back and hitting at her. It's a real cat-fight, and Tony's back in the room trying to calm things down. The two that didn't get their fill look so sore and hard done by, man. With much kissing of teeth they slouch off, their virginity intact. Then, before I know what's happening, two Old Bill are in the room. I hear their radios before I see them. And I reach for something to wrap around myself while I ask them if they're getting a good enough look. Cheek. And as I'm led out the house a few minutes later (at least the bastards let me get dressed) I find out that the front door had been left open the whole time. That was the big mistake. Linton's mother had thought there was murders going on up here and had phoned the police at the same time as the neighbours had complained about rough ragga blasting out on a Sunday morning.

So I was well and truly caught bang to rights, man. And now I is sitting here bored and thirsty and brimming with ideas of revenge. But, I tell you, I've learned my lesson. And this is my advice: if ever any of you bad gal gonna do it five-ways with dem yout', remember to close the bloody door behind you!

England Expects . . .

Julie Savage

England Expects . . .

❖ ❖

On the way down to Portsmouth your sassily ageing man and you had talked about the great romance of Admiral Lord Nelson.

'How wise Sir William Hamilton must have been able to tolerate Emma's sexual enthusiasm, to allow her to fuck not only Horatio Nelson but the Queen of Naples too,' you said.

He nodded. 'The aplomb, Cathy!'

'I'd like to think he loved her sexuality selflessly. Like you, isn't it, my love?' You hugged him as the train rumbled down from London Waterloo.

'I just love you being happy, Cathy. You were made for sensuality,' James said, smiling at you. As usual and despite your years together your nipples melted at that warmth in his eyes. 'And since I can't get it up much these days, the next best thing is watching someone else make you scream with joy . . .'

'Thank you, my darling love.' You kissed his smile, loving the dryness of his lips and the border between their pink erectile tissue and the pale skin of his face.

It was a warm Thursday in April, complete with lambs in the waterlogged fields and white-legged women joggers in last year's shorts. This was joy day: you both organised a day of solid pleasure each week. This week it was your turn to explore your desires: in this case to find out about this sensual woman who was publicly maligned and privately adored.

You both were sitting next to other facing the train's engine and the Hampshire countryside. Familiar as at a fireside, James alternately reading a new sex toys catalogue folded inside *Country Life*, and the *New York Review of Books*. You skimming a 1920s hagiography of Emma Hamilton, Nelson's lover, and glancing over his shoulder at an apple-green silicone strap-on. You so radiant that passengers eyed you as they went up and down to the buffet car for drinks; James so sassy with his greying curls that women fancied him more than when his hair was black – or so he said.

When the train brought you to Portsmouth Harbour you walked across the cobbled Hard, in through the old Admiralty dockyard gates and round the acres of the Royal Naval Museum: the old cooperage, the galleries, the moored historic ships. Then James decided to sunbathe with a glass of Pinot Noir outside the Quartermaster's Arms.

'Go off and have some fun, my darling.'

'And you're going to try and get laid by some tourist, I expect?' I joked.

'Hardly! But now you mention it . . .'

You left him to it and took the obligatory tour of Nelson's famous ship, the *Victory*. To see the place where Emma's lover worked, and died near Cadiz in 1805: the man famous for his flag signal: England Expects Every Man To Do His Duty; his lack of an arm (so she only got half the stroking she needed?); and his famous putting of his telescope to his blind eye and refusing to see an order he didn't like.

Happening upon this vessel, at anchor in a dock near ice-cream stands and the shed housing the retrieved

Mary Rose, was as unbelievable as coming across a lithe and heroic dinosaur in a seedy 21st-century street of apartment blocks. It was as anomalous as a coin from medieval times handed over by a psychic medium. The *Victory's* age and enduring beauty were the main shock. The fresh black hull shone like a magpie's wings. Yellow and white painted flowers high on its prow made the warship look both houseproud and festive.

Immediately you stepped aboard, the stinging smell of new jute and hemp came from the ropes coiled everywhere. The guides, upright men uniformed in snug blue trousers and ribbed navy sweaters, took people round in 20-person posses, strictly. They looked like they've been servicemen themselves: minor officers, bruisers not deck ornaments. Men who know how to handle themselves always attract you, even when you're really feeling quite dykey, as you were that day.

Your guide was a big-boned guy called Spencer whose nose's broken bridge enhanced his tough beauty. He told you all with absolute firmness but humour that visitors had to stay with their guide throughout the half hour it took to see the various decks. Each guide seemed to have his party entranced by that mix of working-class authority and humour. This particular guy clearly relished his hold so much that you wanted to resist him. How dare he seduce you with that striking, melting tone, that wit, that voice that coiled its way round your organs like an uninvited cobra?

His bottom was the heavy sort you liked to fantasise about slamming down on you as he fucked, hard. The sort you could grab on to as you yelled in orgasm. Solid. You made a point of walking behind him so you could watch it as he led you all up the companionway to the orlop deck. Sensing it, he turned round to glare at you but then caught sight of your high breasts and smiled lopsidedly instead. Got him, you thought. Got him! But do I want him?

And then he began telling stories about the ship in a voice with a Welsh lilt. This was the kind of voice you could let yourself be seduced by. But you wouldn't, that day, you decided. Because it was too easy. Because you were with James. Because you also fancied that woman in the grey T-shirt. Because you wouldn't give such a canny git the pleasure.

She walked ahead with the dignity of white women who've learned to carry themselves well through being adoringly fucked by a Caribbean man. Her waist swivelled beautifully as she bent and turned to photograph the brass plaque on the quarterdeck marking the spot where Nelson fell to the fatal musket shot from the mizzen of the *Redoubtable*. He died just eight years after meeting Emma and aged 47, one year younger than James. You wondered what it would be like to roll there on the brass plaque with her, sun-warmed, you both as fleshy delighted symbols of all that the navy abhorred: women, lesbians, sensual hedonism.

This was where the gunpowder was stored, your guide was saying. These cubby-holes were where the officers slept. This was where the loaves for that huge crew were baked each day. 'And it was in a barrel like this, full of brandy, that Nelson was pickled. They had to do something, now didn't they, to preserve him while they carried him back all those long weeks to England. Mind you, I don't know if anyone could face drinking it afterwards.' He nodded at you. You looked away. You were not going to give him the pleasure of a smile.

'And it was in that corner that he lay, fatally wounded, and said those famous lines, "Kiss me, Hardy," and ordered that the nation look after Emma.'

'Which they didn't,' you added, bitter at her penurious, lonely death among her cheap brandy bottles at 27 Rue Francaise, Calais, in winter 1815.

'No, they didn't, madam,' Spencer agreed. And moved on to the mess deck to talk about whips. You found your breasts were swelling under your blue shirt. They were refusing to lie quiescent and ignore him. You were finding it harder and harder to walk easily because your clitoris was so engorged. It was bulging out and catching the purple lace panel at the front of your pants as you moved; your whole mound felt too mountainous to fit inside the jeans any more. You weren't sure who your erection was for: the guide, the woman in the T-shirt, the idea of Nelson and Emma or just the thought of whips.

'The whips,' he said, 'were used when a man was punished for an offence.'

'What might an offence be?' you asked.

'Oh, speaking out of turn to an officer,' he said, grinning. 'Asking questions, for example.'

You registered that you both knew the score: he was telling you that you were doing what he might punish. And he'd punish it happily, and for your pleasure. Maybe there was more to him after all. You looked at his lips. Sensuous, yes, below that impeccably shaved upper lip. He was clearly a man who always shaved, always wore fresh shirts, always did his duty. You glanced at his hands: tough brown skin, promisingly thick fingers, barely tapered at the joints, square clean nails trimmed low enough to not cut any delicate vaginal walls.

'The prisoner was put in leg irons, like so. Then he was given a piece of raw hemp like this. And from it he had to make his own whip. Like these here.' Spencer gestured to a row of them, all clean rope and barely worn leather, so much more tastily workmanlike than the relatively recreational ones you could buy from the on-line discipline stores. You watched his firm broad hand on the whip's tough handle and from the pull in your saliva glands realised you wanted him to be getting it ready for you.

'The prisoner plaited a handle and then all these little

thongs come out of it. The nine "tails" of the "cat". Each thong had a knot at the end, to create a nastier sting. When the man had made his own whip, see, the officer would come down. He'd test the whip, go up and fit a canvas sheath like so.' Spencer motioned, at groin height, the slipping of a condom over a hard, long prick. 'And then the prisoner would be brought up on deck. He'd be lashed to a grating. And there he'd be flogged in front of everyone.'

You'd seen all those old 1960s seafarer movies like *Mutiny on the Bounty* showing heroic golden men with their backs bloody from whippings. But all you could think of was the trail of a whip over your nipples, not lashing you but stimulating you.

The guide was looking at you. Yes, you were having a fantasy of being publicly whipped by him. Could he tell? Your breasts would be bursting out of a white frilled shirt in the hot sun as you were marched to the grating. When your shirt was ripped off to enable the lashing to be all the more direct, every sailor there would want to take your nipples into his mouth, even – especially – the officer who was flaying you. That officer would be like Marlon Brando in *Billy Budd* but meaner. His cock would be huge under those white uniform trousers that had no fly but just those funny flaps that buttoned either side of the pelvis. A huge seaworthy cock that you longed to take into your dripping fanny, there in the sunlight on deck. He'd whip you for wanting it, and then, disarmed by your beauty, relent. He'd put down his whip, undo . . . No, stop it, this was foolishness.

The guide, looking rather puzzled and hostile each time he glanced at you, carried on touring your party round the ship. 'This is the bed where Nelson slept. It swung with the ship's motion.'

And is far too narrow to fuck in, you added to yourself.

'But these cots were made the right size to double as a coffin – and it did. These are the embroidered bed curtains that officers' wives sent to remind their men of home comforts.'

And so on . . . you knowing that if you were married to him you wouldn't want to be domestic with him, but wild. Stuff stitching with ladylike needles: you wanted to clash swords with him. Draw blood. Win. Then be punished for it, just to a delicious level.

All the time you were wondering how you could get him to whip your breasts, just a little, with that cat-of-nine-tails. It didn't seem possible. Such a fantasy aboard one of Britain's most famous public monuments. Masochism on this symbol of glory. It was surely impossible.

He seemed to have withdrawn interest in you, anyway. He wasn't looking any more. But at least he wasn't eyeing up anyone else. The tour ended with what was presumably his usual professional flourish. 'So, ladies and gentlemen, you have now stepped on the same boards as the most accomplished admiral in the world's naval history. You have been on one of the most important ships in the history of the greatest seafaring nation.'

With all the dutifully shepherded others, you climbed down the gangway and off the *Victory*. It seemed that all was lost until you heard his voice call out. It resounded over the cobbled quay.

'Excuse me, madam, I noticed you were interested in the whips. If you come back at 16.45 I could er . . . tell you about them in more detail. Assist you to a greater practical understanding.' His mouth was crinkled, half-lustful, half-nervous.

To try him out you said, 'Oh, I'm not really interested, thank you.'

'A demonstration, if you like?' he proposed. You surely saw the flies on his trousers flare, even though he was in shadow. His shoulders *were* very interestingly

141

forceful. You wanted to cup his square chin, and his hard cock, in your hand.

'OK. A quick one.' You nodded curtly, and then giggled at your own guile. Of course you didn't want a quick anything. What you actually wanted was a slow, slow shafting. And it would kill you to wait another 45 minutes.

But you went away and joined James. When you told him he got so excited at your sensuality that you could see him getting hard. He looked at your excited cheeks, grinned, as usual, and said, 'Go for it, girl. Got your condoms?' and began rooting in his pocket to see if he had some for you. To kill the time you promenaded by the side of the Solent, gazing at the grey battleships in the dockyard and the distant boatyards at Hyde, trying to be an interested tourist, trying to stroll despite your excitment. James watched you licking the pointed white ice cream he'd bought you, up and up. His hand moved to his crotch. 'Whips on your nipples, eh?'

You nodded happily. 'I may be some time.'

He smirked. 'You wish! You think he'll be a match for you?'

'I know it.'

At 4.45 you went back to the *Victory* and there was Spencer seeing off his last posse. He smirked like a master. You suddenly felt like a fragile female outsider – and glad of it. It was his ship, just as the ships he had really sailed on in his days as petty officer were his ships. And in entering it you were in his power. A landlubber.

He ushered you in like a lady. But the minute that the dark shadows of the ship's interior embraced your sunny bodies he came up behind you. He grabbed your breasts, squeezing them hard as if they were East Indian mangoes he was ruthlessly testing for freshness and growled, 'I'll have you locked in irons for looking at me

142

so saucily, girl. And you'll get another twenty lashes for
having breasts so blimmin' gorgeous. And forty fucks
on top for putting me off my job. I could barely speak
for wanting you.'

You shoved your buttocks against his groin and he
pulled you down on the polished wood deck that so
many men had run across in battle, including Nelson
himself.

'No, not here,' you said. 'Tie me to the table and do
it, with one of those whips.'

Spencer pulled you to Nelson's splendid cabin
for'ard, the spring daylight shining in through the rows
of windows across the whole width of the ship. There
he placed you on the end of that 30-foot polished
mahogany table where all the Battle of Trafalgar charts
had been spread and the great captains of Nelson's fleet
had splendidly dined on spiced game night after night
during all those plunderings for the Empire. He tied
each ankle to the foot of that table and you were
stretched out as if for an operation, not a flogging. You
writhed with delight at his knowing that your breasts
were the point, delirious that he would not be wasting
time on your buttocks.

From his pocket in those tight trousers he took up
one of the whips. Your eyes bulged, wondering if his
cock would be as thick and long as that handle. He
trailed it over your lips, then his, and began undoing
the buttons on your sea-blue shirt. Your breasts had
grown large in the white lace bra and he scooped them
out, then kissed and bit your nipples till you were
screaming for a fuck. Your fantasies of the whip were
momentarily forgotten until you caught sight of it again
as he finally relented, stood back, and began undoing
his uniform fly.

'Let me see you,' you begged, reaching out to touch
his trousers and handle that flesh you were always so
curious about. He lashed your hand away lightly with

the whip. 'An extra stroke for insubordination, for looking at an officer.'

But then it was there, erect, naked. A cock hard and solid as his body, standing up tempting you so that you didn't know what you most wanted first, a fuck or the whip. As if to punish you – but only sort of – for wanting the fuck, he took ten paces back, flexed the whip, waited till he knew your whole body was straining for it and began to lash you, softly, on the nipples. Left to right. Port to starboard, stern to prow. Across. Diagonally. Up down. Around your nipples, under your breasts. It stung like hailstones, but warmer. You loved it.

'Please, please, come inside me,' you begged.

'No,' he snarled, and kept on lashing, soft, soft, soft and yet stinging until your nipples were taller than the Eiffel Tower. Then he bent to suck the blood off them. Alternately, he sucked and flicked, gentle, controlled flicks and still you begged: 'Ooh, fuck me, whip me, ram me, lash me!'

He came up close between your legs and began nudging the handle of the whip against the crotch of your jeans. You began rubbing back, up and down, up and down, your brain set askew by the slight side-to-side motion of the ship. Suddenly, breaking your trance, Spencer rammed the handle of the whip up against you, vertically, the tip of its handle pointing towards the ceiling. It pressed against your ready clitoris with such force that you were coming right through your jeans. Just as you were arching, begging for him not to stop, he ripped your jeans and pants down. In he jammed that big, golden cock as you lay there at right angles to him on Nelson's august table. In, in, aah! Again, again, again, and still you were arching to have your nipples caressed by that whip.

'England-expects-every-man-to-do-his-fucking-duty', he bellowed with every thrust. Christ, you thought, this is indeed manful! And you came. Surprisingly you came without him touching your swollen clit. And you came again. And again – the fifth time screaming, your breasts rearing up to place themselves into his hands but he was too busy holding your hips so he could shaft you even deeper.

'Oh, have me, have me!' you yelled.

'I'll bloody have you, girl. I'll have you so high your brains'll fly up in that crow's nest.'

And finally, when you were on roundabout orgasm number eighteen, he came too. And bent over you as you both laughed together.

'Oh, I loved the way you whipped me,' you said as you got dressed, your legs still shaky.

'You deserved it,' he said, grinning. 'You bloody women tourists full of Emma ideas, putting us guides off our duty.' You kissed and tottered as he helped you across the ancient decks, past the cannons sticking out of their gunports that so reminded you of him, and off the ship.

James was not far away, taking in a rope-making demonstration the leeward side of the quay, but when he saw you both coming down the gangway he steered tactfully away. You called him over to introduce him and he saw from your face that you'd had the kind of lashing and rodding you deserved – and more. He put an arm round you to hold you up. As the two men shook hands, James said 'She's a great girl, isn't she? She loves it. Thanks for giving her what she needs.'

Spencer smiled. 'It's the least one of Nelson's descendant's can do. And I happen to admire him for tackling someone as lusty as Emma. Well worth emulating. Would you er . . . like a souvenir?' Spencer offered James the whip.

And on the train going back to London, you locked yourselves in the toilet like you used to do. James took the whip out of his trenchcoat pocket and quickly the whole cubicle smelled of jute as he drew it up and down between your breasts, between your thighs. It was coarse, rasping and beautiful against your fanny, still wet from Spencer. You braced yourself against the wall to arch your body and receive the light lashes all the better. And in the British Rail mirror, hazy with old soap, you gazed dreamily as James discovered that he had all the strength of a flagstaff in him. He licked and sucked at your reddened nipples then rammed you, rammed you with his lovely familiar cock, all the way through Hampshire. The train rocked sideways as the ship had done, but fast, slamming you from side to side. Du dun, du dun, du dun.

And as he tunnelled into you, you couldn't help but dream of the woman in the grey T-shirt. Oh, how you'd like to go for her bottom with that fine, jute whip. She walked like the Queen of Naples. James, you realised, would have loved her too. And found a way to do his English duty to her, too.

Temptations

Airyn Darling

Temptations

❖ ❖

'*T*ell me a story,' she said innocently . . .
    Every time she laughed she glanced over at me,
lovely temptress that she was. I sighed and squirmed
slightly on the couch, trying to pay attention to what
was being said and done by others in the room. *Sliver*
was just cheesy enough to keep our attention, and
certainly bad enough to let us make horrible fun of it as
we watched. She and I kept sneaking these surrep-
titious, bright-eyed looks at each other, though, and it
was beginning to have its effect.
    She was one of those people with whom I felt an
instant and comfortable 'click'; I felt an ease with and
an appreciation of her only moments after we met.
Looking into her eyes, I sensed a likeness; similar
enough to notice, but different enough to keep my
attention, and wonder what was going on in there. She
was . . . I searched for a word . . . 'enchanting'. 'Enthrall-
ing.' Other words that start with 'e'. I felt like I had
found a new toy to play with, and I wanted her all to
myself. Unfortunately, this was not possible for several
reasons. First, there were about seven other people in
the room. Second, and most important, she was there

149

because she was a dear friend's girlfriend. His monoga-
mous girlfriend.

Damn that m-word, anyhow. She was also, for all I
had been told, straight. *Damn that s-word, while I'm at it*,
I thought. I felt like she was flirting with me, but maybe
she was just being friendly. After all, she didn't really
know any of us, and I'm sure she was trying to charm
us all senseless. She was doing a fine job of it, from my
standpoint. She made a comment about the film that I
was about to make myself, and I looked over at her,
smiling and shaking my head. She grinned back and
held my eyes for a moment before settling back into
Fisher's arms and cuddling against him.

I sighed again, watching her watching him. Too many
times, I'd gotten crushes on presumably straight
women, only to be disappointed. Of course there were
the odd few who were curious enough to at least
experiment, some of whom later became bisexual or
lesbian. Danielle seemed to have potential to at least
want to play, just a little bit. I realized I could just be
projecting a naive hope upon her, and so I just settled
back into the soft embrace of the sofa, and contented
myself making pithy comments about the film. My eyes
kept wandering over to her general direction, though,
attracted by what I felt was a gravitational pull. And
damn it if she weren't looking back a lot of the time.

This was just what I needed, oh, by *all* means; never
mind that Fisher and I had dated. Never mind that we
had broken up, and I had started to date his roommate,
Carol. Never mind that Carol dumped me for Fisher.
Leave all that behind, because none of it mattered at
this point, although it does set up the irony nicely. The
thing was that Fisher and Danielle seemed *genuinely
happy* together. How could I put myself between them?
How could I even *think* such a thing? *He wouldn't ever
have to know*, I thought nefariously to myself. Yeah, but
you would know, I chided. Not that I wouldn't be

happy fucking *both* of them senseless, mind you. I still felt a strong attraction to Fisher; it was just not worth risking our friendship over. Having a relationship fail once was one thing. Twice would most likely be another story. It was nice just having a harmless attraction with him now, with no other expectations involved. Now that Danielle was on the scene, she provided another perfect reason for me to maintain my willpower. They were both just so lovely, though . . .

Another sigh. More pithy comments to pass the time.

Helen started rubbing my neck and shoulders, easing away the tension of sitting (with horrible posture) at a desk in front of a computer day in, day out. I relaxed into her touch and nuzzled up against her, letting the sound of her voice soothe my frazzled nerves. It was nice just relaxing, and not having to *do* anything, being surrounded by some of my favorite people on the planet, whom I loved best. She tried to engage me in a conversation about something or another – her classes, her projects, and so forth – and as interested as I was, I couldn't concentrate on what she was saying. Fortunately, she noticed that I just wasn't following, and smiled and scritched my head, while snuggling up against me and laying her head against my shoulder. She finished what she was saying; I murmured an agreement, and we continued watching the film. She got up to get herself something to drink, and sprawled on the floor when she came back, getting comfy. Frank attempted to curl up next to me, but I arranged myself to keep him at a distance, trying not to let my contempt for him bubble to the surface. I shot the back of his head a smoldering glare and silently wished him away. No luck. I sighed. Maybe next time. Dennis made an observation on the film that provoked several minutes of conversation, but I couldn't tell you what it was if you paid me.

Eventually, I lost all interest in the film, and amused

myself with my own sordid little fantasies. They traipsed across the movie screen of my mind, and my inwardly focused eyes devoured the images.

One by one, everyone in the room fell asleep, except for me and Danielle. We kept up the witty repartee for a while, over meaningful glances. We lowered our voices, so as not to disturb our sleeping companions. 'Come upstairs,' she mouthed, and pointed up the stairs. We went into Fisher's room and flopped down on the bed together.

'So. Has Frank driven you nuts yet?' I asked. Frank was one of the most irritating humans I had ever met in my entire life.

She laughed. 'Not yet. I've only spent about three hours total with him. He's a bit trying, though, I have to say that.'

A pause, a little fidgeting on the bed.

'Can I ask you a personal question?' she inquired.

'Of course,' I said, rolling on to my side to face her. 'I'm pretty much an open book.' Here it comes, I said to myself, the part where she reveals her secret desire to be ravaged by a tender and compassionate woman, who understands what she wants. I smiled in confident anticipation.

She paused before asking, 'How come you and Fisher never got back together after Carol?'

My confident smile vanished. *Damn. That's not what she was supposed to say.*

'Well, he and I make better friends than lovers,' I said. 'Sure, he's gorgeous, he's sweet, he's caring . . . but somehow he and I just weren't right for each other.' I shrugged. 'We're both pretty happy where we are now.'

She nodded. 'Just curious.' She paused again, and I nudged her with my elbow.

'What?' I prompted.

'Oh . . . I don't know. Nothing, I guess.'

'Musta been a lie,' I said, mostly out of habit. I really

have no idea why I picked up that useless line from an old friend. Every time someone forgot what they were going to say, or decided not to say it, he said, 'Musta been a lie.' I have no idea why. I didn't even think it was funny. But, linguistic sponge that I am, I dutifully added it to my vocabulary.

At a loss for anything meaningful to say, I did my best to try to make small talk, something at which I am notoriously bad. After a few sentences, I just gave up and fell silent. I picked a spot on Fisher's bedspread, stared at my stubby nails, examined my hair for split ends. I felt her looking at me after a while.

'What are you thinking?'

'Dangerous question, Danielle. I tend to be brutally honest.' I attempted to arch an eyebrow and failed, as usual.

She took a deep breath and looked slightly hurt. 'I can handle it,' she said, somewhat defensively.

I regarded her for a moment, weighing my words. 'I'm thinking I'd really like to kiss you.'

She looked completely surprised, and her eyes darted around the room, trying to find something interesting to look at. They settled on the desk and stared vigorously at the computer. 'Oh.'

'Sorry . . . you asked,' I said with a sad smile.

She glanced quickly at my face, and back away again, and was very quiet.

'I'm sorry if I upset or offended you,' I offered, leaning away from her slightly to give her a little space. 'I'm not going to try –'

She cut me off and said, 'It's OK. It's fine. Really.' She looked at me for slightly longer than half a second. 'Really.'

I nodded and went back to contemplating the wall.

Several minutes passed with nothing said, with an insane amount of tension in the air. I tried to ride it out and let her make the recovery. A few moments longer, though, and I would burst into flames, I felt.

'Why don't you?' she asked softly, still looking away.

I gently turned her face to mine, but did not move closer to her. Her eyes were wide and soft and vulnerable, and she almost looked like she was about to cry, somehow. I slowly leaned towards her, watching her expression, and kissed her softly, briefly, my eyes never leaving hers. I retreated until my face was a few inches from hers. We looked at each other, somewhat solemnly. Finally she made some kind of decision, and reached out, placing her hand behind my neck, pulling me to her. We kissed tentatively again, small, gentle kisses in quick succession, before they became longer, and our lips began to part. We moved closer together, and my hands stroked her back, pulling her into me. I rolled her on to her back and continued kissing her more and more deeply . . .

A burst of laughter from the group jolted me out of my fantasy with a start. 'Well?' asked Frank of me expectantly.

'Erm . . . what?' I asked, blinking.

'How many Baldwin brothers are in the film?' he repeated.

'A hundred and eight? I don't know . . . A fucking lot, no doubt.' Assorted chuckles and they went back to whatever they were discussing. I closed my eyes fully, and leaned my head back against the cushy arm of the sofa, trying to get back into the delicious dream I had been weaving.

Let's see: she asked, I told her, we kissed . . . ah, yes, there we are.

I let my tongue dart quickly into her mouth and immediately back out again. She responded in kind, and finally our mouths gave up any pretense of being separate entities and melted together. Barely audible sounds came from one of us, I wasn't sure which. I tangled the fingers of one hand into her hair, and let the other caress her back and side. She wrapped a leg around me and pulled me fully on to her, and let her own hands run over my body.

A finger poked me in the side, rather hard. I opened one eye, mildly annoyed at the rude interruption. 'You sleeping?' asked Frank. *But of course it's Frank. Who else would violently poke a presumably asleep person to ask if they're sleeping?*

'Yes.'

'Tired, huh?'

'Yes.'

'Yeah, I'm pretty exhausted, too. I haven't been feeling well this week, and I didn't get much work done on my dissertation, and some of my students were complaining about the class. My housemates have coined this really cool phrase about taking a shit that I hope sticks around. Instead of saying "I'm going to the bathroom" or "I'm going to take a shit", we say "I'm going to go lose a few pounds".' He cackled riotously. 'I love that! "Lose a few pounds!" Anyhow, I was talking to my class the other day and . . .'

I let his words fade to a dim buzz in my mind as I firmly shut my eyes and my ears, wondering how one human could be so banal. I tuned in briefly once more to hear him say, 'Oh . . . I guess you're pretty tired then. OK, I'll let you sleep. Hey, Helen, did you hear about . . . buzzzzzzzzzzzzzzzzzzzzzzzzzzzzz . . .'

I took a deep breath. *I will not kill him. I will not rip out his insides and show them to him, while shrieking with malicious glee. Nope. Not me.* So much more soothing to think of other things . . .

I began kissing her neck, her ears, her hair, inhaling the aroma of her body. As I was buried in her neck, I felt an overpowering surge of desire, and I reached under her sweater to stroke the softness of her skin. She sighed and pulled my face back to hers for more kissing.

Her fingers massaged my neck, dug into my shoulders, pulled my hair ... I had forgotten about the sleeping friends downstairs, had forgotten about Fisher, had forgotten that this woman whose tongue was in my mouth was strictly Off Limits.

She pushed against me slightly, and I sat back a bit. She lifted her sweater over her shoulders and took it off. She wore a simple cotton bra with a clasp on the front. She blinked at me uncertainly. I took my own sweater off and began kissing her stomach, stroking her sides, her shoulders, her neck. She licked and sucked my fingers and they passed over her mouth. The growing demand in my nether regions wasn't going to be ignored for much longer. *Be patient*, I growled at them firmly. They backed off. A little. I kissed the flat of her chest, at the base of her neck, and then reverently, lightly, touched the swell of her breast with my lips. I freed my hand from her lips and undid the clasp of her bra. I pushed it to the sides and looked at her as I cupped one breast in my hand, and kissed the soft skin around the nipple, barely grazing the areola with my lips. She squirmed slightly beneath me and moaned quietly. I teased her nipple with my tongue, stroking it softly, then with a bit more pressure, before finally taking it into my mouth and sucking on it firmly. I nibbled on her delicately with my teeth and sucked on it harder.

Our quickened breaths were echoing off the mostly bare walls of Fisher's bedroom. My bra was lost in the scuffling somewhere, and our breasts pressed against each other as our mouths joined together again. She was just unbuttoning my jeans when we heard a noise at the door. We looked over to see a wide-eyed Fisher standing motionless in the door.

'Oh my God,' we both said in unison, as Danielle sat bolt upright, looking mortified and covering her breasts. *Oh shit. This isn't going to be good. Not at all.*

'I ... I didn't know ...' Fisher stammered as he leaned against the doorjamb. He continued staring at us as he sank into a limp sitting position.

I felt ready to cry, and it looked like Danielle was about to as well. My mouth opened and closed, trying to form a series of words that would somehow explain this away as a harmless situation. Nothing to be upset about, everything was fine ... None came stampeding to mind, though. *We're fucked*, I realized. *I have completely and utterly fucked up. What a dribbling asshole I am.*

A few unfathomably uncomfortable moments passed. Each second ticked by with a dull thud in my head once every epoch or so, it seemed.

'Don't stop,' Fisher said suddenly, very quietly.

'What?' we asked him, incredulous.

He didn't say another word; he settled into a comfortable position, leaning against the wall.

'Fisher ... you don't want this,' I said. 'You don't have to ...'

'Don't stop. Please.'

I looked at Danielle, helpless. She was looking at him, probably trying to figure out if he was serious. 'Are you sure?' He nodded, watching us intently.

Apparently, Fisher's a little kinkier than I might have thought. I reached for her, pulled her to me and kissed her lightly, looking into her eyes again, questioning. She answered with a kiss, and pushed me back on to the bed. At first we only kissed, nothing more, being careful not to seem too excited. Gradually, though, I forgot how horrified I had been, and remembered the arousal of only a few minutes ago. This was not difficult to do, given that I had a beautiful, sexy woman lying on top of me, kissing my neck and shoulders, stroking my breasts, and moaning in my ear.

Her back was so soft, her skin supple and smooth. She sat up and looked back at Fisher, who had a dreamlike expression on his face. She undid the button

157

of her jeans and unzipped them before unbuttoning my jeans the rest of the way. We each pulled off our own jeans and underwear, and were now lying next to each other, naked. For a while, we just lay and caressed each other delicately, looking at each other, tracing contours of face and body, testing softness and firmness, caressing with palms, and teasing with light fingertips. I pushed her on to her stomach, and straddled her thighs, massaging her shoulders, easing the remaining tension out of her body. I moved up slightly, so that the fuzz of my remaining pubic hair tickled her bottom, and she laughed. Moving back down again, I kept massaging and caressing, kneading her buttocks, thighs, calves and finally her feet. As I rubbed her feet, I sucked on her toes gently as she squirmed a little. I smiled and pushed her legs apart, stroking the insides of her legs. I positioned her so that the vee of her legs opened facing Fisher. I straddled her thighs again, this time facing her feet, and began kissing the backs of her calves, tracing the tip of my tongue over the curve of her muscles, along the sensitive area behind her knees, up her thighs to the slight crease where her bottom began.

I could smell her now, and longed to bury my face into her shaven puss and cover my face with her juices . . . Back in the real world, someone had turned off the lights, and they were watching the remainder of the film. I cautiously opened one eye, looking around the room, wondering if I'd been making any weird noises as my fantasy took me on its little journey. No one was paying any attention to me, and most of them looked like they were half asleep anyhow. Dennis was snoring softly. I relaxed and figured any sound I made would be more than covered up by the deep bass coming from the SurroundSound system. I shifted slightly in my seat, feeling that I was about wet enough to slide off the damn sofa. I took a deep breath.

Back to Danielle's beautiful body, then . . .

She was rolling over, wrapping her legs around me as she turned to kiss me again. She dipped her head to suck on my nipples. I threw my head back, and she sucked on my neck, biting the tender skin there, making me gasp. I turned my head slightly and noticed that Fisher was rubbing himself through his jeans, and looking for all the world like he was really enjoying this, and not feeling at all jealous. As I watched, he unbuttoned his shirt and took it off.

I moved down her body, kissing and sucking as I went, until I was kneeling on the floor between her legs, my face inches from her wet, hardened clitoris. I uttered an appreciative 'mmmmmm' as I began to part her labia with my tongue. She lifted her hips to my mouth, and I obliged her by swiftly running my tongue over her clit, then down to her vagina, flicking the tip of it in and out of her quickly. She sounded like she was on the edge of orgasm, so I returned to stroking her clitoris with the flat of my tongue, alternately sucking on it and stroking it, sucking and stroking, and finally sucking on it powerfully as her back arched and her hips thrust up into my face as she came.

I heard movement behind me, as Fisher removed his jeans. He came over to us on the bed. I felt his hand touching my back, as my hands gently squeezed Danielle's breasts as the waves of orgasm floated away and she settled back into the bed. She realized Fisher had come over and pulled him down to kiss her. I kissed her thighs and belly, wondering what was coming next, deciding to leave it up to the two of them, since they had the most at stake. Fisher whispered something in her ear, and she sat up, moving to the edge of the bed.

'Your turn,' she said with a wicked grin.

I smiled back, but feigned shock. 'No! No! Not that! *Anything* but that!'

She laughed and pushed me so that I was lying on the bed with my feet propped up on the edge. She tentatively kissed my inner thighs, while probing me with a finger or two, getting the lay of the land. I was also shaven, except for the obligatory nod to puberty: a small patch of hair at the top front. She spread my labia apart with her hands, and touched the tip of my clitoris with a well-moistened index finger, rubbing back and forth slowly. I moaned in appreciation. She moved closer, kissing the outsides of my nether lips cautiously, licking her lips to get the taste of me, testing. I must have passed, as she sank her finger into me and began sucking on my clitoris. I was instantly transported into pre-orgasmic nearly out-of-body experiences. Fisher moved behind her, stroking himself. I watched as he positioned himself behind her, and then penetrated her with a deep-throated sigh. She cried out as he buried himself completely within her, but did not stop her ministrations to me.

Fisher was fucking her slowly. He reached around her hips to gain access to her with his fingers, and began rubbing her clitoris. She momentarily stopped sucking on me and groaned. I raised my head to look at both of them, and was absolutely overcome by the sight of her face between my legs, and him fucking her from behind, rubbing her, reaching underneath her to squeeze her breasts. It was enough to send me straight to the edge, as she began flickering her tongue over my clit again. My cries were getting louder, as were theirs. Fisher's thrusts were coming faster and harder; I could feel her bump against me with each one. Finally, he started to come, which sent me over the edge, too. We both made all the standard out-of-control orgasm sounds, and then slowly returned to our senses.

We realized Danielle hadn't come a second time, and that she was looking like she really wanted to. We smiled at each other, at her, and then Fisher lifted her up so that she straddled him on the bed, as he lay on his back. They kissed fiercely, and he pulled her up so that she was sitting on his face. I sat off to the side and kissed her, played with her nipples, caressed her back, sucked on her earlobes as Fisher's skilled tongue worked on her nether bits. It didn't take her long to start bucking against him, biting my tongue and moaning increasingly loudly. She shook as she came a second time, her cries muted by my mouth as I did my best to devour her completely.

We collapsed into a heap next to Fisher, all of us silent and contemplative, absently running our hands over each other, wiggling when we hit a ticklish spot (except, of course, for Fisher, who refused to be at all ticklish). I wasn't quite sure what to say, if anything. Did anything need saying? The wonderful thing about fantasies is that there doesn't need to be any talking, any explaining, or any real-world consequences ... we could just have fun and I could resolve it any way I liked. I decided it would be nice to have them fall asleep, and have me melt away into the night, leaving them to wake up next to each other, smiling and without regret.

I sighed and pulled myself back into the world of the living room and the rolling credits. People were yawning and stretching, getting ready to leave. Danielle was still asleep in Fisher's lap, and he was looking down on her fondly, playing with her hair. He nudged her gently, and she woke up with a sleepy-confused 'huh?' and generally looked adorable.

Frank made some typical annoying comment that brought me completely back to reality, and I stood up, getting ready to make my exit. Wandering out into the cold wasn't entirely appealing. Not nearly as appealing as making love to a nice warm Danielle, anyhow. Ah well. Sometimes reality isn't as much fun as fantasy life. Every now and then, though, fantasy extends its hand into life, and sometimes becomes reality, too. I hugged Fisher goodbye, told Danielle it was very nice meeting her, and made my assorted goodbyes to the other people in the room.

The air outside was chilling. My leather jacket slowly hardened in the cold, becoming more of a carapace than a coat. I climbed into my Honda, and drove off into the night, my thoughts keeping me at least slightly warm. A nice hot shower, maybe a bath, would take care of the need to reheat myself to the bone. Shower massagers are highly underrated, in my humblest of opinions. Ever since I was eleven, when I had my first orgasm by way of a showerhead, I have maintained a fondness for them.

I switched my brights on as I drove down the deserted dirt road, watching a possum scurry off the road and into the underbrush. Too bad Danielle lived in Kentucky. Perhaps it was for the best, though ... I wasn't sure how much willpower I actually had. It's so much harder for me to resist women than it is for me to resist men. *Whatever happens, happens*, I thought resignedly. My thoughts drifted to past lovers as I drove. I remembered times of excruciating pleasure followed by tender cuddling and soft kisses. I smiled and pulled into my apartment complex's driveway. Gathering up my various stuffs, I walked up to my apartment, greeted two very enthusiastic cats, and headed into the bathroom, shedding cold clothing as I went. I filled the tub with hot water, took the showerhead down from its bracket, lit a few candles, and eased into the almost painfully hot water, relaxing into the otherworldly realm of steam and the sound of water lapping against the edges of the tub.

'Aaaaaaahhhhhhhhh.' I sank up to my shoulders and a pleasant shiver passed up and down my body. The showerhead clunked against the side and bumped into my feet. I reached for it, turned the water on, and opened the drain a tidge, so that I wouldn't flood the bathroom. As the warm water pulsed against me, I began to recall the fantasy all over again, and lost myself in another world of the skin, smells and tastes of a woman I barely knew, but would soon come to know better.

Wild Justice

Jenesi Ash

Wild Justice

❖ ❖

*B*ryn cupped her hands over her aching ears, trying to protect her stressed eardrums as the hip-hop and heavy bass came through the speakers. Her attempt was futile as the angry song reverberated through her head.

The person at the back of Bryn fell heavily against her. Again. Bryn stumbled forward and landed on the guy in front of her. She pushed herself away from him and apologized, but realized her manners were wasted. The guy couldn't hear her. She couldn't hear herself.

Bryn used all her strength as she shoved her way back, her spine slamming into a muscular chest. She jabbed her elbow back fiercely, indicating how angry she was getting with the man.

The stranger pinched her butt in response.

Bryn would have whirled around and slapped the man's face, but she had no room to turn. People on every side crushed her.

Sighing gustily, Bryn craned her head to see the rap group performing on stage. The singers were plunged into shadows as blue rays of light streaked across the arena. Bryn flinched as the crowd screamed their approval.

167

God, she hated being here. She hated this rap group. She hated rap. The only reason why she was at the concert was because her boyfriend got tickets.

Bryn glanced at her boyfriend standing at her left. Kyle's gorgeous face was turned upwards. His body was gyrating to the heavy drum beat.

Bryn's eyes flashed and her mouth twisted as she watched her boyfriend.

God, how she hated him.

She really hated Kyle. Her loathing was all-consuming and destroying her soul. Yet no one knew how she felt. She hid it well under the guise of a loyal, loving girlfriend.

The hate festered deep inside her, its bitter poison seeping through her mind. It killed any sweet feelings or precious memories she had for her long-term relationship with her boyfriend. The hate was new; just two weeks old. It was born when Bryn's stepsister confessed she'd been fucking Kyle.

Confess? That was the wrong word. Gail took great pleasure describing her escapades with Kyle. Gail and Bryn seemed close, but they were never loving sisters. They had a complex relationship built on competition and jealousy.

The sisters competed for parental love and recognition. Bryn always compared her successful career against Gail's glamorous profession. Gail measured her financial success against Bryn's healthy bank account. They always fought over men, although never openly. It was an ever-present undercurrent as the sisters kept a watchful eye on their boyfriends and lovers.

Obviously Bryn blinked. Gail took advantage of the lost concentration. Whether Gail was seduced or was the seducer didn't matter. Her stepsister and boyfriend had betrayed her, and now Gail had seemingly won the sisterly competition as she had gained Kyle's interest.

Bryn's imagination went crazy as she remembered

Gail's revelations. Gail giving Kyle a blow job while Bryn was in the bathroom, preparing for a night on the town. Kyle eating Gail's pussy when Bryn ran down to the apartment's laundry room. The two mating like wild animals in the living room on her birthday while Bryn was passed out on the sofa.

Bryn jerked out of her memories as the guy behind her pushed forward. She kicked back, her lightweight shoe almost flying off as it made contact with the jeans-clad leg. Bryn immediately regretted her brutal response. The guy behind her was annoying, but she was reacting to Gail's confession.

Bryn wished she could have savagely attacked Gail and Kyle. It would have been destructive, vicious and gratifying.

It also would have been stupid.

She knew this even as Gail described how much pleasure she gave Kyle. Bryn purposely squashed down her growing rage as her stepsister relived the sex in explicit detail. Bryn even rolled her eyes over the kinky stuff. She told Gail it was all lies and she didn't believe it.

But she did believe it. Every word. Once Gail exposed the fling, Bryn recognised the truth. Kyle's behavior suddenly made sense. Bryn finally had answers for those nagging unspoken questions.

The night after Gail confessed, Bryn started planning on breaking up with Kyle. She secretly found another apartment and covertly moved her stuff. She wiped Kyle's name off of her financial and legal documents. She was ready to leave.

But something was missing.

Every action Bryn took was meant to protect herself. She was prepared for any problem or surprise. Her systematic, analytical problem solving should make her feel better. She should be proud of her foresight.

She was, but it wasn't enough. She wanted revenge.

She wanted Kyle to hurt like she did. Bryn wanted his ego to be blown away into little pieces so that when he put it back together, it would never be quite the same. She wanted him to feel humiliated and betrayed.

Bryn thought she had planned the perfect revenge. She wanted to carry it out tonight. Dressed in a snug white T-shirt, a denim mini-skirt, flat blue shoes and nothing else, Bryn was going to seduce Kyle's best friend.

Only her plan fizzled. Kyle's friend Freddy couldn't make it to the concert tonight. Bryn was disappointed almost to the level of frustration. Her break-up plan would be incomplete.

Kyle bumped against her and she turned towards him. He was jumping up and down with the beat of a new song. Kyle looked down at her and flashed a toothy smile. Bryn placed a smile on her face as a reply.

God, she really hated him.

She turned away and tried to focus on the scantily clad females dancing on stage. It was next to impossible as everyone around her jumped up and down to the primitive beat.

The stranger behind her was also jumping, his jeans rubbing against the back of her thighs. His belt buckle pressed against the small of her back. She could feel his cock between her buttocks.

Bryn froze as the wicked idea drifted into her brain.

What if she had sex with a stranger? What if she fucked a guy, any guy, maybe even this irritating guy behind her? If she had sex with a nameless man, would she feel avenged? Would her break-up be complete?

Bryn felt a hot blush sweeping through her body at the thought. What was coming over her? She couldn't have sex with a stranger. It was so unlike her. It was senseless, idiotic and crazy.

And yet Bryn couldn't help but think about it.

She wondered how she could pull it off. How could

she seduce a stranger tonight while she was with Kyle? If Kyle figured out what she was doing, what would he do? Would he fight the man, beat her up, or just watch? Would he be angry, indifferent or turned on?

Bryn's heart pulsed heavily to the rap song. Her breathing became shallow as she imagined having sex with a stranger. The idea made her stomach quiver.

What if she had sex with a man while Kyle stood next to her?

Bryn gasped at the vindictive thought.

It seemed so right. After all, Kyle fucked Gail when Bryn was near. He obviously did it for the excitement. He probably found the possibility of getting caught thrilling.

She should do the same to him, only one step further. She would let a man fondle her while Kyle stood next to her. She would fuck a guy and Kyle would be there, not knowing what was happening. When Kyle found out, and Bryn would make sure he found out, he would feel like the ultimate fool. Kyle would know pure humiliation and betrayal. He would know how she felt.

Bryn glanced at Kyle. He was watching the stage, enthralled. His arms were raised as he pumped them to the rhythm of the rap song.

Just looking at him made Bryn want to tear his eyes out. She wanted sweet revenge, but could she let another man use her body like this? Could she be this ruthless?

A hazy vision of Gail and Kyle made Bryn's flittering nerves steady. Yes, Bryn thought. She could definitely be that ruthless. If Kyle could treat her this way, she could respond in the same manner.

Taking a deep breath, Bryn slowly let her rigid posture soften. She stopped trying to defend her space. The crush of bodies nearly swallowed her. Her breasts squished against the man in front of her. The stranger behind now shrouded her body.

171

Bryn fought the instinct to push the bodies away. The stench of sweat was overwhelming. The pressure against her bones was almost too much and she gulped in the hot, stale air. It tasted like smoke and it burned her throat.

The man behind her shifted back and Bryn knew it was time to make her move. Her heart pounded painfully against her ribs as she leaned against the stranger's chest. She waited anxiously to see if the man would push her away or accept her weight.

He seemed to pause for a moment. Bryn's heart was now pulsating in her ears. If this guy rejected her, she was not going to fulfill her revenge. She would leave the relationship with Kyle feeling incomplete and victimized. The stranger had to accept her.

The man relaxed, allowing Bryn's back to relax on his flat chest. Her relief came out in a whoosh. Now the hard part: seducing the stranger.

Bryn kept her eyes focused in front of her as she rested against the man. She felt him rock to the music and she moved her hips the same way. She pushed her butt into him a little, slightly pillowing his cock with her buttocks. His penis swelled and Bryn suppressed a naughty smile.

The rap song increased its tempo as blue, red and yellow lights flashed around them. The stranger's hips rotated to the fast pace and Bryn concentrated on matching his steps. Her ruthless plan and the man's sexy movements was a heady mixture. Her cunt tightened and she tilted her ass.

The man grabbed her hips, grinding his pelvis into her. She countered his move by rolling her hips. His hands clenched. She wiggled her hips. The stranger started rubbing his cock up and down. Bryn felt her pussy grow hot and moist.

She glanced at Kyle. He was dancing, totally absorbed in the music. Bryn considered glancing down at the stranger's hands that rested on her body. She decided against it. There was something decadent about not knowing anything about this man. She had no idea of his name, his appearance, his age. She could feel that he was male, and that was all she needed to know.

Bryn's knees buckled as the stranger's hands crept under her T-shirt. His hands were rough, dry and warm. His palms were large and his fingers were long. The fine hair on his arms tickled her sides as he confidently sought her tits.

His hands boldly cupped her breasts. Bryn couldn't hear it, but she felt his groan of pleasure vibrating in his chest. His enjoyment erased any lingering doubt she may have had about this ruthless plan.

The stranger squeezed her breasts and played with them under the protection of her T-shirt. Bryn knew that if anyone glanced at her, they would obviously see someone fondling her. She cast a quick glance at Kyle, but his attention was still on stage.

The man pinched her nipples and Bryn gasped. He rubbed them with the pads of his fingers until they were hard. Her pussy was getting wet as he played with her body.

Bryn wanted to reach back and hold on to his hips, pulling him closer. She had to fight the instinct. She didn't want to touch him; she wanted him to touch her. Bryn raised her arms, pretending to be like the other concertgoers. The movement allowed the man more access. Her stance made her feel vulnerable as she opened herself up to him.

The stranger lowered his right hand as he continued fondling her breasts with his left. His large hand splayed against her hot stomach before dipping beneath her waistband. Bryn's stomach clenched with anticipation as he teased her pubic hair with his fingertips.

She pushed her pelvis forward, seeking his hand. She didn't want him to tease. She wanted him to grab, to pull, and to yank. Her clit was trembling and she could feel this wild need centering in her cunt. She spread her legs as wide as she could without falling over.

The man finally rubbed his fingers lightly through her moist hair, the friction causing Bryn to shudder. He pinched her nipple hard in response. She moaned shakily, curling her outstretched hands into fists.

The stranger was practically on top of her as he rubbed one finger against her. He then used two. Bryn found his fingers tantalising. He didn't just rub continuously. He was gentle then rough. He used short and long strokes.

Bryn's body began to tremble as he stuck his finger into her cunt. He pumped it in and out, in and out. Bryn's world focused solely on the man's hand. The music around her became background noise. The people smashing her seemed so far away. The rainbow of colors flickered around her like a crazy kaleidoscope.

Desire swirled in her womb. Her neck and shoulders tingled. Her ankles and legs burned. Her breasts grew heavy with a fiery sensation. Her nipples puckered as liquid fire streaked through her body.

Bryn cried out as an orgasm hit her hard. No one heard her shriek as she surrendered to the violence inside her. Her body convulsed, her legs twitching helplessly as her breasts jiggled against the man's hand.

She sagged against the stranger, her body still quaking from the aftershocks. His hot breath stirred her hair and tickled her ear. One of his hands was still clenched to her breast while the other stroked her cunt.

Bryn became increasingly aware that the man's body vibrated with need. His cock dug into the small of her back. His touch was becoming coarse and rough. The man was quickly losing control.

Her surrounding drifted back. The rap group was saying something, but Bryn couldn't make out the words. It sounded like a piercing shriek to her. The lights flickered and danced, but she wasn't aware of the colors. The people around her still pressed against her and she couldn't remember why.

Kyle! Bryn twisted her head to find him. He was right next to her, his foot pushing against hers. His face was partially hidden in shadows, the dancing lights eerily flickering above him. He was yelling, punching his fist to the stage, as if his opinion of the song could be heard.

Satisfaction trickled through her spent body. Her revenge would soon be complete. Bryn smirked as she watched Kyle shouting, his face contorted. God, he was such an idiot. What did she ever see in him?

The stranger removed his left hand from her breast. Bryn felt the loss immediately and whimpered. She craved for his touch. Her complaint died on her lips as she felt him fumbling with his belt.

Bryn's pulse quickened as the man unzipped his jeans. She could feel his every move since his body was pressed against her back. His cock sprang out and she was gasping for breath, unable to contain her wicked excitement.

He kneaded and massaged her wet and throbbing pussy. He scrunched up her skirt with one hand, her bare ass exposed to the hot air. He held her tight as he shoved his cock deep inside her.

Bryn groaned as his penis filled her completely. He was so large that the fit was almost too tight. She squirmed and both his hands bit into her naked hips, ordering her to stop. She immediately complied.

The man pulled out slightly before ramming back in. Bryn groaned again, arching her back, splaying her outstretched hands. The stranger was deeply embedded inside her and it felt delicious.

Bryn turned her head to see if Kyle was aware of what was going on. He was dancing like the music filled him, jerking his arms and head wildly. He tilted his head toward her and opened his eyes.

Her heart stopped beating. Her breath was trapped in her lungs as Kyle looked at her. Her skirt was bunched up, her naked ass exposed, her cunt filled with a stranger's cock. The man was slammed up against her and was beginning to pump. Bryn swallowed hard, the action hurting her suddenly dry throat.

Kyle's eyes were wide, his mouth open. He yelled something, shaking his fists. Bryn thought she was going to pass out, that her half-naked body would crumple to the ground.

Kyle turned to the stage and shook his fists, shouting. He jumped up and down as the band's most popular song began.

Bryn stared at Kyle, incredulous. She thought she had been caught, but Kyle wasn't aware of her scandalous appearance. He looked right at her while she was being fucked by another man and didn't even notice. Sure, it was hard to see anything from the waist down while they were crushed together, but his chinos were brushing up against her bare hips! He was standing right there!

Bryn turned to the stage as the group danced the intricate choreography. She arched her throat back and laughed. Her laugh cleansed her bitter soul and freed her troubled mind. She stretched her arms above her head as the stranger gripped her hips and repeatedly shoved his cock into her wetness.

She reveled in his fast, crude pace. She pushed against his savage thrusts. She swayed against his gyrating pelvis. She accepted his wildness and gained power from it.

Bryn soon became as untamed as the stranger. She could feel an orgasm building inside her. It was unlike any she had ever had. Her body was imploding. Her insides felt like they was caving on to her womb.

The man kept ramming inside her, gaining momentum. The music around her was building to a crescendo.

The lights flashed around her faster and faster until they became bolts of lightning. The audience bounced to the beat, their bodies pounding into each other.

Bryn's body shook as the man hammered into her. Her breasts slapped against her body. Her hair fell over her face in waves. Her legs were about to collapse.

The stranger plunged into her cunt and Bryn went to pieces. She screamed as the orgasm blew her mind away like scattered leaves. Her body silently howled from the passionate fury before going blessedly numb.

The man yelled in her ear as he convulsed inside her. She sagged against him, the heat of his body scorching her overstimulated skin. His hands remained on her hips, loosening his commanding grip.

They remained connected for a moment before she found the strength to pull away. Her legs wobbled as she straightened. The man removed his cock from her and she tugged down her denim skirt.

Bryn's heart was thumping. Her pulse was erratic. Her breasts felt bruised and she could feel the stickiness between her thighs.

She had never felt better.

She couldn't wait to get home. The presence of the man behind her grew dim as she started planning her next move. How should she reveal this fling to Kyle? While he was eating her pussy, or while he was jamming his cock inside her? Maybe during the afterglow of a good hard fuck.

Bryn didn't think the timing mattered too much since she had already experienced her special brand of wild justice.

Shoreline

Lesley Wilson

Shoreline

❖ ❖

*F*or days and nights we have lain together, entwined like sea creatures, sucking each other, binding our bodies together as if they are made of something other than inflexible human muscle and bone. We need to be inside each other, wrapped around each other, consumed. We make love until we are raw or liquid or blissful. We hardly eat. Our sustenance is the taste of ourselves. We rarely sleep. We rest on each other's bodies, tranquillised by our scents. Although we never speak of it we know our situation is desperate. Sometimes we go to the crudely hung shower and cling together while the uncertain force of the water trickles tepid then gushes hot on our skin, perhaps to wash away our passions, stun us apart. But then we lie on towels while the sun climbs to the small window on the roof, pounding our love into each other while the old wetness goes and a new wetness comes. We know this can't last. We are not alone in our small place of wildness and ocean. Others will try to find us. Perhaps we need to find them. We found each other so easily . . .

ANYA

His silhouette, the tall dark strength of it, seems to merge with the rest of the rock on which he sits. As I approach I see that he moves slightly, back and forth towards the sea. In my fatigue the shape is made crazy, a strange horn-like mass stuck on to the black stone, swaying.

My nightdress clings to my thighs in the dawn breeze. The smell of me comes through, unwashed, musky from the long night of broken sleep. So often I awake, the sheet twisted hard and damp around my waist and tight between my legs, my hand always there, my fingers always wet. Alone in my dreams I bring myself to orgasm and I don't know why.

ERNST

I don't look up although I hear her. Her breath comes fast and she makes soft moaning sounds as if something hurts. Then she stands over me so I can't ignore her. She looks drugged, sleepwalking, but her skin is white and her legs are long. Around her eyes she has the darkness of exhaustion. She fixes me with those eyes – crazy glittering green eyes. They command attention. But I don't want her.

'Go away,' I tell her. It's not difficult although the sound of my voice sounds strange. I have been alone here so many weeks. Then she stares through me as if she doesn't want me either and then I feel the familiar anger rise, the tightness in my chest, the heat behind the eyes. But suddenly she turns and walks towards the sea. Her hair swirls wildly against the sky. The after-scent of it comes through the ocean tang. It is both repulsive and intoxicating.

As she strides against the wall of water her legs are barely strong enough to withstand the power of the waves. In seconds her thin dress is transparent, her frail body pounded back and forth, her high buttocks clasped by the foam that licks at her. She is going in too deep and I know she will not swim.

ANYA

This dream is more vivid than most. I am being dragged from the depths of the ocean. The heaving waves are taking my dress. It is ripped and coiling in ribbons. I put my head back and my hair is sucked in by the sea. I don't see the sky but two dark eyes looking down at me. His face is expressionless but beautifully sculpted as if in stone. I feel his hands under my body, pulling me back. The coldness of the water sharpens my senses and I think for a moment I am not dreaming. But back in the shallowness he picks me up and carries me against his chest and everything's hazy again. My wet face and hair loll against his tight dark skin. I taste it. I want to drown inside the salt and warmth of him. The hardness of his arm under my knees makes me want to feel more of him. I squirm, push myself more into him. He makes a sound of annoyance, grips me to him tighter. Despite my chill and numbness it starts again, the slow pleasurable ache between my legs.

ERNST

'You can't want this, surely. God, woman, you're half dead.' I can't stop my voice trembling or stop myself staring at her writhing body.

Twice now I have grabbed her wrists and pushed her gently back on the sand as she has thrust herself towards me or tried to pull me down. I try to quieten her but her head twists back and forth in refusal. She says the same thing over and over again.

'I want you now. Take me. Bring me to life.'

As her slender body struggles beneath me, strips of cotton

cling to her slight firm curves and tiny rivers of water trickle down her flesh. One small breast is fully exposed, her pink-brown nipple large and high with cold.

'Touch it. You want to, don't you?'

This time, when I meet her eyes, she stares directly back. The green of her gaze becomes hot. I feel myself uncoil like a snake, become hard. My blood pounds till I'm sure I feel her hand on me, caressing and persuading me to throbbing erection. Sweating now, and sick with desire, I look down to see that her hands are nowhere near me although my erection is obviously visible inside my shorts.

I gasp to see both her hands between her own legs, urgently, one on top of the other, her fingers pressed hard and sliding back and forth, her legs spreading wider and wider, tearing another long slit in her dress. Now the soft ginger hair between her legs is exposed, her fingers working furiously then slowly revealing glimpses of the oily pink flesh and its glistening growing wetness.

'Come down to me. Come down to me, now.' Her soft plea is irresistible.

Her arms reach up once more. I smell the musk and salt from her fingers. I hold her wrists and kiss the taste of her. Her fingertips quiver. On the sand her hips arch slightly. I can't resist.

Slowly I move between her legs. But I am on my knees, still cautious. A slight rain falls and the grey summer sky stains yellow. I put my hand flat on her stomach. I stroke her gently, being careful not to put any weight on her. She is fragile. Now her whole body shudders. Her face is very pale.

'You'll get cold,' I tell her, and the words sound stupid. I continue to caress her abdomen, my thumb edging towards the top of the soft tangled hair on her mound.

'Then cover me. Please.' There is a sob in her voice.

I hold her quivering arms down at her sides on the sand and come forward to take her in my mouth. She sighs as I put my face to her, forcing her mound up to me, making me lick and taste more and deeper of her juice. I taste the sea *from her, and her desire flows on my tongue. Her long nails tear at my wrists. She wants to push my tongue further inside her. She wants my head in her power. She wants to come.*

'I'm cold. I'm so cold.'

She is telling me to cover her, fuck her completely.

I lift my face from between her legs and move over her. I kiss her damp eyelids, her parting, quivering mouth. All the time she searches my eyes. Until she makes the sign, I nudge myself gently between her legs, teasing not quite entering. But I am growing crazy with the need of her, having to slow again and again as the urge to pound into her and release my desire becomes almost unbearable.

'Now?' I ask her. 'You want me now?' I know I sound desperate.

Just when I think I can't stand it any more, that she must let me inside or my seed will burst on to her thigh or the sand, a strange bewildered look comes into her eyes and she frowns. Her eyelids flicker then they close and her head falls limply to one side. Abruptly I move back from her, trembling, half-kneeling on the sand. I glance around, which is absurd, for surely there can be no one else lurking on this island. There are no signs of life to be seen or heard, only birds crying overhead and the crash of waves. So I pick her up. Although I kneel I pick her up easily. She is as light as a child. Tormented with lust and ashamed, I take a further look around then place her legs around me. I am exposed to her. She, wet with desire, is exposed to me. She falls like a rag doll on my chest, her arms flopping over my shoulders. I want her so badly. I hold up her head and cover her peaceful white face with kisses. She doesn't respond but my erection almost of its own accord seeks out her pink moistness.

'I'll bring you back to life,' I whisper against her cheek but without hope.

Then strangely, although her eyes remain closed, her lips open in a smile.

'Yes,' she murmurs. 'Yes.'

*With one easy movement I am inside her. But I go slowly
at first, afraid that I might rip her slight body apart. I clasp
her small buttocks and hold her hard to me so that her special
place is massaged by the root of my cock. In a half-sleep and
now clinging damply to my back, words pour from her
mouth.*

*'Ripen me, open me, rain in me. I am weak, much too
weak.'*

*I thrust harder inside her. I feel her knees tighten at my
waist.*

*With my fingers spread wide at the base of her spine I
clasp her to me until she writhes on me, the walls of her cunt
squeezing my cock. She throws her head back, animated, but
her eyes remain closed. Her mouth opens wide as she gasps
and sobs and sighs her mounting excitement. Now she is
trembling hard and pushing herself into me as if she can't get
close enough. With delirious pleasure I try to bring her to
orgasm before I let go and reach my own. The sand beneath
us is wet and I half turn to see a large wave rush towards us.
We topple as the wall of water comes to its peak and crashes
over us. I pound into her as the incoming tide falls back. The
foam fizzes and melts in her hair. She cries out in surprise or
fear or ecstasy.*

ANYA

There's a white curtain of the thinnest material over the
window and it's full of sun. The square of light hurts
my eyes. The walls are made of heavy timber but look
frailer and fresher in the light. It must be near noon.

I am lying on a bed of rough blankets and coarse
sheets but beneath my cheek I feel a pillow of the softest
satin. I can smell perfume from it although I haven't
used scent for years. Suddenly I realise that my hair is
damp and full of sand. I must have wandered again. I
have no idea how I got here but there's something lived
in about the hut-like dwelling that makes me feel I

might not be alone on this island after all. My heart beats fast.

He enters the room quietly through a partition of tinkling, coloured beads. He is a dark, tall, strong-looking man and the softness of his approach seems incongruous. He sits on the bed naked but for a pair of sun-faded shorts. I smile at him with delight and amazement and he smiles back.

'You're the man in my dreams,' I tell him. 'The only one I ever saw the face of.'

'What do you mean?' He looks puzzled.

'Every time I go to sleep men make love to me – at least, I feel them but I never see their faces. Not since I've come here. You're the first.'

'Why *did* you come?'

His hand reaches down to take a lock of hair from my cheek. The gesture feels right, almost as if he is not a stranger. It's the sort of thing my husband used to do. A long time ago.

'I ran away. I thought I'd be alone here. My husband was a soldier . . .'

I don't explain further. Recounting the story makes me sad and, anyway, few people understand. To my surprise and alarm the man gets off the bed abruptly and goes to stand by the square of light, his back to me.

ERNST

She escapes because she is married to a soldier. I escape because I am one. We both think we are alone on this island. I don't know whether to laugh or be angry. I consider sending her away, getting rid of her, when suddenly I feel her hand upon me. Her fingers caress my shoulder, hesitate, then trace a tingling line down my back. At the base of my spine her palm rests and she massages me and I become less tense. Then as I sense she will, she reaches her expert fingers round to my front to steal inside my shorts, to stroke and tease my erection till I feel the glaze of my wetness being slicked like oil again and again on the throbbing head of my penis.

'Shouldn't you be doing this to your husband?'

I mean the words to sound condemning, bitter, but the intensity of my desire shudders through them.

'He couldn't make love to me. Too much fighting,' she sighs. 'No, you wouldn't understand.'

I look down to see her kneeling before me. Her fingers work expertly. But her eyes are not the eyes of a manipulator. She is a woman desperate for passion.

'I'll beg if I have to,' she says, and her hands rest a second. Her lips move nearer and nearer the tip of my cock. An immense heat moves through me. She glances up. Her eyes are pleading.

'You don't have to beg.'

As I shudder with the exquisite torment she laps into my body, I know I can refuse her nothing.

When she wraps her pale mouth around me, when her tongue plays like the flicker of a magic snake all the gunfire I have ever heard, the aching limbs I have carried, all the terror in all the eyes are soothed and melted away by the velvet motion of her mouth.

When my seed explodes into caverns of her angel face, when I see her eyes shine with hope and the glisten of my wetness on her lips, when she drinks down my seed as if she's dying of thirst, there is no hope for me, but all the world of hope for us.

I reach down and take her hands, lift her to her feet and bind her against me. There is room for two on this island and room for dreams but no nightmares.

Outmanoeuvred

Juliet Lloyd Williams

Outmanoeuvred

❖ ❖

Shannon eased her body slowly over her right leg and felt the muscle at the back of her thigh stretch. She did the same over her other leg, then routinely went through the other stretches, warming her body, preparing for the exercise to come. Beside her Laura was doing the same and grinning widely. Shaking her head, Shannon couldn't help smiling back. 'Ready?'

Laura straightened and stretched her arms high over her head, pulling her T-shirt taut across her chest. 'Too right I am.'

There was a tap on the window behind them. 'Good luck,' Louise mouthed and gave them the thumbs up.

'Let's do it,' Shannon said.

They kept the pace slow to allow their muscles to warm properly. The roads were empty; the early morning and slight drizzle keeping everyone in their beds. At her side Shannon could hear Laura breathe, hear the slap of their feet on the pavement as the pace picked up. A warm glow settled over her body in spite of the weather. She lifted her face to the moist air and felt the dampness cool her. She smiled, thinking she would love to take off the rest of her clothes and feel the coolness

191

settle on her hot body, to feel the dampness prickle her skin, bud her nipples, arouse the heat between her thighs. She shook her head. Not now, though, now they had to run.

The road rose slightly and became a gravelled path as they reached the start of the mountain. For a while they ran silently along the mountain path, feet crunching on the gravel, sometimes squelching in the occasional patch of mud that hadn't dried out in the past couple of sunny days. Ahead the path forked: one led to the small lake, the other into the trees. Shannon jogged to the right, following the path into the darker covering of trees. Behind her Laura followed.

Only the whisper of the breeze shifting the trees and the birds' early-morning songs disturbed the silence. Calm and still. Just the two of them.

Ahead a bird screeched loudly and flapped into the sky, disturbing the other birds so that they all soared into the air, squawking unhappily. Had they disturbed them, Shannon wondered briefly, or were they still too far away to bother the birds? Was it something else? What?

It took a couple of minutes to reach the place the birds had been and, looking around her, at first she could see nothing out of the ordinary. Then, out of the corner of her eye, she saw something move. For several seconds she couldn't make the shape out, then she realised. A man, partially hidden by the trees and barely noticeable until he stepped from his hiding place on to the path into full view of the two women. Behind her Shannon heard Laura inhale sharply. A man in fatigues. Army. A snapping twig, a rustle of leaves to the side of them and more male bodies lined the way. All soldiers.

Shannon felt a surge of excitement shoot through her. How many were there? Her first impression was five, maybe six, but she didn't stop to count them; she carried on running, straight towards the first man, who remained motionless. With trees lining the path it would be difficult to pass him. As she drew closer she was able to see him clearly: tall, muscular, a harsh lived-in face and a grin almost as wide as his shoulders. Lust raised its head, making her heated body hotter. Would he move? Or would he stay there?

He folded his arms across the broad chest and widened his feet. He wasn't moving. Laura moved closer; Shannon could feel her touch her shoulder briefly. Then she understood why – the other men had fallen into step behind them and she could hear their feet pounding closer and closer. Her heart stepped up a beat and she moved faster, aware of the adrenalin rushing through her system. A few yards away the soldier stood, unmoving except for his eyes as he watched the men gain on the women, and the wide grin as he ogled the two female forms.

As she drew closer, Shannon saw the challenge in his eyes. A challenge she couldn't resist. To her left she noticed a gap in the trees and decided to take it. The ground sloped sharply away beneath her feet; it made her legs ache as she struggled to stay upright on the slippery grass. Behind her she heard Laura gasp. Turning briefly, Shannon saw Laura held by a couple of men, and judging by the grin on her face she wasn't finding it at all unpleasant.

'The other one's mine,' the man blocking her path yelled. He swore as he followed Shannon through the trees. Above her harsh breathing and the pounding of her heart she heard him gain on her. Smiling, she slid further down the grass, using the tree trunks and branches to keep her balance. He'd have to work to catch her.

Branches caught at her as she passed, snagging her clothes and her hair. Her feet thumped against the ground and her arms flailed in front of her, trying to clear the way. He was closer now. She could hear him breathing, feel him behind her. And it was exquisite. The thrill of sexual excitement, of being chased, was exquisite beyond belief. Jogging alone made her horny. How many times had she masturbated in the shower on her return? The hot glow, the rapid thump of her heart, the pressure between her legs were so sexy. Anyone who didn't find exercise sexy must be mad.

A hand caught her arm. Wriggling, she tried to free herself without stopping. The fingers loosened and she was free. For a second there was nothing, then a huge arm clamped around her waist and she was wrestled to the ground with a sweaty, male body landing heavily on top of her.

Before she could struggle or even find her voice, a large hand slid between her thighs and captured her groin. She moaned in pleasure and he squeezed hard. Pure bliss. The pain receded and pleasure took over as her body shook with orgasm, leaving her writhing beneath his hard body. Even as the tremors died away, he kept his hand on her mound, squeezing gently, squeezing every last drop of pleasure from her.

'Horny bitch,' he murmured, his mouth mere inches from hers. 'Aren't you?'

She couldn't speak, could barely catch her breath. Her hand found his cock through his trousers and gently closed around the swelling. 'Horny bastard,' she gasped.

He laughed, loud and confidently, and hauled her roughly to her feet. 'We're a pair well met then.'

With one hand firmly wrapped around her arm, he dragged her back up the banking. Long silvery sighs of pleasure and masculine grunts met them. The noises made the hairs on the back of her neck tingle and arousal, barely assuaged by her earlier orgasm, started to flicker once more. As they came up over the banking she could see a naked Laura on her hands and knees, breasts and body swaying as one soldier thrust into her from behind, his hands clasped tightly around her narrow waist. Another soldier kneeled in front of her, holding her hair in one hand, forcing her head up. In his other hand he held his prick and was teasing her open mouth with it. And from her moans she was enjoying every second of it. Another two men looked on.

'Caught the other one, sarge,' one of the men jeered, who was watching the action with his flies open, rubbing himself frantically. The youngest of the group merely looked on in amazement as the sergeant turned Shannon to face him and dragged her T-shirt over her head, then dropped it on the ground.

'Feisty one, this,' he told them as he dragged her breasts over the top of her bra. 'And she's mine first. Isn't that right?' he murmured in her ear. He didn't move as he waited for her response. Shannon could only nod in acceptance. In the back of her mind she appreciated his offer of a way out but she wanted this as much, maybe more, than he did.

The way he was talking made her squirm. It was almost as if she wasn't there. That she didn't matter to him. All he cared about was the pleasure he would take from her body. It was a new and brilliant sensation to be thought of as a mere sex object; it was something she had never experienced before. She knew then there was nothing she wouldn't do. And it thrilled her so much she nearly came.

'See,' the sergeant was saying, 'she's so horny she'll come if you touch her tits. Try it, Private.'

His language, crude and so male, made her squirm even more. Then she was roughly turned around, with her arms held tightly behind her back. The youngest soldier took a hesitant step towards her.

'Go on, lad,' the other soldier encouraged. 'Think of it as part of your education.'

His face paled as he moved towards Shannon. Her

body began to shake as she imagined his hesitant fingers on her body. Was he a virgin? How old was he? Probably not twenty, but a virgin? A movement to the side caught her eye. The soldiers had finished with Laura and she'd flopped on to her back with her legs together. The sergeant had noticed it too for he said, 'Keep her legs open.'

Laura complained most vocally as her legs were prised apart.

'They're to be available at all times for whatever we want,' he continued. His harsh voice made Shannon weak with longing. The tension was unbearable. Why didn't the young one touch her? He was so close she could feel his breath on her but still he did nothing.

Slowly his hand reached out to tentatively touch her erect nipple.

'That's it,' one of them encouraged.

One finger trailed over her nipple, teasingly unaware of how it made her squirm and made her even wetter between her legs. Encouraged by her gasp, he cupped her breast and weighed it in his hand. When the sergeant nodded, he tightened his fingers and squeezed. Her mouth fell open and she began to pant and mewl with pleasure.

'She's going to come. Squeeze both of them, lad, and watch her come.'

Both hands dragged her breasts further out of the bra and closed over them. He tightened his fingers and she wriggled, trying to get closer.

'Keep still,' the sergeant hissed in her ear, 'or I'll have you punished.' He bit her earlobe, making her squeal. The lad stopped and watched them carefully.

'Please,' she moaned.

'Right!' the sergeant snapped. 'Punish her.'

The men whooped excitedly.

'Get her blindfolded.'

Her arms were still clasped tightly around her back

and something dark covered her eyes. Then it fell silent. There was a rustle as someone stepped closer. Laura's gasp sent fear hurtling through Shannon. Fear of the unknown heavily tinged the pleasure. What were they going to do?

'Gag that one,' the boss ordered. 'Phil, stick your cock in her mouth to shut her up.'

Shannon heard Laura moan happily as Phil obviously did as he was ordered. Her mind filled with images of Laura on her knees, sucking Phil's cock, of the punishment she herself was due. Could she take any more stimulation?

Her arms were released for a few seconds then dragged over her head and tied to a branch above her. The branch was too high and she was forced to her toes. Her arms ached, her legs ached, but still nothing happened. It was too much.

'Just bloody well do it!' she yelled. No sooner had the words left her mouth then a hand struck her breast. He'd slapped her. The swine had slapped her. Anger more than pain made her scream.

'Go on, scream. No one will hear you,' the sergeant taunted before nipping her ear once more.

Rough hands dragged her shorts to her ankles. There was a loud swish and something hard and rough connected with the soft flesh of her buttocks. Stripes of pain burned through her, mingled with pleasure. After four lashes her tight shorts were dragged roughly up over her warm buttocks, enclosing them in the tight material, and the man whipping her moved in front.

'Might as well warm the tits up as well,' the voice murmured. He waited indeterminately long seconds before carrying out his threat. The flesh on her breasts was softer than her buttocks and stung more. Her nipples burned like fury, but it made the pleasure sharper, more urgent.

'Now touch her, lad. See how she likes pain with her pleasure.'

Someone, the youngest, moved before her, and the hands cupped her stinging flesh once more. The slightest touch there made her want to moan with pleasure; she was so much more sensitive. He tightened his grip and squeezed, gently at first, till her body strained at its ties, then becoming tighter and harder. Her stomach coiled, readying itself for the release to come. She squeezed her thighs together, much to the men's amusement and ribald comments. One breast was released and she moaned in dismay, only to gasp happily as a wet mouth replaced it, cooling the heated flesh. Being suckled and squeezed hard, she came with a huge cry of pleasure.

Her body still shaking, she was quickly untied. She collapsed in a heap but barely had time to catch her breath before she was shoved on to her back and her legs splayed. There was a rumble of laughter from the men; she stiffened, unable to see what was happening. Something cold touched her nipple and was quickly removed. Her mind filtered through all the possibilities but she couldn't think of what it could be.

Fingers grabbed the material between her legs. It was wet from her juices and he knew it. She felt his head touch her thighs, heard him inhale deeply, felt him rub his nose to the wetness, savouring her excitement.

'Enjoying yourself?' She wanted to deny it but how could she? He'd touched and smelled the evidence of her enjoyment.

'Now let's see exactly how turned on you are.'

She lifted her hips for him to drag her shorts and panties down but he didn't; he merely laughed. He tugged on the material, pulling it away from her groin. She tensed, aware of every sound, every movement. There was a ripping sound – her shorts. He was tearing the seam at her groin. But instead of ripping it as she thought, he was cutting it. When he'd finished, he sighed and pushed her thighs further apart. Tearing along the seam wasn't good enough: he'd cut a chunk out of her shorts and panties. She could feel the air cool and damp at the junction of her thighs. From mound to anus there was a two-inch rectangle of material missing. Enough for them to see all of her. But seeing wasn't enough.

A cock thrust into her, hot and hard and deep, through the gap in the material. Even before he spoke she knew it was the sergeant who was thrusting so wickedly into her, twisting his hips, making her ripple around him. Every inch of her ignited once more at his lunging; she hadn't thought it possible. It was so strange to be wearing shorts and be fucked at the same time.

'You love it, don't you?' he murmured in her ear. 'Love every dirty second of it.'

His words were driving her wild. She wrapped her arms and legs around his hard body, pulling him closer. His breath mingled with hers, his face merely inches from her. She wanted him to kiss her, to drive his tongue into her mouth as his cock was driving into her pussy.

He teased her, nipping her ear, biting her jawline, making her moan, making her squeal. Slowly his mouth edged closer to hers, his tongue circling her lips then plunging inside to toy with hers. He tasted of coffee, strong black coffee, and strong male. Then he was gone. She groaned in dismay.

'Want to come now?' he muttered.

He wasn't having it all his own way, Shannon decided. She tightened her internal muscles around him, smiling when he groaned loud and urgently. In the background she was aware of the cheers, the mutter of the others. So what if they were watching – it added another dimension to her pleasure. Being watched and fucked. She'd give them something to cheer about. She trailed a hand over the clothed muscles of his back, down past his shirt. Rucking it up, she dug her nails into his muscled flesh, revelling in his moans and the marks she'd leave there. Both her hands clasped his buttocks, pulling him tighter towards her. Her one hand moved closer to his anus, and he knew it. He snarled as she let her finger tickle the sensitive skin and scratched the puckered hole.

'Damn you,' he gasped, then bucked into her hard and came, his snarl of pleasure drowning out the other raucous noises. His body was heavy on her as he lay there for several seconds, too dazed to move. Slowly he shifted from her.

'Don't move,' he ordered. 'Legs open. Private, get between those legs and taste her.'

Shannon couldn't see the private's face but could imagine only too well what a picture it must have been, for the others laughed.

'Go on, lad. Taste a pussy. Lick the sarge's come from her.'

'Get your face between her thighs.'

'Lick her out.'

'Make her come again.'

The teasing seemed endless but gradually Shannon heard him shuffle towards her. She held her breath as she felt him slide between her legs, his clothing rubbing previously unknown sensitive areas. His hands on her clothed thighs made her jump. His hands shook as they stroked the smooth skin underneath, transmitting his nerves to her as he slowly moved closer to his goal. The nervousness heightened every touch. Tentative fingers smoothed the ruffled curls at her groin, feeling the rasp against his skin. Her whole body began to throb anew. Her two earlier orgasms were forgotten – all she could feel was the tentative touch of his hands at her groin; all she could remember was the sergeant's mind-blowing thrusts deep inside her. Now she needed more. She needed the private's hands on her, his tongue tasting her, worshipping her. And because it was new to him then it made it better for her.

His fingers parted her sticky sex lips. She heard his swift intake of breath. Her mind reeled as she saw herself through his eyes – saw the red, glistening folds of flesh, swelling under this man's gaze, saw the wetness trickling from her pussy mixed with the sergeant's come.

'Get to it, lad.'

The others were losing patience with the innocence now, wanting action. She wanted to yell at them to give him time, let him take control. Indeed, he wasn't going to be rushed. When the next man jeered, Shannon felt him turn to the watchers.

'Fuck off!' he yelled.

Good for you, Shannon wanted to say. You stick up for yourself. It worked, for the men fell silent.

His fingers slid over her wet flesh slowly, tentatively discovering each fold, each nook, each movement drawing Shannon into a swirl of pleasure. More confident men had drawn less of a response from her. Some were so sure that they paid no attention to what they were doing, as they went through it by rote. This man was enjoying every sensation, taking in every inch of her and revelling in it.

'Do you like this?' he asked as his fingers slid over the nub of her pleasure. She moaned and he laughed softly to himself. 'You do? And what if I do this?' His tongue replaced his finger and she stiffened. 'You like that a lot, don't you?'

Shannon could only nod as words failed her. Her mouth was dry, her limbs heavy with sensation, her mind numb with pleasure. His tongue traced every inch his fingers had, then circled the entrance to her vagina. Slowly his tongue lapped at the juices, both hers and the sergeant's, and she heard him moan in enjoyment.

'I knew you'd like it, lad,' a voice murmured close by. 'How does she taste?'

'Un-be-liev-able,' the lad replied.

'Slide your fingers into her. See how tight she is,' the sergeant encouraged.

He did as he was told and Shannon tightened her muscles around them. He sighed happily.

'Like to feel your cock in there?'

'Yeah!'

'Then shove it up her and make her moan. You'd like that, wouldn't you?'

Shannon nodded her head vehemently.

There was a rustle of clothing. Then the touch of a heavy cock against her thigh. Automatically she reached for him; he was hot, velvety smooth and rock hard. She couldn't wait to feel him inside her.

'Lift her legs over your arms. Don't let her control anything,' the sergeant urged.

Her legs were raised, hooked over his arms.

'It'll be better, deeper like his.'

She was so wet, so open to him, he slid in easily. Ecstasy. His hesitant movements sent chills down her spine. His thrusts were erratic but touched the very fibre inside her. His breathing increased, becoming interspersed with low moans. Everything increased her pleasure. He was nearly there. Now to make it really special for him. She slid her hand between their bodies and found her clitoris. As he plunged into her, she rubbed her clitoris and felt herself fall headlong into pleasure. His gasp as he felt her contract around him pushed her further into ecstasy, then he stiffened and came with a long moan.

'God, that was fantastic,' he murmured when he could breathe again. 'I could feel her come around me.'

'This one's an expert, aren't you? We're not finished yet. Phil's desperate to get his cock into you. He's fucked your friend in the mouth and up her arse. And she loved every dirty second of it. Now it's your turn.'

The blindfold was ripped off. Shannon blinked in the bright light. All around her there were bodies in various states of undress. Laura was curled on top of one soldier, fast asleep. Shannon smiled: no stamina, that girl. She was pulled to her feet, and she wobbled as her legs almost failed to hold her. Phil (she assumed) stepped towards her, his cock spilling out of his enclosed fist.

He backed her against a tree, and stepped between her open legs. Dragging one leg past his thigh, he rubbed his cock along her pussy. Then, without a word, he pushed into her. The tree was rough against her back and she savoured the scratchiness against her skin but she wasn't there long as Phil made her wrap her legs around him and then turned and walked away. Each step brought her down hard on his cock, driving him deeper into her.

Then he stopped. Why? His hands slid down her back to her buttocks, holding them open. She felt her breath snag in her throat. Something cold and metallic slid into her. The tip of a tube of cream: someone was lubricating her arse. The cream was cold then her sensitive flesh started to tingle. She wriggled in Phil's grasp to try and assuage the tingle but it didn't work.

Someone gently touched the curve of her spine, tracing a finger over her vertebrae. It made her shiver. Phil's cock twitched inside her. The cream tingled. A tongue traced the path the finger had made. Wet and hot. She twitched. The cock jumped. The cream burned.

'I'm going to have you up that nice tight arse of yours in a minute,' a voice taunted. The sergeant's. 'But first let's see how you like this. Something to cool you down.'

She stiffened, wondering what 'this' was. It was cold and hard as it touched the rim of her arse. She felt the resistance of her anus give to allow the intruder entrance. It was cold, very cold. It sent a shiver through her. It wasn't very long or thick but when Phil bucked his hips she felt it move inside her, wiggling from side to side, touching the sides of her rectum, making her bowels quiver. She couldn't help moaning at the sensation of being filled in both orifices.

'Like it? Like having a knife handle up your arse?'

Arrogant swine! She couldn't deny it – she was enjoying it. It was gently removed from her, only to be replaced by the tip of the sergeant's cock, which was much thicker and longer than the handle of the knife had been. Slowly he pushed into her, just an inch. The coldness was replaced by heat. She moaned low and urgent. He was a lot thicker than the knife handle. Beads of sweat puddled on her brow. Phil thrust and she was pushed backward, slowly and inexorably, on to the sergeant's thick cock until he was in to the hilt. She was squashed between two men, two cocks filling her in the basest of ways. Phil thrust first, his face crunching in pleasure, then the sergeant drew back and thrust into her. One after the other, never stopping, never breaking the rhythm that was tearing her apart. One after the other they pushed into her, pushed her pleasure beyond its limit. Hard male bodies rubbed against hers, making her yield to them. The sensation was indescribable. She was full of hard men; their sweat teased her nostrils, their moans filled her ears, their bodies thrust hard into hers. Orgasm crescendoed over her, driving everything else away, and replacing it with a pleasure that made her scream.

She came around to find herself wrapped in one of the men's jackets. She snuggled closer to the warmth, the scent hitting her nose – it was the sergeant's jacket. Beside her Laura stretched and slowly stood up. She passed Shannon her once white T-shirt that was now covered in leaves and dirt. Shannon struggled into it then realised they were alone.

'How long have they been gone?'

'Not sure,' Laura said. 'About ten minutes. You all right? I've never seen you like that before.'

Shannon closed her eyes, remembering the sensations the morning had brought. She shivered. 'Exquisite. Absolute bliss. What a morning. Come on, we'd better get back.' She looked down at the gap in her shorts. 'Good job this T-shirt is long.' Laura grinned.

They walked back slowly, their energy spent, savouring the memories, the feel of sated flesh. For Shannon the sensation of being clothed but having a naked pussy was strange, her sex lips rubbing together as she walked.

Louise was waiting for them. 'Were they there?' she demanded as they stepped into the living room. She smiled at Shannon's nod. 'I told you they would be. Well? Tell all.'

Shannon sank on to the sofa and slowly parted her legs to reveal her naked flesh. Louise's snatched breath made her smile. 'It was brilliant.' She rubbed her hand against her sore flesh. 'Superb.'

'What's Sergeant Croydon like?' Louise asked, barely able to tear her eyes from Shannon's revealed pussy.

'Divine! He fucks like the devil.' Shannon caught Laura's satisfied smile. 'Doesn't he?'

'It certainly looked that way to me.'

Shannon rose. 'I'd better get a move on. But first things first.' She picked up the phone and dialled. When it was answered, she said, 'Captain James here. Get Sergeant Croydon in my office as soon as he gets back from manoeuvres. There's something I have to give him.' Her hand touched the jacket he'd left wrapped around her. There was something else besides the jacket he deserved. The picture formed in her mind – Sergeant Croydon draped over her desk, naked arse up awaiting the slap of her ruler. And maybe she'd take her vibrator along, to see how he liked it with something up his arse.

After this morning she could have him up on a charge of insubordination. She knew what she preferred – and what he did too.

Meeting the Bitch

Jean Roberta

Meeting the Bitch

❖ ❖

On the day I was supposed to see Georgina again, the air was as warm and moist as a cunt that has gone hungry for too long. It was a typical Canadian prairie summer day, heavy with the promise of thunder. A hot breeze whispered around the edges of buildings like a neighborhood gossip.

I knew my skin was beaded with sweat when I climbed the concrete steps of the bungalow I had shared with George for three years. When I left her, I vowed never to share my life with another butch game-player, a confused bundle of clashing desires.

Before I rang the bell, I wondered for the umpteenth time why I had agreed to this meeting after George had shown me what she was full of. And after I found out that I was the fool who didn't know as much as I thought I did.

When George and I first started spending nights in each other's apartments, we talked for hours about what we wanted and how we defined ourselves. Discovering what turned us both on, we realized we were both attracted to each other's dykey spunk, the core of invert/pervert rebellion that drove everyone else around us crazy. We bared our souls to each other – or at least I thought so at the time. For a while, I couldn't imagine either of us needing more than we could give each other. And then George started spending time with the kind of woman she once said she couldn't trust.

The door opened. 'Bobbie,' murmured George, standing in the doorway with eyes downcast as modestly as a geisha's. 'I'm glad you came.' There was still something boyish and fey about her, as though she were playing the role of Peter Pan. I'll never be innocent again, I thought, but you'll never grow up.

I stalked silently past little George in her clean white T-shirt and jeans. I had come here to see George's new girlfriend at close range.

My rival looked like my worst fears made visible. I thought her black spandex shorts and little red high-heeled sandals were the height of gutter style. I caught a fast glimpse of tight cleavage and carefully tousled sun-bleached hair flung over bare shoulders before my need for self-control forced me to drop my eyes. My head spun. I could hardly believe that my George would invite me to meet this theatrical tramp, this joke of a woman, in my old home. But I had to believe it. And I had to behave in a way that my dyke conscience could accept. My goddess, I yelled in my mind, why have you forsaken me?

'Bobbie,' the tramp asserted in a smoky voice, 'I'm Sarah.' She sounded slightly amused. She was actually stretching out her long fingers to shake hands with me. I had never seen such an obvious femme make such a straightforward masculine gesture. I wondered whether my held-in rage gave me the aura of a dangerous woman who needed to be appeased.

Trying to see myself through the eyes of the two anxious women who waited for me to speak, I felt clumsy and out of place. I knew I lacked the ageless and genderless grace of George, the 35-year-old teenage buck, and the sultriness of her new playmate. My own average-sized body felt leaden in the heat. My last sight of myself in a mirror had shown short wavy hair that looked as brown and ordinary as wood. My skin looked sallow next to George's pale face, but my Metis* genes showed up more in the shape of my eyes and my mouth.

I wondered whether George had told her new girl-friend that I was a non-practising alcoholic; the mere idea made me feel drunk with rage. At that moment, I just knew that cool white dykes and sun-bleached blonde bimbos were taking over the world, attracting all eyes and soaking up all love. I could have cried, but I was not femmy enough to do that in front of others without feeling stupid.

'Bobbie,' said the tramp, 'would you like some lemonade?'

'Yeah, OK,' I muttered, almost snarling. I suddenly laughed, releasing enough of my tension so I could stand still and remain law-abiding. 'What are you two trying to prove?' I burst out. George was paler than usual. 'Did you really think inviting me here could make up for what you did to me? Did you think I'd tell you that everything is all right now and the three of us could be friends?' I hoped neither of them would ask why I had agreed to come. I didn't know how to explain it.

A knowing look of pity filled George's clear blue eyes. 'She doesn't live here, Bobbie,' she told me. 'You know I never wanted you to move out,' she insisted, forcing herself to look at me. Her gaze wavered, trembled, shivered, but remained desperately fixed on my hot brown eyes. 'I never wanted to hurt you.'

The urge to rip her apart like a hungry wolf tearing

* French-Canadian term, equivalent to 'mestizo' or 'half-breed,' indicating a mixture of white and aboriginal ancestry.

into a rabbit was so strong in me that I could hardly restrain it. Don't do it, shrieked the voice of my conscience. Do you want the cops to come get you?

The touch of a hand on my shoulder made me jump. 'Do you hate me, honey?' Sarah asked confidentially. She had the gall to snicker. 'I can't really blame you, even though I never wanted to steal her away from you. I never wanted to cause trouble between you, Bobbie. That's not my game.' Her greenish eyes flickered over the black shirt that hugged my chest. 'I know how you feel,' she tried to soothe me.

I grabbed her by a shoulder and pushed her away from me. 'Fuckin' hardly,' I spat. 'You bloody well don't know how I feel. George never lied to me until she started sneaking out with you.' George wouldn't look me in the eyes. The wind outdoors had picked up speed, and it was moaning around the sides of the house like a woman in pain. I could see angry grey storm clouds through the front-room windows.

George and Sarah exchanged glances. I felt as if tentative, invisible hands were gently sliding up under my shirt, circling my breasts to feel their size, sliding over my tense back and down my shorts, reaching for the slough between my legs. Were George and Sarah, the new couple, in cahoots to weaken my will? The thought made me furious. 'I'm leaving,' I snarled.

I was stunned by the pleading look in Sarah's big eyes. 'Don't go, Bobbie,' she begged me like a lover, like the hungry pussy she obviously was. 'Just stay for one glass of lemonade. I want to tell you my side of it. You haven't given me a chance.' I recognized a grain of truth in what she said just as I caught a whiff of her perfume. The scent floated into my nose, slid down my backbone and spread itself into my hands and my crotch.

I let George ease me into a chair while Sarah went to the kitchen for lemonade like a good hostess. George even began to rub my upper back with one hand before she felt my lingering anger and jerked away from me.

The click of Sarah's heels on the tile floor announced her return. Handing me a glass of lemonade, she actually kneeled at my feet. 'I always wanted to meet you, Bobbie,' she cooed, looking fearlessly into my eyes. I warned myself that I was being conned, but I couldn't resist touching her honey-colored hair. After a few strokes, I grabbed a handful of it near her scalp.

'Didn't you know George had a partner?' I asked, sounding more anguished than I intended. The truth dawned on me. 'You like couples, don't you? You don't want a relationship, you just want to play games.' My voice seemed to affect her like the crack of a belt, and she flinched.

'Please don't blame me,' she begged. Tears trembled just inside her lower eyelids. 'I can't handle another serious relationship right now. I've been through too much. I just want a good time with friends I can trust. Friends who won't judge me, and who know I'm not a troublemaker.' Tears began sliding down her cheeks. She looked so adorable that I had to fight off the impulse to hug her.

Now that she had started explaining herself, Sarah couldn't stop. 'I didn't always know I wanted a woman. I had to go through some horrible relationships before I figured it out. Now I can't turn it off. I was attracted to George from the first day I met her, but I didn't know about you until she told me. And then I guess you didn't seem real to me until I saw you. I never wanted all this to happen.' George looked as guilty as a convicted murderer. I could see her struggling not to touch Sarah, who remained on her knees. My clit was beginning to demand attention. The contrast between my shrinking anger and my rising desire struck me as funny, and I laughed.

I grabbed Sarah by both shoulders, shaking her gently. 'You really deserve a spanking,' I told her.

'That's what I want,' she whispered, her voice barely audible.

George gave Sarah a look of pride and sympathy. The air between them seemed to hum. I was appalled, but I was excited. Without more words, I grabbed the top of Sarah's spandex shorts and rolled them down over her hips, taking her panties down at the same time. She gracefully stood up so that I could pull her clothing down past her knees, exposing a triangle of light brown hair that looked like a patch of late-summer grass. After stepping out of her shorts, she lifted her striped halter top over a pair of bouncing breasts crowned with dark nipples. She seemed eager to pass my inspection.

I stood up to hold her around the waist, and found her skin moist and yielding. She weighed less than I expected, and I had no trouble pulling her across my lap on George's chesterfield. Without thinking, I began slapping Sarah's firm buttocks so that they shook slightly. The sound of my right hand striking her skin was incredibly satisfying. 'Poor slut.' I chuckled under my breath. I could hear George gasping in time to Sarah's moans.

When both her ass cheeks were bright red, I forced myself to stop. My victim made no move to get off my lap, so I ran a hand lightly over her hot ass. A sense of shame was creeping through me. 'I don't usually do this,' I muttered into one of Sarah's small pink ears, 'but you asked for it.' I was trying to convince myself that I wasn't a pig. She struggled to stand up, and I helped her.

Sarah's eyes were wet and her face was as red as her behind. She seized my head in both hands to give me a long kiss. 'Forgive me?' she whispered. I didn't know what to say, but when I searched through the feelings in my guts, I didn't find any trace of resentment left. I hoped I had driven away her guilt. I squeezed her shoulders to answer her question. I wanted to squeeze her poor ass, but I thought that would be going too far at this stage of the game. I'm not a lady or even a gentleman, but I am a Canadian.

George took the risk of running a hand through my hair from back to front; this was one of her gestures. 'I missed you, Bobbie,' she told my neck. She tweaked both my ears, then lowered my head to give each of my nipples a wet kiss through my T-shirt. I couldn't sit still. 'Baby, baby,' she crooned, squeezing me. That was her word, and she always said it in a 1950s rock-and-roll voice. I was dangerously close to crying, so I ducked my head to bury my nose in George's closest armpit. I loved the smell of her sweat.

Sarah playfully grabbed my T-shirt and pulled it up. I co-operated by moving away from George and raising my arms like a kid being undressed by her mom. Sarah grinned shamelessly at the sight of my small, firm breasts. 'No rings,' she remarked casually, licking her lips. At first I wasn't sure what she meant, and then I was speechless at her suggestion. 'You'd look good with rings,' Sarah advised me. 'At least one. Through here.' She pinched a nipple.

I had always thought of that kind of adornment as a specialty of masochistic male queens, but I felt fairly sure Sarah didn't see me in that role. I realized that I still barely knew her, and this thought made me uneasy. 'I'm not the hardware type,' I mumbled.

George had deftly removed my shorts during my conversation with Sarah, and she positioned my bare back on the dusty wool of her chesterfield. My sweaty skin objected. 'I need something underneath me,' I complained.

George laughed and scampered into the bedroom, returning with a sheet. 'We can mess this up,' she assured me and Sarah. 'It needs to be washed anyway.'

A spasm of disgust passed through me, but I couldn't afford to be choosy. I let George slide the sheet underneath me, then I spread my legs as an invitation to her. Sarah held my head in her lap while George began licking my belly to my tingling slit. I wanted her so much I could hardly breathe.

I wanted to feel George's tongue with no barriers in the way, and I was not disappointed. Just as it nudged its way in between my outer lips, we were all jolted by the crack of thunder. Rain began pelting the roof as George gently pulled my thighs apart and began circling my clit with wet kisses. I felt as if I were falling down a deep well while watching the stars. George's thin, hard, purposeful fingers soon followed her exploring tongue. Downward and inward she went, searching for feelings I had tried to hold safe inside myself for weeks. The torture was exquisite.

Sarah rubbed my scalp. 'Oh, honey, I know that feels good,' she purred in my ear. 'She never stopped wanting you, Bobbie. We both want to make you happy.' One of her hands cupped one of my breasts. I grabbed her hand, either to stop her or encourage her, I wasn't sure which.

George had two and then three fingers inside me, and it felt like the old days, like the time of our honeymoon. I wanted her to reach in deep enough to touch my heart. My eyes filled with tears. 'You shit,' I gasped, laughing. George's mouth was busy, so I knew she couldn't talk back. Her revenge was to flick me with her tongue and nibble me carefully with her teeth, never giving me a rest. I came hard.

George came up for air, grinning. 'You OK, man?' she asked me.

I felt as if I would never catch my breath. 'What d'you think?' I gasped. 'Fuck.'

'I did, my baby,' she joked. She seemed to glisten

with satisfaction. I wasn't feeling exactly the same, but I had needed what she gave me.

She cuddled me, stroked me. 'Bobbie, man,' she sighed. 'You a helluva woman. I missed that taste, you know.' She held me. A ball of grief sat in my stomach even though I felt her love. I knew that we would never again be the way we were, but I also knew that I hadn't lost her. 'Temper, Bob,' she murmured. 'Jeez.'

'I'm honest,' I snarled quietly. 'I let you know how I feel, and I have reasons. Do you think that's wrong?'

'No, no,' she soothed me. 'Oh God, I don't blame you for your feelings. They're kind of intense sometimes, but that's you.'

I thought of something else. 'George,' I demanded, 'are you sure you don't mind sharing Sarah with me?' I knew it was insensitive to talk about her as though she weren't there, but I've never claimed to be a born diplomat. 'You found her first. Don't you feel she's yours?'

George squirmed. 'I like sharing her with you,' she replied, almost under her breath. 'We always used to do things together. I know you like her and she likes you too.'

I glanced at Sarah, who was watching us both like a kid eavesdropping on her parents. I laughed. 'Come here, you bad girl,' I ordered, pulling her around me so I could see her. I let my hands slide over her breasts. 'George, how do you do it?' I asked. I was curious. George turned paler and didn't answer, so I asked Sarah. 'How do you like her to do it, honey? I know you're not too shy to tell me.' She wrapped her arms around my neck and gave me a long wet kiss.

George found her voice. 'She squirts,' she bragged, running a hand along one of Sarah's hips. 'If you play with her G-spot, she comes that way. She could wet the whole bed, baby. You have to see it.' George's words were accompanied by the sound of rain pounding on the roof.

'Let's carry her,' I advised my partner, holding Sarah around the shoulders. George grabbed her legs, and together we carried her into the bedroom as she squealed with delight.

We laid her on the bed. I buried my nose in her tangle of sweet-smelling hair, then began massaging her springy breasts. I circled her nipples with my tongue, then sucked as hard as I could. I had a feeling that Sarah was the kind of woman who could come just from that. I raised my head to look at her. 'It's like feeding a baby, isn't it, sunshine?' I laughed.

'Oh yes,' she sighed. Interesting, I thought. She is a mother. For a moment I wondered what it felt like to give birth. I wondered why the breeding process hadn't left any permanent marks on Sarah's body, and then I wondered what to look for. I decided to think about it later.

George was slowly kissing her way down the brownish line from Sarah's belly-button to her damp nest of hair. Sarah was moaning. George looked up. 'She had an interesting life, baby,' she told me. 'She's tougher than she looks.' I admired a small tattoo of a bluebird above Sarah's left breast; it was right under my eyes.

George suddenly stood up, rummaged in a bureau drawer and came back to the bed holding a shiny object. 'She likes this,' George told me, grinning. I looked closer, and saw that it was a small vibrator. 'If you want her to go crazy,' George instructed, 'you have to use this in the right places.' She must have noticed the look on my face because she quickly handed me the gizmo. 'You want to try it?' George asked me slyly. I glanced at Sarah, who was panting. I knew I would have to watch the scene I had imagined for so long.

'No, man,' I answered quietly. 'I want to see how you do it.' I studied one of Sarah's shoulders. 'I want to watch you, honey,' I told her. She stretched herself smugly.

George was already tickling a protruding pink clit which looked wet and swollen. Sarah's hips were dancing. George had trouble holding her pussy lips open with one hand while she used the other to ease her magic wand into the mouth that drooled for it. She squatted over Sarah to gain some leverage. The woman was loud and dramatic, thrashing and moaning all over the bed. I had expected a performance like that from her, but by now I wasn't offended.

Wanting to leave my own mark on Sarah, I slid up her neck and gave her a hickey. I slid down to squeeze her nipples and whatever else I could reach. I surveyed her smooth belly and noticed the gold ring in her belly-button. 'No tit rings,' I remarked, only a little sarcastic. 'Or collar. You need more accessories.'

All too soon, her voice rose by an octave and several decibels as she screamed in climax. George and I both held her as her breathing returned to normal and she awkwardly turned from side to side to give us sloppy kisses. She was like a friendly cocker spaniel. I could tell from the wetness of the bedspread that she was not well trained.

I led my two playmates into the bathroom for a cool shower. I still felt a twinge of something like hurt pride, but I could stand it. Like the wool upholstery on George's chesterfield, that feeling had the power to keep me alert. I wouldn't have given up the day's adventure for a lifetime of monogamy. When I thought of that, I realized that it sounded straight and boring anyway.

Under the massage of the water, I washed George's back and shampooed her hair while she kept her eyes closed and her face upturned. I felt I was reclaiming her. Sarah handed me whatever I needed without being asked. I rewarded her with playful pinches on her butt and thighs as she squealed and tried to hide her curves behind little George.

'Sarah,' I told her softly, 'I still have to get much better acquainted with you.' In response, she picked up my nearest hand and sucked on my fingers as though they were something private and sexual – as in fact they were. Untried possibilities hung in the air of the little house that felt like my home again.

Esthely Blue

Mary Anne Mohanraj

Esthely Blue

❖ ❖

My toes curl and release. I am lying with my back against his chest, with my ass against his groin and him slowly going limp inside me. I am catching my breath, slowing down, listening to my heartbeat fill the room. I am waiting for the right moment to shift away; though it would be nice to cuddle, I'm dying of the heat. Yes, long enough, and in one movement I slip a little forward and he slides out and only our toes are touching now, way down at the bottom of my bed. And I look down the curve of my body, smiling, down the faint moonlit bed, down my thighs to knees and calves, looking for my toes – they are not there. Ankle, heel, and emptiness.

I can't feel them, either.

My heart thumps loudly. I blink, and my toes are there, returned, and I am tempted to put it down to a trick of the light, but . . . Well. Nothing to be done about it right now.

'You OK?' He seems concerned.

'Mm . . . how 'bout you?'

'Oh, fine.'

We've cooled a little, and shift, so my head rests on his shoulder.

'I can't stay the night.' He's apologetic. 'I wouldn't be able to sleep.'

'Ssh . . . that's OK. Thank you . . . It was lovely.'

He chuckles. 'Thank you!'

I am tempted to ask him, if, during the act, he happened to notice any odd flickering, but decide against it. A little too intimate a question – I'll save it for Mark or Peter.

'So, you do this often?'

I smile. They always ask. 'Not so often. But occasionally, when the mood strikes . . .'

'And Mark . . .'

'Has his own diversions. And friends.' I don't mention Peter. Mark is usually enough to explain, the first time round.

'You don't get jealous? He doesn't?'

'Hmm . . . he says he doesn't. I do, sometimes. But I'm not sure that really matters. It hasn't been enough to stop me.'

'Interesting.'

The moonlight slides across the floor. We talk, about little nothings. The bed is left entirely in darkness, and now it is my desk that shines palely in the night, doubly illuminated by the moon's light and flickering computer screen. Swirling screensaver, cool blues mixing into greens. Finally, he gets up, peels off the condom, cleans up, gets dressed. He sets my alarm for me: 6 a.m. Deadline tomorrow – mustn't oversleep. Then he sits by me until I start falling asleep, kisses my forehead softly, slips out. Sweet boy.

I keep my eyes resolutely closed, until I fall completely asleep.

I won't be visiting Mark for a few weeks. My flight's booked for the 22nd. In the meantime, the work for the new magazine has assumed nightmare proportions. Every hour seems to bring fresh complications. If I had known how much time this would take, would I have started it? A little late to worry about it now: the first issue's due in three weeks. Sometimes, as I'm typing, my fingers seem to flicker away, but the words keep appearing on the screen, and since I touch-type, I'm not really looking at my fingers anyway. Maybe I need new glasses?

I'm on the phone while I work, talking to Katherine. 'Oh, I'm sorry, sweetie. Yes, that's terrible . . .'

Her boyfriend's causing trouble again. I make appropriate noises as that's all she needs. This is a recurring theme, and it no longer needs all of my attention. I know my lines. 'No, I wouldn't take that either. You should talk to him.' She starts crying: time for reassurance. 'Aw, c'mon. It'll be OK . . .'

While I murmur, I type. She'll never know. A brief pang of guilt, stifled.

'Dear Mr Rossiter-Parks, thank you for your kind submission to our new magazine. I'm sorry to have to inform you that . . .' I really need to take the time to set up a template and automate part of this. More efficient in the end. Tomorrow. I'll do it tomorrow. In the meantime, I can do this kind of letter in my sleep. Heh. Now *that* would be efficient. 'Please do feel free to submit to us in the future . . .'

Her sobs quiet a little. My cue. 'You know he loves you.' Her sobs get louder, making it hard to concentrate. 'Look, it *can't* be that bad!' Whoops. Not too exasperated. She'll just get more upset. Soothing. That's the way to go. 'I think you're great, kiddo, and I'm sure he does too . . .'

I've been sitting quite a while in one place, and my neck has started to hurt. I reach up to switch the phone from one ear to another, and my hand isn't there. My forearm ends at the wrist. I freeze, and Katherine weeps on, while I stare at the computer through the space that should have been filled by my hand.

I bite my lip, hard. I draw blood.

Then my hand is back. Just as if it had been there all along, almost as if it had planned this. Just a little excursion. A rest, perhaps? Have all of my body parts been doing this all along, behind my back? Ducking out when I wasn't looking? Maybe I haven't been paying enough attention to my body lately. Maybe it wants some exercise? I *have* been skimping on my sit-ups, after all. Just haven't felt like I had the time for the full workout in the mornings.

I haven't heard anything Katherine has said for minutes.

'Kiddo, I've got to go. I'll call you back tomorrow, OK? Sorry! Bye.'

I hang up the phone. She was still crying. My lip is still bleeding. I have not taken my eyes off my hand, but it seems pacified. It stays right where it's supposed to be. My heart is thumping – a few toes were one thing, but I need my hand. I can't type without it, and if I can't type, then the magazine will go under, and it's not just my project – people are counting on me, it's my responsibility. Not to mention that I won't be able to make my damn rent . . . Was that a flicker?

OK, OK. Deep breaths. Calm. Just calm down.

I pledge that I will do my exercises every morning, OK? I wonder if saying this in my head is enough, but it would sound so silly to say it out loud.

I get up and close the door. 'I pledge that I will do my full exercises every morning.' I add an 'I solemnly swear' just in case. I would have liked to start with 'I, Sita Mathuri, being of sound mind and health . . .' but that seems a bit risky, since I'm not certain of either.

I go sit at the computer again. Eyes fixed rigidly on the keys, which means that I make far more errors than usual, I start typing names again. Everything will be fine.

I call Mark, but he's neither home nor at the office. He could be anywhere – the boy tends to wander. No voicemail either. I consider sending him e-mail:

Mark. Disappearing rapidly. Send help.

Or maybe:

Sweetie, I regret to inform you that I am losing my mind. Since I know you love me for my mind and not my body, please let me know if you'd like to dissolve this relationship . . .

Perhaps something like:

I'm not sure what's going on, but body parts are going AWOL. Would like to discuss this with you. I know it sounds mad, but maybe it's just some strange disease. Hopefully not communicable. Come soon!

I settle for the ever-useful:

Call me, please. Soon.

That should worry him nicely; I think that's what I wrote the last time I broke up with him. Or maybe that was the time before last. In any case, I could use some company in my misery. I log off and go make dinner. I watch my fingers very carefully when I chop. I can't afford to lose any.

Peter's here for dinner. He got delayed in traffic, which explains why he wasn't here to help chop. He's nothing if not prompt. We have curry and I have wine. A couple of glasses. He doesn't drink.

'So? Tell me about last night.'

'Last night?' What? Has he guessed? I hadn't quite worked up the nerve to tell him yet . . .

'The one you took home from the reading. Pretty boy – so, how'd it go?'

Oh, him. Right. 'Oh, fine. He didn't stay the night, but we had a nice time.'

'Think you'll see him again?'

'Don't you think I have enough on my hands with you two?' A little sharper than I meant.

He looks surprised. 'Well, that's hardly stopped you before, has it? Wasn't your record five, concurrently?'

'Yes, and I neglected them all. Two of those lasted less than a week as a result.'

'So, even you have limits. Glad to hear you admit it.' He sounds a little bitter. I haven't been able to spend much time with him lately – so busy. What does he expect? Besides, it's not like he has tons of time either.

'I have plenty of limits. I have as many limits as anyone.' Ridiculous. Why am I snapping at him? 'Look, let's just go to bed. We can do the dishes in the morning.'

Once in the bedroom, I am suddenly shy. Stupid, after all this time, but I don't know how to tell him, and I don't want to meet his eyes. I pick up clothes and put them away. I straighten books on the shelves until he comes up behind me and slips his arms around my waist. I stiffen, then relax into his arms.

'You OK?'

'I'm sorry, I'm just kind of cranky. It's been a long day.' I twist around so I'm facing him, his arms still loosely wrapped around me.

'Anything in particular?'

I kiss him instead of answering. I don't know what to say. I raise my hands to cup his face, and he pulls me closer, his mouth opening against mine, his fingers starting to dig into my back, soon so hard that it hurts a little, the way I like it.

We stumble towards the bed. We fall on to it. My mouth is now on his cheek, his neck, digging under his shirt, my fingers unbuttoning as fast as they can. It's one of the best things about sex with him, the way it blazes up out of nowhere, burns me up so I can't think, can't slow down even when he wants me to – and does he really want me to? He's egging me on, his fingers shoving up my skirt, sliding into me, and I'm glad Mark got me out of the habit of wearing underwear years ago 'cause I can't wait for it. I'm squeezing my thighs around his hand, I'm slamming down as he slams up and rising and rising, with my whitened fingertips digging into the bed, arched and ready to scream . . .

. . . and it's gone.

Not gone the way it is when you get there and fall over the top and down the other side. Definitely not that kind of gone. It's almost as if someone had dumped a bucket of ice-water on me at just the wrong damned moment – except that then I'd have felt the ice at least. I'd be cold and shivering and wet. And I am wet and shivering, but only on my skin, only cooling sweat, 'cause what's between my thighs is absolutely nothing except for Peter's hand, wet and slippery and hanging there in air.

Peter's face is chalk-white. He looks like he's about to have a heart attack. Then everything suddenly goes back to normal and his hand has disappeared between my thighs again, except that I am not on the verge of coming any more. I am not even close; I am about as far away as you can be, and I am not happy. Peter slowly pulls out his hand; even if he'd wanted to keep going, he could tell that I didn't. He pulls it out and wipes it on the sheets and then looks up at me.

'OK. What's going on?'

'I don't know.'

That's not going to satisfy him. It doesn't. I tell him everything, starting with last night's toes and proceeding through missing fingers and a disappearing hand and ending with today. And as I do, I get more and more scared – and more and more angry. Toes I could deal with. Even fingers or hands: I can always dictate, right? Voice recognition software gets better every day. But if I can't have sex any more 'cause the relevant parts have chosen to wander off at the crucial moments

. . . My fingers are digging into my thighs. They hurt. I am hurting myself. I am hurting my body, which is not behaving at the moment. I am wondering what will happen if I try to actually tear away some skin. Will it disappear before I can? Would it come back?

The phone rings.

It's past midnight. It must be Mark. Peter goes outside to smoke a cigarette and think. I pace back and forth as I tell the story again. It's easier than I expected. It usually is, talking to him, at least once I get started. Unfortunately, he doesn't have the answer for me. I try not to let him hear how disappointed I am. I doubt I fool him, but he lets me pretend. It's been a rough day, after all.

Peter comes back in. I tell Mark I'll talk to him tomorrow night, and hang up the phone. Peter pulls me into a hug.

'You should go see a doctor.' He's using that 'I'm-not-nagging-but-you-know-this-is-a-good-idea' voice. I hate that.

'What can a doctor do?'

'This might have happened to someone before. I'll see what I can find on-line, but in the meantime, you should see an expert.'

I consider arguing, but he will be impossible until I give in. He was like that about my wearing seatbelts, and remembering to take my thyroid medicine, and going to the dentist. I think I give in just to get him to stop nagging – but he doesn't care as long as I do it.

'Drive me?'

'Of course.'

He holds me tight all night. I wake, once or twice, and he is still holding me. It doesn't really help, but it doesn't hurt either.

Peter calls the following morning, and somehow gets me an appointment. I think he bribed the secretary. He waits patiently while I do my exercises. I've already lost faith in them, but I did swear. I keep my promises.

The doctor is very beautiful, with short black hair and ice-blue eyes. I try not to check her out too obviously as she goes through the routine physical, checks my pulse, palpates my breasts . . .

'Well, you seem pretty healthy. What seems to be the problem?'

I can't say it. I just can't. I stare at her, and she at me. Her cheerful expression grows concerned, but she waits patiently. This room is too big and cold and white. I want a blanket, but you can't ask a doctor for that. My teeth are chattering. She says nothing, and finally, I have to speak.

'Could I borrow your pad? And a pen?'

I write it down. It's always easier to write. 'Parts of my body keep disappearing.'

She reads it, and her eyes only widen slightly. Good doctor – well trained.

'Parts of your body keep disappearing? Which parts?'

I tell her, and watch her expression subtly shift. This isn't going to go well. I can tell.

I argue with Peter in the car going home. He thinks I should do what the doctor says; slow down a little, try to decrease stress, maybe talk to a counselor. Unfortunately, none of my body parts acted up in the office, and I know what the doctor was thinking, with her sharp blue eyes and pointed questions. 'The poor girl is over-committed, in more ways than one.' 'She's so tired and stressed that she's imagining things.' It would have been ridiculous to bring Peter in as witness, and she'd probably just have decided that he was over-committed too. He's not been sleeping well, and he looks exhausted. Still, there aren't any bits of *him* disappearing. I'm getting scared.

Peter drops me off with a hug and makes me promise

to call him if anything else blinks out. For a moment, I don't want to let go. I hang on tight. But I can't hang on to him for ever – besides, I told Mark I'd call him. And I owe Katherine a call, still. I let go, kiss his cheek, and head inside.

It's easier telling the story the fourth time. I'm not sure why I bother, though. Katherine reacts as expected. She's been convinced for years that if I just picked one of them, settled down with Mark or Peter, got married, etc. and so on ad nauseum, then I'd live happily ever after. She's read too many romance novels. She's fixed up the problems with her boyfriend since we talked yesterday, which means that she's even more convinced that True Love (tm) will conquer all. If I swear monogamy to Mark (or Peter), then all my problems will be solved. No more disappearing bits.

Even if that were true, it wouldn't be worth it.

'That's not an option. I love both of them. No, Kat, I can't tell you which one I love more. I don't know. Well, I'm not you, am I?'

She eventually gives in on that one, but then shifts her attack. Surely I can at least stop bringing pretty boys and girls home for a night? Sure I could, but why should I? What can that possibly have to do with this? We argue for hours. Usually she's less persistent than this – after all these years, you'd think she'd have given up entirely. But now she has new ammunition. We argue until I am ready to weep with frustration. Finally, I just hang up. She'll understand. I'll call her back next week and apologize; I just can't cope with any more right now.

There is work waiting for me, but I can't look at it now, I can't. I just can't.

I call Mark.

* * *

I meet Mark at the airport; he's bought a ticket and come out early, two whole weeks before my scheduled trip. I feel better as soon as he arrives; stronger. Solider.

Nothing had disappeared in the few intervening days, but I'd been looking a bit translucent. My housemates had mentioned that I seemed pale; one of them made me dinner last night, out of the blue. She kept trying to get me to drink carrot juice. I'd started staying inside; in bright sunlight, I could see the veins and arteries through my skin, the blood pumping away, the muscles stretching and flexing. It didn't seem to be dangerous – my hands could still type, my legs could still walk – but it's just unnerving. I'm so glad to have Mark with me.

I slide my arm around him, hold him tight. Definitely better. I don't mention it until we're home, until the bus has deposited us down the street and we've walked up the last few blocks to the house. Luckily, he travels light. We slip inside, dodging housemates; he's not the gregarious type, and lately, for all their kindly concern, they weary me.

'I think you should spend more time alone.'

Mark doesn't usually give advice, even when asked. He must be actually worried.

'I feel better. Now that you're here.' It sounds appallingly mushy, but he's used to that from me.

'I can't fix it for you.'

'Shh . . . I know.'

We talk for a while, and then go to sleep. No real answers yet. Difficult to have answers when you're not sure what the question is. Is the doctor right? Is Peter? Am I stretched too thin? And if so, is there anything I can do about it? Is there anything I'm willing to do?

In the morning, I wake to sunlight coming in the window, and tentatively hold a hand up to it. I can't see through, even a little. Totally solid and normal.

Relieved, I turn to wake Mark up, but he looks so peaceful. He hates being woken. At least I can make it a pleasant waking.

I slide further under the sheets, slip down to gently breathe on his hip, his thigh. If I do this just right, I can get him hard without waking him. Once, I even made him come in his sleep; that was satisfying. I'm not particularly interested in trying to repeat that, though – my nipples are sore and my thigh muscles are tight. I want him, and I want him awake. I breathe in deeply; the scent of him always turns me on. I blow gently on his hardening cock, I lick down the length of it, I rub my thighs together as I take the head in my mouth. I rub my cock against his leg. What?!

He's awake. I'm very awake. We sit up. I yank back the sheets, and there, below my belly, nestled in a little nest of fine blonde hair, is a pale cock just like his, shocking against my dark skin. I can't help it – I gasp out loud. You might call it a shriek. Not that I haven't fantasized a little about having a penis – what woman hasn't? – but to have his . . . And it is his, exactly. Our eyes flick back and forth between our groins, comparing. Twins! Mine softens just as his does, it relaxes into exactly the same shape. We don't say anything; we just sit there, staring. It's there for at least a minute before it slowly fades out, and my own, more discreet, genitals fade in. I feel a little better, but still . . .

'Well.' My voice is shaking. I take a deep breath. 'Peter has been complaining that I start sounding like you when I've been talking to you a lot. Maybe we shouldn't be surprised.'

'I don't think being near me is going to be a solution.' He sounds relieved.

'No.' What if it had been my head that faded out, to be replaced by his? Or even my heart . . . 'Still, if I could figure out how to control this, to do that again, the possibilities . . .'

'Do you think you can?' He has an unfortunate predisposition for asking difficult questions.

'Well. No. Probably not.'

'You don't want to just disappear bit by bit, and you don't want to turn into me. I think you should at least try going away. Away from everyone.'

'But the project –'

'Will survive without you for a few days.'

He's right, of course. Maybe that's why he so rarely gives advice – so that when he does, he can be right.

I borrow some camping gear from the housemates, send out e-mails to the appropriate people, change the message on the machine: 'Gone fishing; back Wednesday.' I take out some money, buy groceries, pack the laptop, try to remember what I've forgotten, grab my medicine, and finally head out. Peter drops me off at the trailhead. I promise I'll call every night and let him know that I'm OK. He's not much of a woods person; I think he thinks I'll be eaten by bears. There are no bears around here.

By the time I hike in and wrestle with the tent and gather wood, I'm so exhausted that I don't even worry about being able to see the fire through my hands. It's kind of a pretty effect, actually: flickering reds and golds glowing under my brown skin. I feel a little guilty about not having written anything, but console myself with the fact that I only have three two-hour batteries for the laptop. If I don't type tonight, then I can stay another day. I curl up in my blanket and go to sleep.

Third day. I didn't type anything yesterday. I didn't flicker either. Skin's opaque this morning, and the lake is beautiful, if cold. I swam naked at noon yesterday. I think I'll go in a little earlier today. I could swim for hours here; days. When I finish, there's a meadow nearby, and my blanket makes a perfect place to curl up and bask in the sun. I've got a lot of bug bites, but it doesn't seem to matter. I've run out of books, too. I could always write my own – when I run out of paper, there's bark, right? I could learn how to make ink out of something. Bug blood, maybe, or fish guts. Of course, I'd have to catch a fish for that.

That's a bit of a problem, actually. I didn't really bring enough food to stay past tomorrow afternoon. When I hike back out this evening to call Peter, I could ask him to bring more food. Maybe I'll do that. It's nice here. Quiet.

Peter looks worried.

'You sure you want to stay longer? Do you have enough batteries?'

'Plenty – don't worry.' It's not as if I'm using them.

'This should last you a few more days. You ... you do look better. Healthier.'

'Glad to hear it. I'll see you Saturday, then?'

'Umm ... OK. Guess that's it, then.'

'Yup. Listen, it seems a little silly to call every night. I'm fine out here. I'll call if there's a problem, OK?'

'Well, OK.'

'Bye, then.' I heft the now-heavy pack on to my back and turn away. He leans over to kiss my cheek before I'm out of range. I let him, and smile.

'Bye,' he says, as I walk away.

The sun is so warm and the insects buzz above the grass tickles as the breeze blows it against my damp skin the sky is a thousand shades of blue and i will count and name them all before sunfall before night because when night comes then i will have to count the stars and there are so many this is my one two three day of naming blue

icicle blue
Mark's eyes blue

computer screen blue
atlantic blue
my favorite jeans blue
esthely blue

I made that last one up entirely esthely the color
where midnight runs into deep sea lit with sunlight
blues esthely esthely esthely

Peter finds me. Peter finds me and cleans me up and
takes me home and holds me until I am myself again.
He tells me that my skin had turned green. Not transparent or translucent; very there – oh, definitely there.
There, like a tree is there, a tree reaching up into the
esthely sky, alone in the night but solid and rooted in
the earth.

I don't think I was meant to root quite so deep.

I don't have an answer to the questions, but I have a
plan to keep me whole. This is the plan.

1. Schedule time for Mark and Peter. Schedule time
   for work. Schedule time for friends. Schedule time
   for play.
2. When I start feeling a bit translucent, drag someone with me to the woods. Don't talk to them, or
   at least not much, but make sure they bring me
   out again before I take root.
3. Repeat as necessary.
3a. If this doesn't work, panic.

The first issue is coming out on time, it looks like. Or
only a few hours late, at any rate. Katherine is engaged.
Huzzah – that should keep things calmer. Tomorrow I
go to visit Mark, thank the gods. And my housemates
have made dinner for me, which is nice. My toes are
tingling a little – that's the first sign, I've learned. It's
OK, though. It'll be a couple of hours before anything

actually disappears, and I'll have time to take a long walk first and count the stars. That should hold it off for a while. It's just like remembering to take my meds.

This isn't quite how I expected things to go. But I don't know if that matters.

I'm not giving up, not yet.

If I hadn't come this way, I'd never have found my shade of blue.

*Hades and
Persephone*

Ainsley Gray

Hades and Persephone

❖ ❖

*I*n a sea of black leather, I am wearing a white cotton dress, made in Mexico. Do I look at all innocent, or only delusional, like the ghost of a flower child from the sixties who is unaware of the passage of time? I also remind myself of dead women artists whose strangeness has been admired since they disappeared from the world: Emily Dickinson, Frida Kahlo. When I woke up this morning, this dress seemed like the only appropriate thing to wear. I wasn't fully awake.

This is snack and mingle time, between workshops and demonstrations. Two long tables in this big room are covered with lunch meats, buns, cheese, pickles, olives, raw vegetables and dip, pretzels, potato chips, desserts, coffee, tea and juice. The organizers of this event have provided for all the appetites of the participants. I don't feel included as a consumer. I feel both conspicuous and invisible.

My eyes are drawn to the small, sassy roundness and redness of the cherry tomatoes on the vegetable tray. Strictly speaking, they don't belong either. I eat half a dozen, one after the other, and their tart flavor lingers in my mouth.

A determined baby dyke in leather pants and heavy metal strikes a pose that demands attention. Her artificially red hair is fiercely short. I bet she has a tattoo somewhere of flames or a dripping dagger. She has obviously done everything she could think of not to be cute, but there it is. She looks 23 at the very oldest, and she is aiming at me from across the room. Who else would want an old virgin? While becoming Head Vandal at some school for troubled youth, she probably had lurid fantasies about her English teacher, equal to the most fevered outpourings of Coleridge and Swinburne.

She comes right up to me, close enough that I can smell her breath (beer, coffee, cigarettes and some faintly metallic smell behind a mint advertized as supercool), and she lets the silence build. 'Hello,' I say. I'm so tempted to ask her age that it is hard to resist. I know that the unspoken rules of this place require that she tell me the truth. This also works in reverse: she could ask mine. I won't go there first.

My first woman lover was ten years younger than I, and that seemed unusual to me at the time. I never guessed then that as I aged, my suitors wouldn't, or not necessarily. I wonder why the term 'chickenhawk' has no equivalent when obviously the condition exists. Lesbian watering holes are full of hawk fledglings, the down still fluffy on their chests, their harsh voices cracking like those of teenage boys, flapping their newly powerful wings at ripe hens.

But then, attraction has much to do with convenience. In my day, young women didn't 'come out' into queer identities at age 18, 21, even 25. And what now looks like a titillating feminine style, to be put on like a dress, was taught to us as Manifest Destiny. I digress.

She reaches with both hands to find my nipples beneath the thin cotton of my dress and my bra. She begins squeezing and rubbing them in lieu of conversation, not being the courtly type. 'They're getting hard,' she tells me. So is her sarcastic tone, but it's OK. I've met a lot of kids. 'Are you ready for me?'

I laugh, despite knowing that this is the very thing to bring out her bloodiest or most incoherent. 'You could have come out of me, you know,' I remind her, 'instead of looking for a way in.' If she wants me to call a spade a spade, I'll oblige. 'But yes. I've been waiting for you.' Even her pretensions are a turn-on, or maybe I'm just warped. After all these years and in this milieu, that possibility occurs to me.

'What's this for? You don't need it, mama.' She seems annoyed at something other than my previous remark. She finds my bra unnecessary, although it isn't giving me any protection. She abruptly turns me around to find the buttons up the back of my dress. She unbuttons them from the top as though doing something for me that I should have had the sense to do myself. I feel cool air on my back as she unhooks the closing of my bra. My breasts feel like animals set loose from confinement as I breathe deeply.

'That's better,' she chuckles, reaching inside my dress to torment my nipples directly. Her hard little fingers know how to vary the sensations, from teasing and suggestive to the impersonal cruelty of a mammogram. 'So why do you wear the damn thing?' she demands. I have trouble concentrating on her question and forming a reply, which is why she wants to talk now.

'Prevention,' I explain. My nipples feel so long that I wonder if they will ever return to their usual modest size. Electrical currents are running from each of them through my belly to my clit. 'Don't want them to sag.'

She is not impressed. 'So do chest exercises, princess,' she snarls into one of my ears. 'Push-ups would do you good.' When? Now? I didn't sign on for that.

We are attracting some attention, but we have not drawn a crowd yet. I suspect she would prefer to do this on a crowded street corner for maximum drama.

Several participants are sitting and crouching at the feet of their owners, who feed them from the food table. These domestic groupings attract even less attention than we do.

She seems determined to shrink my ego while expanding my tits to the fullest they have been since they overflowed with nectar of the goddess. She can't prevent me from noticing that of everyone in this room, she is the one who has not withdrawn from me for an instant since she first saw me. 'Don't you like them?' I flirt.

That gets me a double twist and pull that makes me gasp. A few more heads turn, and a few slow smiles are aimed at her and at me. 'Smartass question,' she tries to growl demonically, for my ears alone. 'Don't ask what you already know.' She steers me from behind in the direction of an empty table at the back of the room. I am growing wet, and my breathing quickens. Whatever is coming next is going to raise the stakes.

As I expected, she bends me over the table and raises my skirt. What she finds under it seems to try her patience more than anything else so far. 'Awww,' she groans. 'Pantihose, bitch?' If this isn't a rhetorical question, I don't know what is. I note that she chooses to break her own rules.

I take a deep breath, my face against bare wood. 'Control top,' I explain. 'I need the help.'

'No shit,' she mutters. 'But not that kind.' I imagine a regime of early-morning stomach crunches for the following year; I'm optimistic. My best revenge, I tell her silently, would be to watch you live on. And on, as you feel yourself being slowly pulled back into the earth you came from. Just wait, dear child.

Her battle plan seems to be to take me fast, hard and publicly to establish the terms. She seems to think this method of possession would work better than a slow seduction. I'm not convinced that she is right about this or many other things, but I am willing to hang on for the ride. Meanwhile, my underwear is cramping her style in a way I didn't foresee when I dressed to make a first impression. (But it worked!)

She grabs two handfuls and rips. Now we are really attracting the audience she has been wooing all along. She tears the nylon off me in the style of a scandalous Victorian actress playing a mustached villain, and I try to step out of the shreds as gracefully as possible. This involves kicking off my shoes, so I am left standing on bare feet. 'Don't move,' she murmurs into my hair. She wants to be the magician while I am either more or less than the assistant: the top hat, or top's hat, out of which anything can be pulled.

She tugs at my panties, which cling to my bush for a brief moment from damp affection. She pulls harder, and they slide down my legs. I now feel hordes of people staring at my ass, which has seen firmer days. I assure myself that I will soon be too distracted to care. Like her, though, I enjoy an audience.

I can hear a collective sigh as her hard fingers tunnel in, exploring my wet folds. My hungry lower mouth responds with frenzy, wanting to be fed. She can feel my magnet trying to pull her in deeper, and she laughs with delight. She pushes forward and withdraws, then repeats the motion, grazing my clit in the process and showing off for the witnesses who can all testify that our marriage has been consummated. I sense that this is not the main course of the feast, only the cocktail sausages on display.

'Do you think she's wet enough?' she asks an onlooker.

A deep male voice responds: 'Let me check.' I wonder whether she knows this guy. She guides one of his big hands to my opening, where one finger (the middle, I think, which seems fitting) proceeds with surprising gentleness into my slick cave. He carefully tickles a sensitive spot, and I am afraid I will come too soon. As he pulls out, he tells her something I can't hear. The crowd responds with scattered laughter over moans and gasps. Someone is definitely being fucked, but it's not me at this moment. I feel lightheaded.

I hear a zipper being pulled down. For a split second, I wonder irrationally if I am going to be left like this, wet and exposed, while my suitor fondles a more suitable playmate, having lost interest in a slit without a face. The crowd seems quieter, and I don't know why.

Her fingers spread me open and some hard, smooth object nudges its way in. I can guess from the way it is being pushed that she is wearing a strap-on. The whole crowd seems to feel my relief, and I could swear they all exhale at the same time. I haven't taken on anything this size for years, but my hungry cunt hasn't forgotten how to welcome a guest. Noises that can't be held in are rushing out of my mouth.

'Did you . . . think . . . you wouldn't get it?' she pants, and the sound of her exertion tickles me beyond reason. She is breathless from fucking me. I am breathless from being fucked. Who could have predicted such equality?

This feels like reverse labor: I am taking her in and in because she is now mine, even if her choice of me was as whimsical as an unplanned conception. I wonder what it feels like on her end: is she getting enough stimulation to come? I certainly am, but this doesn't mean I will be able to do it while being watched.

'Don't hold back,' she warns. I panic. I can't let go on command! This is a disaster! She reaches around the front of one of my thighs to find my swollen clit. She traces circles and figure-eights on and over it, like a schoolgirl doodling on the title page of a new textbook. The combination of girlish delicacy and hard thrusting is somehow greater than either thing separately. I gasp as my first spasm grips her phallus. Her breathing quickens and grows louder as my spasms reach a peak.

When we have both calmed down enough to separate, she backs away, withdrawing the thing she probably thinks of as her Daddyhood. I rise up enough to glance backward. Its skin looks like black leather, smeared with fluid. A cock to match her pants, what a fashion statement. A hand slaps one of my ass-cheeks. It feels male, but I can't be sure it is the same hand that checked my wetness. It feels like the hand of one of her assistants.

When I see her again, she is removing the harness that held her tool in place. She slides the pants off her hips with such speed that I can see how badly she needs my attention. She sits on the table as I kneel in front of her. She spreads her legs apart, arching her back beautifully.

I inhale the smell of a warm pink sea-cave as I stretch out my tongue to get a taste. She is hot, rich and just salty enough. She holds my head in place as I lick my way into her wet folds and suck her excited clit almost to trembling hysteria. She controls her impulse to buck and scream by gripping my head. She is flowing with nectar, which is my reward. I could do this for ever, but she couldn't. I feel a hard spurt inside her, and my face is suddenly drenched with her juice.

I try wiping my face on my sleeve and my skirt, but there just isn't enough fabric to absorb her tribute. I can't help smiling, like a dirty-faced kid who has just eaten a watermelon and doesn't care who knows it. Someone hands her a handkerchief, not a Kleenex. She wipes herself with it and returns it to a woman who folds it carefully. I feel a pang of discomfort or jealousy at this evidence that someone else feels entitled to such a souvenir, which my suitor is willing to grant.

Her greenish eyes are searching my wet face and disheveled brown hair as though she has never seen me before. She has pulled up her pants and tucked herself in. She gestures for me to turn my back to her. I do, assuming she will button up my dress.

She pulls up on my cotton bodice, and I am afraid she will rip it apart unless I raise my arms so that she can pull the dress over my head. My bra is still unhooked, and my panties and shoes are scattered on the floor. I pick up the remains of my ensemble as though picking up shells while wandering naked on a beach. It feels luxurious. There is scattered laughter and approving glances from those members of the audience who aren't completely distracted by their own activities.

She pulls something out of a pocket. By instinct (how else?), I kneel in front of her as she fastens a narrow leather collar around my neck. It looks so modest and useful that I suspect it must be the apprentice version of something more serious which could be earned later on. She attaches a leash to a ring in the collar, and leads me out of the room with it.

She leads me into a lavatory which says 'Ladies' in black gothic script on the door. She seems as amused as I am. She leads me into an atmosphere of floral air freshener over disinfectant, and lo, there are mirrors everywhere. She holds me to her, pressing herself into me in a way that feels possessive and gracious at the same time. I breathe in the smell of some butch cologne mixed with the female sweat on her neck as we see ourselves, melodramatically entwined, duplicated in mirrors that reflect us to infinity. I know that she needs desperately to break the lushness of this moment with sarcasm. 'You must be Persephone, lost maiden,' she sneers softly. 'Kidnapped and ravished,' she adds smugly. 'You can't go home again.'

'Lost for years in mortal time,' I assure her. 'And you must be Hades, lord of the underworld.' She nods slightly in gentlemanly acknowledgement, but ignores the sarcasm in my voice.

I am afraid to ask her what I want to know, but not

knowing feels unbearable. 'How long will you keep me?' I ask quietly.

'As long as I can,' she sighs. 'I can't promise to train you.' She sounds amazingly world-weary to me until I remember how I felt when I was about her age. 'I'm not sure how much time I'll have in the next few months. I'm going back to school and I have a new part-time job.'

I can almost feel the Hand of Destiny touching the back of my neck, sending chills down my spine. 'Where?' I ask.

'A bookstore,' she mutters as though she can't imagine why this would interest me. 'Elysian Books.' So she is going to be the new trainee I've been promised. Apparently it has not occurred to her that many women of my age have risen to the level of our incompetence in our places of work, regardless of how we appear elsewhere. I can almost hear the laughter of the gods.

'If you want me near you, my lord,' I tell her, trying to sound submissive, 'I won't be far away.' She presses her lips to mine, pulls my tongue into her mouth and nibbles it. I can feel the variety of fears she is trying not to show me or herself. After she releases me so we can catch our breaths, I ask: 'Do you think you'll recognize me above ground?'

She pinches one of my ass cheeks, playfully but hard. 'Do you think you can hide from me?' she demands.

'No,' I chuckle, the laughter almost bursting out of me, 'or vice versa. We'll see.'

'It gets worse,' she threatens, casually running her fingernails down my back.

'It gets better,' I respond.

An Inside Job

Catharine McCabe

An Inside Job

⊰ ⊱

Rita was deep in a dream, living it as vividly as if it were reality. She was lying naked on a low pallet in a small, airless hut, somewhere in the vine-covered gullies in southern Mississippi. Her shimmering, auburn hair was long, straight and fragrantly woven with flowers of jasmine and honeysuckle. The imposing, large black African woman had attended to it for almost as long as it had taken her to arrange the offerings on the voodoo altar and light the candles that now furiously burned around her.

The flames heated up the closeness of the cabin until Rita felt like she was suffocating. She tried to close her slender, widespread legs but they were held apart by the voodoo spell the woman had begun to weave. Rita was lashed to the small bed more securely than any number of straps could have done. Her softly furred pubis was trickling with moisture that had begun to seep between her legs, and her dark-brown, hardened nipples were tingling as the words of the spell drew the spirits into her body.

It was Rita's face that held the black woman's gaze as she continued to exhort the Invisible Ones to enter the

253

girl. Rita's lips were softly parted as she breathed in the mingled, heady scent of her flower-woven hair and her moist, open sex. Her eyes were closed in rapture, the lids trembling whenever the loa touched those places deep within her core that caused each tautly stretched nerve to vibrate and become charged with ecstasy.

Like tentacles of fire, the voodoo spirits wound through Rita's mind, stroking the pleasure center deep within her brain until every fiber in her body was tense with the need to climax. And still the African woman chanted her words, the exotic, foreign sounds falling in a soft, breathless cadence over her bare skin, guiding and directing the Invisible Ones to stroke the dark, secret places in Rita's body.

A willing captive, yet writhing in need, Rita wholly surrendered herself to the licking tongues of the spirits as they wickedly plundered between the soft lips of her sex and feasted hungrily on her swollen clitoris, pulling at it with soft, sucking tugs. Then, while they slowly penetrated her depths with their combined fullness, her hips bounced uncontrollably against the cot in response to their relentless pounding. The Invisible Ones' laughter echoed in Rita's drowsy mind, taunting her in their heightened state of lust, and reminding her that she had once been their charge in another lifetime.

'Kitty' had been her name, and now, while in the spirit, she still answered to it. She had been a young woman whose gracious life had been intruded upon, like so many others of that era, by the War of the Rebellion. When the Union army had begun bombarding her home she had escaped death by hiding below ground, taking shelter in the darkness of a root cellar. A Confederate soldier seeking food had been caught in the crossfire and also sought refuge there. They were forced to hide together for the entire day. As they listened to the terrifying barrage of mortar fire above, he took her. At first she was unwilling, but only at first.

Then, once the day and the battle had passed, he seemingly abandoned her, leaving her ravenous for his body.

Bess's own role in those turbulent days was primarily the reason that Rita, now within the shelter of deep sleep, had called to her. Rita had no way of her own to contact the voracious loa. In another time the priestess's knowledge had been vital in order to use the emotion-hungry spirits to bring Kitty and Michael back together and to wreak havoc upon those who had done Kitty harm. Once called, they continued to hover around Kitty's soul and chose to follow her from lifetime to lifetime, never straying very far.

'Michael!' Rita breathed her rebel lover's name from her former life and Bess smiled and nodded her head. The voodoo queen had been awakened from a century of spiritual slumber and had beckoned Rita to travel backwards in time, over 120 years, to the place where she needed to be in order for the black priestess to practise her magic.

Michael, himself aware of the power of Bess's black art, held the loa in great respect. Out of his love for Kitty, and with the help of the spirits, he had also bound his soul to hers, vowing to never leave her. His reappearance as Richard in Rita's current life brought them both incredible joy.

Now, at Bess's urging, Rita had become the required sacrifice needed to persuade the Invisible Ones to fulfill her deepest desire – to hide, small and unnoticed, within Richard's body in order to experience every atom of sensual pleasure he felt as he made his way through his day. Then, as she slowly stretched and grew within him she would feed his pleasure back to him more irresistibly than he had ever known, giving to him what the loa had given her – hour upon hour of endless, uncontrollable erotic delight while he tried to work or play or sleep.

In the bed they shared, Rita twisted and tossed as the spirit-filled dream consumed her, pulling her deeper and deeper into Bess's haunting enchantment. Richard, naked and sprawled by her side, muttered in his sleep and drew Rita to his chest in order to soothe her. However, Rita's spiritual travel had unleashed a torrent of erotic energy; her compelling need became the sumptuous feast the loa had to have in order to replenish their energy. Consequently, her dreamy rapture became heightened and extended by them, built up and drawn out much further than the ordinary orgasm of an unattended soul. When Rita's wish to fill her lover's body with endless pleasure reached the Invisible Ones, the fiercely charged orgy was inevitable.

In the enveloping blackness of Rita's mind she heard the hollow, deep sighs and erotic groans of the spirits as they pleasured themselves deep within her. They took the woman from climax to shuddering climax until, hours later, she became too weak to respond to their urges. After one last, winding caress the loa took their leave, spiraling into the night to hover, to watch, and to see how she used the gift they had given her.

The resultant changes were already becoming dynamically apparent. Rita woke and, hovering over Richard's body, her hair streaming across his chest, she began to caress his skin with her fingertips. She watched herself with amazement as her soft, supple body sank against his larger frame, only to be slowly absorbed by him until nothing remained of her at all. The bargain had been met.

It wasn't unusual for Rita to be at work early. Yet, when Richard woke up and found she wasn't snuggled beside him, he felt disappointed. This morning his erection was nearly bursting with the need to plunge into her tight cunt. His hand strayed to his enormous stiffness, and rolling on to his back he closed his eyes and began to conjure up her face in his mind. Buried under his skin, Rita's essence immediately flamed into hot awareness as she felt him touch the head of his cock and begin slowly rubbing the welling drops of pre-come down its length. In his subconscious Richard felt a small shudder run through his body, and he could have sworn he heard her familiar sigh of arousal as his fingers closed more tightly around his rock-hard shaft.

Maybe she's still here! he thought as he quickly got out of bed to follow the sound of her voice. His fat cock bounced against his stomach as he walked through the house and out on to the large, redwood deck overlooking the Malibu coast. He glanced down at the beach below; with the exception of a few gulls and a sandpiper, the sandy stretch in front of their house was empty. Calling her name over the sound of the surf, he walked back through the living room and into the kitchen; but no one was there.

Back in the bedroom Richard stood in the center of the floor, wondering what he had heard. As he turned back toward the bed he glanced at himself in the mirror and he nearly lost his composure when he saw his reflection. There stood the usual tall, muscularly handsome man whose hand still fondled and stroked his swollen cock. It had become a dark, dusky red as he held it in his palm and slowly pulled it. His blond hair fell in unkempt locks across his forehead. His tanned face was still creased with soft lines left by the pillowcase. His blue eyes were still fogged with sleep. But what amazed him and nearly left him speechless was the other face that seemed to be hidden within his own. Rita was there.

Richard turned around to look for her, but she wasn't behind him. When he turned back to the mirror, there she was again, her familiar features blending with his own, although no more distinctly than an incoherent shadow. She was blurred and fuzzy, and she was smiling back at him. As Richard continued to stare at himself, he began to see her in the rest of his reflection. Her form had stretched and lengthened to fill his own, although she retained her curving slimness where the rest of his image was filled with rippling biceps and quads.

'Go ahead!' the face urged him. 'Feel yourself!' He took his hand off his prick and slowly ran his fingers over his face, trying to touch her while he touched himself. He felt her soft lips as they rested just underneath his own, and when he took a deep breath, she chuckled. 'I smell your salty cock,' her voice echoed in his head. She sounded tiny, far away. Yet, he could feel her breathing within him. He could feel the cadence of her chest rising and falling within his own; could feel her breasts pushing against his as her hardened nipples stroked his from the inside out.

'Run your fingers over your chest,' she whispered. Doing as she asked, his hands left his face and came to rest against his small nipples.

'You know what to do, Richard. Don't be afraid. Touch them like you'd touch mine.' His fingertips began to tingle and when he lightly stroked his tiny nubs, the nearly electrical charge he gave himself shot from his chest to the tip of his cock. It jerked against his belly like a wild animal and he immediately gripped himself and furiously began to masturbate. He rapidly stroked himself from base to tip while he watched Rita's face, hazily reflected within his own, grow more and more aroused. Her features softened and her lips parted as she became forced to breathe harder with him.

Richard fell back on to the bed, still tightly holding his throbbing penis, still rubbing himself and smearing the slick drops of wetness up and down his shaft. He closed his eyes in pure, unadulterated pleasure. Whenever his fingertips encountered the head of his cock, he heard her sighs of bliss. Running one finger around and around the swollen tip, he felt her give a delicious shiver. His opening was weeping freely, soaking his finger with as much lubrication as he felt when he toyed with her cunt. When he looked down at himself he could faintly see the image of her swollen clit. As he continued to rub his cock, Richard moaned to the ceiling.

'Oh, God! Rita! What have you done?' he cried, his voice nearly cracking with emotion.

'I'm within you,' Rita answered, with more calmness than she actually felt. 'Everything you feel, I feel. Everything you do to yourself, you do to me, and when you're ready to come, I'll take up where you leave off and let you experience what I feel when you touch me,' she explained, her voice closer now, soaking through his body like a warm shower. Richard laughed aloud as he lay stretched out on the bed. His hand slowly continued the motion, his usual grip feeling more like her tight, wet sheath than the warm enclosure of his own palm and fingers.

'I'm astounded! This is incredible! You really are inside me!'

Lightly pinching his nipple with his other hand, Richard made her gasp with delight, and when he did it again he felt her clitoris leap underneath the tips of his fingers as he continued to circle them around and around the tip of his cock.

The double sensations were wildly arousing and, before he knew it, he was as close to orgasming as he had ever been in such a short stretch of time. He felt his cock begin its initial, jolting pull as his balls drew up tightly between his legs. Her fuzzy lips were soft, engorged and slick. He could feel them as soon as he cupped his testicles and gently held them against himself. He rubbed a finger against the base of his cock and thought he felt her cunt open to accept him as he pressed his fingertip back and forth over his thick channel.

The decision to prolong his climax and remain in control was made too late. Hearing her gasping sobs within his head, he rolled over on to his side and began working to bring his cock to a spurting, jerking end. Rita's swollen clit nearly burst over his finger as he slowly rubbed the head of his penis. Although he would have liked to lie there and bask in the afterglow, he felt compelled to keep stroking himself. He could still feel the swell of her consuming pleasure as it lay gathering within the core of his body, like an erotic itch that demanded scratching. Her tiny moans were proof that she needed his stimulation. She was almost there – so close he could hear her gasps and feel her belly tense. His abdomen tightened in response and his feet flexed involuntarily as her toes begin to curl.

'Oh, please, please don't stop – just a little more!' She pleaded with him for release.

Richard's fading orgasm was instantly reignited and quickly spiraled with Rita's, his balls suddenly unloading more streams of his own thick jism as he felt her heat coil tighter and tighter inside his cock. Within a split second her climax came in a riot of sensations that nearly caused Richard to faint. The spasms between his legs were huge and rolling, sending wild impulses to his brain to be translated into something he didn't understand but knew would completely consume him.

When it was over, Rita lay within Richard's exhausted body and felt his muscles slowly release and relax as he began to drift off to sleep. His eyes closed, darkening her view of the room, and when she tried to wipe away the feeling of trickling semen between her legs, he clamped his hand over his penis and halted her movements.

'Time to sleep,' he mumbled thickly. Smiling to herself, she let his body take them both under.

After an hour Richard woke up, the frantic messages from his bladder causing him to hit the floor on a run. Reaching the bathroom, he guided the hot stream of water into the bowl.

'I thought you'd never wake up!' Rita blissfully sighed as he continued to fill the bowl with their combined foamy urine. Richard laughed at the thought of her having to hold her water until he was ready to go.

'Let me hold it,' Rita said as her fingers took over Richard's hand, and with a small, wicked laugh she began to play with his soft penis as he slowly dribbled to a stop. 'Now what?' she asked when he was finished, and as Richard stood there he grinned and looked down at his hand. 'Shake it,' was all he said.

Richard flushed the toilet and turned to look in the bathroom mirror at Rita's reflection.

'Suppose you tell me how you got inside of me,' he stated, a little worried that this bodily marriage might be permanent.

Rita, her hand still teasing Richard's growing cock, began to tell him about her desire to crawl inside him and feel what he felt. 'I dreamed about Bess last night and she called me to her. I told her my wish, and before I knew what had happened, she had me naked and restrained on her cot, calling to the Invisible Ones to use me as her offering. She told me, "You have to pay the price!" When I finally became too tired to be of any use to them any more, the bargain was sealed. I was in heaven and in hell at the same time.' Richard heard her story as if she were talking from a distance, but he felt her fingers stretching and pulling his cock until he was suddenly undeniably hard and ready.

'How do you get out of me when the time comes?' he asked.

'I don't know,' Rita answered, 'but when the Invisible

Ones have helped me achieve what I wished for, then it will be over.'

'The spirits are nothing to trifle with, Rita. You must have wanted this very badly to waken Bess and the loa.'

'Mmm! Oh, yes. I wanted this more than anything.' Her hum of pleasure filled his mind. 'Look at yourself!' she exclaimed, and Richard looked down, amazed at the size and hardness of his erection.

'Do you like it, being inside me, experiencing me?' he asked, his voice filled with lust and wonder. He began to rub one finger around the tip of his cock as Rita continued to slowly stroke his shaft. He could feel her becoming aroused by what he was doing. 'Oh, yes!' he heard her sigh and he felt her legs spread further apart as they pressed against his outer thighs. Without warning, his belly loudly growled a reminder that they hadn't eaten breakfast yet.

'Are you hungry?' he asked as he walked back to the bedroom. He had decided to get dressed and try to get through the day in a somewhat normal fashion. 'Yes!' he heard her respond. Looking in the mirror he saw her face looking back at him, her eyes shining with a mixture of worry and amusement.

'This isn't going to make you mad at me, is it? I mean, I didn't ask you if it was OK,' she said, hoping he wouldn't become upset with her as the day progressed.

Richard pulled on his jeans and zipped up the fly. Grabbing his T-shirt, he pulled it over his head and tucked it in the waist of his pants.

'Look at it this way,' he said as he dressed. 'We might learn something about each other's feelings, and since we've been through so much together already I doubt this will pull us apart. Anyway, I know exactly where you are at all times now!'

* * *

To most people eating at the restaurant, the solitary man sitting in a booth by the window didn't seem a bit unusual. However, one woman kept glancing in his direction, her wide-eyed gaze running the length of his body, taking in his hard, muscular legs and broad shoulders before settling hotly on the obvious bulge in his jeans. Grabbing her coffee she made her way over to where Richard sat, and without introducing herself, sat down across from him. Rita let out a warning growl in the back of Richard's mind, but Richard decided to ignore her for a moment and see what the woman wanted.

'Hello there,' she breathed, as she leaned across the Formica to take a packet of sugar from the holder. Her hand lightly brushed the top of his as she drew it back across the table, and her eyes held his in a meaningful glance before she opened the small envelope and poured the grainy contents into her coffee. 'I noticed you were eating by yourself. Do you mind if I join you? I just hate eating alone.'

'Well, I guess not,' Richard said, feeling a slight uneasiness in the pit of his stomach. Again Rita let out a low growl. He looked at the woman and then looked around for the waiter, hoping to have his order taken before too much time passed.

'I just hate eating alone!' Rita's voice echoed in his mind as she mimicked the woman who had assumed that he was free. Richard smiled a little at his lover's jealousy and decided to feign indifference to her mood. He stretched his hand across the table and shook the newcomer's.

'I'm Richard, and you are . . .' he asked as he watched the woman lick her lips a little and settle into the booth more comfortably.

'Carla,' she said, drawing back her hand and placing the mug to her lips. She puckered her bright pink mouth into a tiny, round shape and blew gently across the top of the coffee mug before taking a small sip.

'Have you ordered?' he asked, looking back around for the waiter who was cleaning the table where the woman had been seated.

'No,' she responded. 'I really just came here for the coffee.'

'And to pick up men!' the voice inside Richard's head muttered angrily. 'Go ahead then. See what she wants, but don't forget you're mine!' Rita whispered hotly as she gently began nudging him between his legs. Then, suddenly, her hands were all over his cock and he couldn't help but squirm as he felt his growing hardness pressing against the tight leg of his denims. Realizing Rita was going to be merciless, he shifted in his seat and tried to adjust his erection so it didn't look quite so obvious.

'You sure seem nervous,' Carla said as she watched Richard change positions several times before finally settling down.

'I'm OK,' he stated, suddenly wishing he were anywhere but there, but now that he'd allowed Carla to sit down, he had no other choice but to finish what she'd started. Besides, she was pretty, in a coarse sort of way. He could see the outline of her nipples underneath her low-cut, hot-pink spandex top, and when she raised her arms to straighten her hair, her breasts rose with them and threatened to spill out of the opening. She wasn't wearing a bra. Suddenly his erection became his own undoing as he realized just how turned on he was getting while he watched Carla toy with her hair.

'I'm going to turn this meeting into a lesson in misery!' Rita laughed. He could feel her tongue lightly licking his own in soft strokes, and her fingers were rubbing her nipples within his chest as he sat there and tried to keep control. He could feel her arousal. The fabulous sensation of her cunt becoming juicy and swollen radiated deep within his balls. His hands were in his lap and he pressed his fingers against himself, mashing his cock against his leg. He smiled when he heard Rita's sharp intake of breath.

Ah! Who's miserable now? he thought to himself, and she immediately half sobbed, half laughed, 'Not fair! This is my experiment! You're not supposed to get us turned on and then get it on with her!' But Richard realized he was decidedly in control at this point and continued to torment Rita by lightly scratching the head of his penis.

'Do you want to go somewhere else?' he asked Carla. Inside his head he heard Rita's hiss of surprise, and he inwardly shushed her.

'Sure!' Carla replied, fluffing her hair for the last time before standing up.

'No! Wait! We haven't even eaten yet, and I'm starving!' Rita cried, her belly growling with unabashed hunger, but Richard was too intent on looking at Carla's tight, round bottom. Her pink top was cropped short and suddenly Richard was dying to wrap both hands around Carla's narrow waist as she bent over to straighten one leg of her shiny capri pants.

'Oh, for heaven's sake! She's a hussy with absolutely no class at all!' he heard Rita scream as she struggled to regain the ground she had lost.

Relax, he thought. This is going to be fun for both of us. I'm still yours, and I still love you. She's an experience for us to enjoy. Just think about what you'll feel while you're inside me! He heard Rita's racy thoughts as she ran the arrangement over in her mind and, groaning inwardly, he glanced down at his front. Rita had stained his jeans with her growing wetness. I knew you would see it my way! he thought again, and opened the door for Carla.

Richard caught the woman's wink as she walked past him, then he took her hand and led her to where he'd parked his truck. As soon as she slid on to the seat and made her way to the center she reached over and began to stroke Richard's erection.

'She doesn't waste any time, does she?' Rita exclaimed as she felt Carla's hand roaming up and down Richard's penis. 'The little hussy sure knows where to rub!' Richard felt Rita's long legs try to spread further apart so she could feel the woman's fingers stroking her clit.

Richard pulled Carla to him and cupped a huge hand around one of her soft breasts. It felt heavy and good and warm. Rita took the initiative, and closing Richard's thumb and index finger around Carla's large, pink nipple, she pinched it until the woman began to moan. When Richard's mouth slanted across Carla's, he let Rita enjoy the exploration, feeling her tongue slide along his.

'Mmm! She tastes good,' he heard Rita whisper in his mind. Then Richard took control of Carla's tongue and sucked it into his mouth. Carla was beside herself as Rita continued to gently pinch her nipple.

'You'd better get us out of here before we get arrested,' he heard Rita whisper, and turning the key the truck roared to life.

'One last kiss,' Richard said as he covered Carla's mouth with his own. This one's for me, he thought as he softly sucked Carla's lower lip, feeling his cock leap against his jeans as she continued to stroke him.

The kiss was rapidly progressing into something much longer and deeper when a sudden wave of hot current raced through him, starting at his feet and running through his balls. Richard jerked as if he'd been touched by some unseen electrical prod. As he pushed himself away from the woman to look for the source, Rita's voice screamed inside his head.

'The loa! They're trying to take control! We need to get home!' She reached for the end of Richard's cock and began to rub herself with his fingertips. 'Oh, God, hurry! I can't hold them off!' she whispered, her voice tense and suddenly fading.

'I don't live too far from here,' Carla started to offer, 'but if you want, we can go back to your place.'

Just as Rita had been crazy for food, the thought of all of that erotic energy so close at hand made Richard and Rita nearly wild for the feast. They could hear the heavy, obscene laughter of the hungry spirits growing louder as he wheeled the truck into their driveway.

Getting out, he reached inside the cab and pulled Carla out of the truck, holding her off the ground. His hands grabbed her hips as he pulled the woman to him, the pressure of her huge breasts nearly driving him crazy as she rubbed herself against his chest. Richard ran his fingers between Carla's legs and as he felt how wet the woman had become he heard Rita's far-away scream for him to hurry.

The loa had taken over Rita's senses and had expanded and magnified every sensation until she was nothing more than a bundle of erotic nerve endings. Richard had never felt so hard and ready in his life, and Carla had suddenly become a rag doll, her body limp with unchecked desire as he continued to rub and press the division between her legs. The lips of her cunt lay in two distinctly swollen lumps beneath the tightness of her pants.

'Please!' Carla panted, her body trembling against Richard's as his finger found and pressed her clitoris back and forth underneath the seam. Putting his arm around her shoulder he half led, half dragged her to the door, unlocked it and pushed her inside.

Before she was halfway through the opening Carla had already nearly undressed. She had stepped out of her slides and had pulled her top over her head as she walked through the entryway. Rita's heart pounded in Richard's chest as she watched the woman continue to strip before Richard's eyes. Carla's body was gorgeous, long, lean and supple.

When nothing was left but her panties, Richard kneeled in front of Carla and jerked them down over her hips until they were tightly bunched around her knees. Rita's touch trembled slightly as she took Richard's hands and dragged his fingers across the woman's hairless cunt. Her pouting cleft barely hid the tip of her bright red core and he quickly separated her sticky love lips with his thumbs. In the next instant his tongue found her clit and began to lightly lick it up and down. Carla grabbed his head and pressed her body against his roaming mouth.

'Pull her pants all the way off. I want to feel how wet she is,' Rita whispered, her voice tense and shaking. Soon, Carla's underwear was in a small heap on the floor, and his fingers had parted her thighs so he could do what Rita asked. Without hesitation he drove two thick digits into the woman. Carla whimpered and braced herself. Richard heard Rita's moan inside his head as she felt the woman's heat and wetness envelop her fingers through his touch. It was quickly becoming too much.

'Hold on to me, baby,' he muttered, and Carla steadied herself against Richard's shoulders. She moved her hips against him as he rotated his hand and began to finger-fuck her.

'Let me taste her – oh, Richard! Please! I have to do it!' Richard heard Rita's plea before it was covered by the loa's harsh laughter. Placing his mouth on Carla's cunt, Richard felt Rita take his tongue and began to pleasure the woman as only another woman could, slowly and ravenously. Carla screamed when she felt this, and looking down at Richard's head she placed her hands behind his ears and held his face tightly against her.

'Where did you learn to eat a woman like that? Oh,

God!' The only response she heard was the lush, wet sucking sounds of Richard's mouth as he continued taking her.

Fully controlled by the spirits, Richard slid his tongue downward, increasing the pressure against Carla's cunt as he quickly plunged it within her. Carla's hips jerked back and forth against his face.

'I'm almost there! I don't think I can last much longer!' Carla cried, her voice becoming loud and shrill. Richard's body shuddered with each movement of his head, his turgid cock twitching and jerking against his groin.

'Take her! Take her now!' It might have been Rita's voice, but the quality was that of the spirits. It was demanding, harsh, and it seethed with need.

Richard lifted his head long enough to tell Carla to lie down, shoving her in the direction of the couch. As she crossed the room he took off his clothes, ripping the shirt buttons through the buttonholes and trying to crawl out of his jeans without unzipping them. His cock was dripping, throbbing, red, angry and enormously full. The loa had taken charge of all of them, and when Carla saw the frenzied look on Richard's face all she could do was spread her legs wide apart and hold open her swollen cunt.

Her knot was protruding well beyond her cleft and her thighs quivered as frantic bolts of pleasure began to center and expand between them. Nuzzling her with his nose Richard uncovered her swollen core, and then his tongue zeroed in on it like a heat-seeking missile. The dry, hissing voices of the spirits burst into Richard's head and began whispering.

'We're going to have this woman together! All of us! She's ours! You are ours! We won't leave until we take what we need!' The loa crawled around in Richard's mind, burrowing into his brain until their thoughts became his. They twisted around his penis and probed his gut with silky, arousing strokes. With their exacting touch they brought his rod to the bursting point, and he mutely realized all control was lost.

Now firmly in charge of Richard's mind, the Invisible Ones spewed hotly charged, erotic suggestions to Rita, and Rita's only answer was a deep moan as Richard rose to his knees and slid his body up against the edge of the couch. Unable to fight them, Richard allowed the loa to rub his cock between Carla's fat juiciness, making him stroke himself against the woman's engorged knot. His cock then quickly moved towards her hole, guided by the hands of the Invisible Ones.

With a tremendous shove they plunged his rod into Carla's body. Richard's shout of rapture was hoarse; however, the subsequent, harsh grunts of pleasure were those of the spirits. Carla's body was now physically joined with Richard's and the orgy had begun.

The laughter of the Invisible Ones was raucous as the loa fused Richard and Rita's sexes tightly together, making her one with him. Her body shuddered and responded inside his while he slowly pumped in and out of Carla's opening.

Using Richard's eyes, Rita looked down at Carla's body. Carla's fingers were riding her clit, circling and swirling around it in tight movements. Richard snarled for her to keep masturbating and Carla could only moan as the loa whipped through her body in a raging whirlwind filled with mind-blowing sensations.

On his knees at the edge of the couch, Richard drew Carla's hips more tightly against his loins and wound her legs around his waist. Holding her bottom cheeks in his strong grip he gritted his teeth and began to pound himself into her, feeling the tightness of his balls draw everything upward as the pressure inside his body quickly built. Rita's climax earlier that morning was his first real taste of the depth of a woman's orgasm, and now it seemed she was quickly headed for another one as he relentlessly drove himself deep into Carla's sheath. He could feel Rita shudder each time he stroked himself within the other woman's gripping body.

'Kiss her and suck her tongue! Kiss her and let us feed!' The loa's commands were automatically carried out. Richard bent to take the woman's mouth with his own, only to find Rita's tongue wildly stroking both his and Carla's.

'Harder! Oh, please! Do it harder!' Richard heard Carla's strangled groan, and as he regained his grip on her hips, she suddenly began to climax in hard, shuddering jerks against his thrusting cock. He gasped and cried out as he felt Rita's second orgasm ride on the heels of Carla's. It was shockingly hard and fast, racing throughout his body in shattering waves.

Inside Richard's body, Rita felt Carla's spasms grip the entire length of Richard's swollen penis, and her cries echoed into the atmosphere as each jolt of pleasure crashed through her. The loa, demented and insatiable, cackled as they continued to inexorably draw out and feed upon the fantastic sensations.

'You wanted to experience Richard's body! Are you satisfied? Have you received what you wanted from us?' the loa hissed, filling Rita's mind with their coarse, lewd grunts and echoing laughter.

Rita mewled and whimpered, her body totally given over to them as she tried to respond. Her thoughts were not coherent, but her body finally knew what it was like to be a man and literally fuck another woman. Tongues and fingers would never compare with having a rock-hard erection and feeling the stretch of a tight, elastic sheath.

Richard heard Rita's cry of ecstasy as his own climax overtook him. Carla's head thrashed wildly against the pillows and her fingers kept up their mad tattoo against her clitoris as she continued to orgasm hotly around

Richard's throbbing cock. She looked at him, eyes streaming with tears, sobbing at the raw pleasure she felt. The loa were causing her ecstasy to reach unbearable heights.

Richard's cock remained hard and pulsed with energy as the Invisible Ones wound their silky enchantment around his balls and his brain. With a loud shout he climaxed again, his rod leaping and jerking within Carla's grasping cunt as she lay unresponsive on the couch. Her body was completely spent.

When his orgasm finally faded, Richard released her. Carla rolled off the couch and lay on the floor, her legs limp and splayed wide as Richard's seed ran out of her body and on to the thick carpet. Carla weakly turned her head towards her pile of clothes. It was over. It was time for her to go, and the loa were compelling her to dress and leave.

Without bothering to show her to the door Richard wandered back to bed and crashed on the mattress, his mind and body in a state of total exhaustion. About an hour later, when he woke up, Rita lay sleeping beside him. He bent over and buried his face in her hair before kissing her on the back of her neck. She smelled faintly of candle smoke. Moaning slightly, she turned over and hugged him before sinking back into her dreams. Bess was there, calling her, and Rita went willingly.

The Leather Lover

Georgina Brown

The Leather Lover

❖ ❖

Sandwiched between the gleaming glass of high-rise offices, the old market where traders used to sell fruit and vegetables was now given over to stalls selling hand-painted glass beakers, Indian cottons, joss sticks, chickpeas and all manner of spices.

Personal assistants, recruitment specialists and refugees from computer help desks browsed among the ethnic mix of food, clothes and utensils, each item likely to form part of their evening's escape from the rushed reverie of their day job.

In a way, that was exactly the effect the dog collar had on Mandy. She had fingered the oriental silks, imagined them cool against her skin. She had sniffed the air and swallowed the smell of incense mixed in an atmospheric pot pourri with the rich aromas of myriad spices. All of them inspired her imagination and urged her to buy, but the dog collar stopped her in her tracks.

Mentally her body was already naked because she had been imagining the feel of the silk around her breasts, over her belly and fluttering gently against her buttocks. Leather decorated with metal studs was an easy progression though she had never worn one before, but then, she had never seen this one before.

It was just over two inches thick and decorated with shiny metal studs. Usually these studs were chrome pretending to be silver, but these were different. Like the buckle and the leash ring hanging from it, they gleamed like dull gold. The inside of the collar was lined with gold velvet.

'Lovely, isn't it, dearie?' said the woman behind the stall. 'What sort of dog do you have?'

Mandy answered neither question but merely ran her fingers over the soft leather and felt the slightly pointed fierceness of the gleaming, metal studs.

'How much is it?'

There had been no real need to ask how much it was. Whatever price, she would have paid it. Tucking it under her arm she took it back to the office with her and as she walked she felt its hardness against her breast and her flesh tingled. Not once did she question her sanity in buying it. She only thought of how she would look standing naked in front of a full-length mirror tonight, the buckle and the leash ring gleaming at her throat. A moist wetness eased between her legs. Her flesh swelled – erect flesh fuelled by her own erotic fantasy. She rubbed her thighs together and almost groaned out loud – not the sort of thing to do in a crowded lift on a workday lunchtime.

So fixed was her mind on the object nestling beneath her arm, that she hardly noticed the man who got in the lift beside her until he asked her what floor she wanted.

'Three,' she said.

He pressed it for her.

The fact that she had recognised him as Harvey Pillenger, the Chief Executive and a man rarely seen by a peasant such as her, hardly registered. There were far more pleasant thoughts on her mind, no matter the rugged looks and sexy eyes and the obvious aphrodisiac of power that he exuded. Her mind was fixed on the dog collar and what had possessed her to buy it.

Perhaps because she was distracted was the reason she swung her bag around too quickly when it came time to exit the lift and make her way to her desk, her computer and the e-mails she knew awaited her. Whatever the reason, because she did that, the paper bag tilted to one side. The dog collar fell out and, as is the law of chance when least expected, it tumbled straight on to the feet of the Chief Executive.

She gasped and rushed to grab it.

'Sorry . . .' she began

'I'll get it,' said Pillenger.

'No . . .'

Her protest was ignored.

His hand got there before hers. He picked up the dog collar and handed it to her. 'That's a handsome collar.'

'Yes,' she said, aware that her face was getting hotter and that she must be approaching the colour of best-quality salmon. She snatched the collar from him and stuffed it back into the bag.

His hand landed on her arm. 'Are there many break-ins in your area?'

Taken off guard, she blinked open mouthed as she looked up into his face. 'No,' she said. 'Why do you ask?'

He nodded at her reclaimed package. 'I thought you were dealing with big crime and needed a big dog.'

Feeling a fool she shook her head again. And why was he looking at her like that? He'd hardly registered her before. Could the dog collar be having the same effect on him as it had had on her? Worse still, had he guessed that she would be wearing it herself?

'Thank you,' she said, shaking herself out of the embarrassed stupor she had sunk into. 'I have to go now.'

She could feel his eyes following her as she hurried

away. *Act naturally, you fool!* Head erect, she slowed her steps. She must appear confident, as though buying a thickly studded dog collar and having no dog was the most ordinary thing in the world.

When she got back to her office the sensual and the more conservative side of her character went into immediate conflict. At one point, just after she'd considered things over a cup of black coffee, she even tossed the collar into the wastepaper bin. But its presence seemed to call out to her, beckoning her to feel its sensual texures again, to imagine its decadent softness gripping at her neck, taut leather and hard metal contrasting with her skin. As a flush of pinkness returned to her cheeks – with excitement this time rather than embarrassment – she retrieved it.

'Damn it,' she said, though not too loudly. 'If I want it I'm going to have it!'

Just for once, the journey home ran to schedule; the train was on time and there was a bus waiting patiently at the other end.

Food was the last thing she needed once she was inside the one-bedroom flat that was big enough for two though she hadn't so far resorted to advertising for a flatmate. Her stomach could wait. Living didn't just mean eating.

At last, in the privacy of her own bedroom, she took it out of its bag and set it down on the bed. Then she stared at it, trying to divulge the secret of why it was obsessing her. It gleamed like some icon beckoning worship. And that was the way she felt about it. She worshipped it, she liked looking at it, and shortly she would feel its firm grip around her neck.

Slowly, so she could savour the preliminaries as well as the actuality, she took off her clothes, folded them and laid them on the chair at the side of the bed. With trembling hands she took hold of the dog collar, undid the heavy buckle and held it full stretch before her.

Though nothing touched them her nipples tingled with anticipation and something resembling a current of electricity ran through her pubic hair. Carefully, she placed the collar around her neck and buckled it.

She instantly liked the feel of it and the knowledge that however vicious the collar itself might look, it was soft on the inside.

She sighed. The time had come. Now she wanted to look at herself, to see the effect of leather and metal against the softness of female flesh.

The mirror was old, full length and garnished with bunches of grapes and cherubs with full cheeks and equally round bottoms.

She stared at her reflection. Raven-black hair fell to her shoulders. Her eyes were shining and her flesh seemed to glisten as if someone had brushed her skin with a coating of the same kind of glitter she'd used on her cheeks before attending a party.

I look radiant, she thought. I look more alive than I've ever looked, and I feel ... A long sigh shivered through her body.

She ran her hands over her breasts, rolled her nipples beneath her palms.

'I feel excited,' she said to her reflection. 'I want more.'

Her belly was firm beneath her exploring hand, the skin soft, the effect narcissistic. Of course she loved herself. Why shouldn't she? Making love to oneself was not shameful. Indeed, it was gratifying. She could please herself what she did, her actions originating from the private fantasies within her mind.

She ran her hand down over her belly and fingered the luxuriant hair that formed a deep and dark triangle between her thighs. Pushing one finger between her moistening slit, she slid it through the slippery flesh then brought it back again and gently – because she wanted to take things slowly – she rubbed at her clitoris which swelled and seeped with fluid beneath her touch.

With her other hand, she played with her breasts, pinching them, kneading them, flattening them against her body because the look of the leather almost willed her to do that. She was its slave. She would be anyone's slave who saw her in this because, she realised, that was what the collar demanded. Demand ruled her. She needed another player in this scenario. Her own company was no longer enough. But it was too late for that now. Who did she know who indulged in leather? It wasn't something you asked people.

There was no alternative. For now she would have to imagine that someone else was here playing her game, someone else was here giving her orders.

She cocked her head to one side as if listening for a silent command.

'I won't do it!' she said because she understood only too well there was no satisfaction in such a game unless the submissive showed some spirit.

She hooked her finger into the bronze leash ring that hung at her throat and pulled on it until she was down on her knees, obedient to her imaginary master.

'Now you're going to do whatever I say. You will endure whatever I do.'

As she said the words, her fingers worked against the plush wetness of her sex, rubbing her clitoris with experienced fingers until she knew that to do any more, she would come.

'And you mustn't do that,' said the voice of her imaginary master. 'Because I am not ready for you to do that. I have things that I want you to do first.'

In a daze of tantalising arousal, she fetched the things she needed. First there were the clip-on ear-rings that had weighty silver daggers hanging from them. Then there was the stone obelisk she'd brought back from Cairo. At present it formed a useful housing for the kitchen roll. Her mind more set on masturbation than mopping up, she slid it off and tossed it over her shoulder. The last item was a black silk scarf that she fetched from her bedroom drawer.

She cried out as she clipped the ear-rings on to her nipples. Their touch was tight and cold and the daggers were heavy.

'That's it! Cry out! I want you to cry out,' said the voice in her head.

Every inch of her body registered the fact that the heavy ear-rings were gripping her nipples in their metal grasp. They were getting as hard as the metal that gripped them.

Just as before she forced herself back down on to her knees, though this time she went down a little further than before. The heavy stone obelisk, '*A present from Egypt*' etched along its base, was between her legs. The further she eased herself on to its slick coldness, the further it penetrated until she felt only its square, fat base against her flesh.

'Now your hands,' said the master she had created in her mind.

She looped the silk scarf through the ring, tied one end around her left hand, the middle around her right hand, then pulled the remainder through the ring and looped it back around her left hand so both hands were tight up against the metal ring.

'Now ride it!' said the unseen voice.

As she stared at her own reflection, she bounced up and down on the cold neck of the obelisk, its main body thudding against the engorged arousal of her aching clitoris.

Her breasts bounced and the clip-on ear-rings with the hanging daggers jiggled and gripped so it really did feel as though someone was pinching her, milking her to suit themselves.

The vision she saw stared back at her, the face

flushed, the eyes bright with excitement. She could do nothing to stop this because she did not want to stop it. Her hands were tied to the collar, high above her breasts, and yet she wanted them tied behind her back. Her nipples were caught in tight metal clamps, yet she wanted them to be more restricted, to have them feel as though they were prisoners of someone else and no longer hers to attend to.

Between her legs, the obelisk was sliding in and out, fucking her, and bringing her to a climax. And when it came, when it made her body tense, her back arch, and her sex seep with juices, she made herself a promise. There would be more of this. More leather. More sex.

Harvey Pillenger was standing in reception the following morning – and the morning after. This had to be more than a coincidence.

He turned and smiled at her. 'Good morning, Miss Mayhew.'

'Good morning, Mr Pillenger,' she replied with some surprise. He knew her name.

He had nice eyes. She noticed that much. Wrinkles appeared when he smiled. He had character. A man of experience.

She walked on and couldn't help smiling to herself. The dog collar had affected him as much as it had her. It was no surprise when she was called to his office later that morning.

'I need a new PA,' he began. 'One who can cater to my every need.'

This did not surprise her. But she had to treat him seriously. 'Will I get a salary increase?'

His eyes narrowed as he smiled. 'A bonus too if you outperform my expectations. Which I am sure you will. You seem very capable.'

Capable. She wanted to laugh at the word. She could see in his eyes what he really wanted. It was all down to the dog collar. He loved leather too.

'May I think about it?'

He looked surprised but quickly smiled with the confidence of one who is used to being in control. 'Of course you may.'

That lunchtime she went to the market again and headed for the stall from which she had bought the leather collar. She fingered the leather leashes and chains, the thin strands of leather that she presumed were for the smaller members of the canine world.

The stall holder recognised her. 'Hello, dearie. Nice, aren't they?' she said, nodding towards the thin leather strip she was holding. 'Let me show you the best way to use it. Come inside.'

Mandy followed her in but said, 'I don't really think –' She had been about to say that she didn't have a small dog. She didn't have a big one either, but that was hardly the point.

'This works best, dearie,' said the woman.

To Mandy's surprise the strip of leather opened at one end. The woman slid her hand through and jerked on the leather. It closed tightly over her wrist. She did the same with the other end.

'You see, dearie? It's self-adjusting. You can manage it all by yourself.'

She grinned up at her and for the first time Mandy noticed the knowing twinkle in her eyes.

'I see,' she said slowly.

'That's the thing about leather, dear. It's a solitary affair. You enjoy it for itself.'

As her eyes got accustomed to the dim alcove behind the stall, Mandy saw just how varied the items hanging from nails and bulging from boxes were. More leashes, more chains, belts and girdles, and bridles that were definitely not made for horses.

'Take this as a gift from one leather lover to another,' said the woman, winking knowingly as she rolled the fine strip of leather in her hands then pressed it into Mandy's hand.

That afternoon she e-mailed her reply to Harvey Pillenger. Yes, she would take the job. He replied that he wanted her to take up her post within the week. She was in no doubt as to what he wanted from her. 'But you won't get me,' she muttered to herself, smiling as she typed her response. She'd found the love of her life. Leather! Its softness, its strength, could never be equalled by a mere man or even by mere sex. Nothing, she told herself, could change her mind.

The first week was uneventful if eyeing each other up and getting to know each other's ways could be called that. It was on the Wednesday of the second week that he asked her the question she'd been waiting for.

'I want you to work late tomorrow evening. I thought it only fair to give you notice so you can arrange your diary accordingly. I wouldn't want to intrude on your personal life.'

Personal life! She smiled to herself. 'I can do that,' she replied. Poor man. He didn't know she already had a lover, one that dominated her quality time and made her do things no man could make her do. He couldn't know that whatever sexual overtures he might have in mind would be rebuked because he couldn't live up to the lover she already had.

'I want to show you something special,' he said on that Wednesday evening, when everyone else had gone and the cleaners were coming in, bashing and banging with their vacuums, their polishers, their mops and their buckets.

'An Italian restaurant?' she asked, perhaps a little too confidently.

He frowned, looked deep into her eyes and shook his head. A secretive smile creased his mouth. 'I didn't think you'd be interested in food. Not yet.'

Silently he led her to his car, a silver-grey Mercedes convertible.

'We won't be long getting there,' he said as they pulled away. 'I'll take you to supper afterwards.'

'I don't want to be too late,' she said with an air of cool detachment. 'I've got to take the dog for a walk.' She fancied he looked at her as if he knew she was lying. But she couldn't help saying it. There was no dog. There was only the leather dog collar and the aching dampness between her legs. Imagine what I could be doing now if I was at home, she thought. The collar would be around her neck. Perhaps she'd bind her breasts with the other bits and pieces she had, squeeze them together so her nipples thrust forward like dark-red bullets. Perhaps the ear-rings again. Perhaps clothes pegs, or bulldog clips or . . .

She was suddenly aware that Pillenger was talking to her.

'We're here.'

She stared at the house before her. Classy and coun- trified. Everything a man of means could hope for – red brick, Georgian and flanked by barns and outbuildings.

'This way.'

She did not object when he took her by the hand but she did feel the urge to say something now instead of letting him down later.

'Look,' she said as he opened a small door into a building that looked like a barn, 'I'm not into having sex with any –'

'No,' he said.

She didn't object as he pulled her in through the door into semi-darkness.

It was the smell she noticed first, the subtle aromatic smell of long cured hides supple with age and generous applications of saddle soap and leather polish. Her mind sent the message to her body. Her flesh tingled as thoughts of sexual indulgence spread along every nerve.

Suddenly there was light. It was provided by a series of green-shaded wall lights, old but functional. They hardly registered. Her eyes were filled with the sight of bridles, harnesses, leashes, saddles and collars, none of which looked suitable to fit a horse.

'I think they'll fit you,' Pillenger said in answer to her unspoken question. 'Now be a good girl and take your clothes off. And if you do it quickly I won't fasten the harness too tight and I won't smack your pretty bottom too hard with a good leather thong. Then again, perhaps I might, anyway.'

She shook with excitement as she did as he asked. There was no reluctance because she knew what was happening. He was here. Her leather lover was here.

BLACK LACE NEW BOOKS

Published in July

PRIMAL SKIN
Leona Benkt Rhys
£5.99

Set in the mysterious northern and central Europe of the last Ice Age, *Primal Skin* is the story of a female Neanderthal shaman who is on a quest to find magical talismans for her primal rituals. Her nomadic journey, accompanied by her friends, is fraught with danger, adventure and sexual experimentation. The mood is eerie and full of symbolism, and the book is evocative of the best-selling novel *Clan of the Cave Bear*.

ISBN 0 352 33500 9

A SPORTING CHANCE
Susie Raymond
£5.99

Maggie is an avid supporter of her local ice hockey team, The Trojans, and when her manager mentions he has some spare tickets to their next away game, it doesn't take long to twist him around her little finger. Once at the match she wastes no time in getting intimately associated with the Trojans – especially Troy, their powerfully built star player. But their manager is not impressed with Maggie's antics; he's worried she's distracting them from their game. At first she finds his threats amusing, but then she realises she's being stalked.

ISBN 0 352 33501 7

Published in August

WICKED WORDS 3
A Black Lace Short Story Collection
£5.99

This is the third book in the *Wicked Words* series – hugely popular collections of writings by women at the cutting edge of erotica. With contributions from the UK and USA, these fresh, cheeky, dazzling and upbeat stories are a showcase of talent. Only the most arousing fiction makes it into a *Wicked Words* compilation.

ISBN 0 352 33522 X

A SCANDALOUS AFFAIR
Holly Graham
£5.99

Olivia Standish is the epitome of a trophy wife to her MP husband. She's well-groomed and spoiled, and is looking forward to a life of luxury and prestige. But her husband is mixed up in sleazy goings-on. When Olivia finds a video of him indulging in bizarre sex with prostitutes, her future looks uncertain. Realising her marriage is one of convenience and not love, she's eager for revenge!

ISBN 0 352 33523 8

To be published in September

DEVIL'S FIRE
Melissa MacNeal
£5.99

Destitute but beautiful Mary visits handsome but lecherous mortician Hyde Fortune, in the hope he can help her out of her impoverished predicament. It isn't long before they're consummating their lust for each other and involving Fortune's exotic housekeeper and his young assistant Sebastian. When Mary gets a live-in position at the local Abbey, she becomes an active participant in the curious erotic rites practised by the not-so-very pious monks. This marvellously entertaining story is set in 19th century America.

ISBN 0 352 33527 0

THE NAKED FLAME
Crystalle Valentino
£5.99

Venetia Halliday's a go-getting girl who is determined her Camden Town restaurant is going to win the prestigious Blue Ribbon award. Her new chef is the cheeky over-confident East End wide boy Mickey Quinn, who knows just what it takes to break down her cool exterior. He's hot, he's horny, and he's got his eyes on the prize – in her bed and her restaurant. Will Venetia pull herself together, or will her 'bit of rough' ride roughshod over everything?

ISBN 0 352 33528 9

CRASH COURSE
Juliet Hastings
£5.99

Kate is a successful management consultant. When she's asked to run a training course at an exclusive hotel at short notice, she thinks the stress will be too much. But three of the participants are young, attractive, powerful men, and Kate cannot resist the temptation to get to know them sexually as well as professionally. Her problem is that one of the women on the course is feeling left out. Jealousy and passion simmer beneath the surface as Kate tries to get the best performance out of all her clients *Crash Course* is a Black Lace special reprint.

ISBN 0 352 33018 X

If you would like a complete list of plot summaries of Black Lace titles, or would like to receive information on other publications available, please send a stamped addressed envelope to:

Black Lace, Thames Wharf Studios,
Rainville Road, London W6 9HA

BLACK LACE BOOKLIST

All books are priced £5.99 unless another price is given.

Black Lace books with a contemporary setting

THE NAME OF AN ANGEL £6.99	Laura Thornton ISBN 0 352 33205 0	☐
FEMININE WILES £7.99	Karina Moore ISBN 0 352 33235 2	☐
DARK OBSESSION £7.99	Fredrica Alleyn ISBN 0 352 33281 6	☐
COOKING UP A STORM £7.99	Emma Holly ISBN 0 352 33258 1	☐
THE TOP OF HER GAME	Emma Holly ISBN 0 352 33337 5	☐
LIKE MOTHER, LIKE DAUGHTER	Georgina Brown ISBN 0 352 33422 3	☐
ASKING FOR TROUBLE	Kristina Lloyd ISBN 0 352 33362 6	☐
A DANGEROUS GAME	Lucinda Carrington ISBN 0 352 33432 0	☐
THE TIES THAT BIND	Tesni Morgan ISBN 0 352 33438 X	☐
IN THE DARK	Zoe le Verdier ISBN 0 352 33439 8	☐
BOUND BY CONTRACT	Helena Ravenscroft ISBN 0 352 33447 9	☐
VELVET GLOVE	Emma Holly ISBN 0 352 33448 7	☐
STRIPPED TO THE BONE	Jasmine Stone ISBN 0 352 33463 0	☐
DOCTOR'S ORDERS	Deanna Ashford ISBN 0 352 33453 3	☐
SHAMELESS	Stella Black ISBN 0 352 33485 1	☐
TONGUE IN CHEEK	Tabitha Flyte ISBN 0 352 33484 3	☐
FIRE AND ICE	Laura Hamilton ISBN 0 352 33486 X	☐

SAUCE FOR THE GOOSE	Mary Rose Maxwell ISBN 0 352 33492 4	☐
HARD CORPS	Claire Thompson ISBN 0 352 33491 6	☐
INTENSE BLUE	Lyn Wood ISBN 0 352 33496 7	☐
THE NAKED TRUTH	Natasha Rostova ISBN 0 352 33497 5	☐
IN THE FLESH	Emma Holly ISBN 0 352 33498 3	☐
ANIMAL PASSIONS	Martine Marquand ISBN 0 352 33499 1	☐
NO LADY	Saskia Hope ISBN 0 352 32857 6	☐

Black Lace books with an historical setting

FORBIDDEN CRUSADE £4.99	Juliet Hastings ISBN 0 352 33079 1	☐
A VOLCANIC AFFAIR £4.99	Xanthia Rhodes ISBN 0 352 33184 4	☐
SAVAGE SURRENDER	Deanna Ashford ISBN 0 352 33253 0	☐
INVITATION TO SIN £6.99	Charlotte Royal ISBN 0 352 33217 4	☐
A FEAST FOR THE SENSES	Martine Marquand ISBN 0 352 33310 3	☐

Black Lace anthologies

WICKED WORDS	Various ISBN 0 352 33363 4	☐
SUGAR AND SPICE £7.99	Various ISBN 0 352 33227 1	☐
THE BEST OF BLACK LACE	Various ISBN 0 352 33452 5	☐
CRUEL ENCHANTMENT Erotic Fairy Stories	Janine Ashbless ISBN 0 352 33483 5	☐
MORE WICKED WORDS	Various ISBN 0 352 33487 8	☐

Black Lace non-fiction

THE BLACK LACE BOOK OF
  WOMEN'S SEXUAL
  FANTASIES
	Ed. Kerri Sharp
	ISBN 0 352 33346 4
		☐

- - - - - ✂ - - - - - - - - - - - - - - - - -

Please send me the books I have ticked above.

Name ....

Address ....

....

....

.... Post Code ....

Send to: **Cash Sales, Black Lace Books, Thames Wharf Studios, Rainville Road, London W6 9HA.**

US customers: for prices and details of how to order books for delivery by mail, call 1-800-805-1083.

Please enclose a cheque or postal order, made payable to **Virgin Publishing Ltd**, to the value of the books you have ordered plus postage and packing costs as follows:

UK and BFPO – £1.00 for the first book, 50p for each subsequent book.

Overseas (including Republic of Ireland) – £2.00 for the first book, £1.00 for each subsequent book.

If you would prefer to pay by VISA, ACCESS/MASTER-CARD, DINERS CLUB, AMEX or SWITCH, please write your card number and expiry date here:

....

Please allow up to 28 days for delivery.

Signature ....

- - - - - ✂ - - - - - - - - - - - - - - - - -